# FREE FALL

### A JOHN CEEPAK MYSTERY

## Chris Grabenstein

PEGASUS CRIME
NEW YORK  LONDON

*For Seaside Heights and Beach Haven, NJ—*
*the two towns that inspired Sea Haven*
*and suffered so much when Hurricane Sandy hit the Jersey Shore.*

This book is a work of fiction. The names, characters, places, and incidents are products of the writer's imagination or have been used fictitiously and are not to be construed as real. Any resemblance to persons, living or dead, actual events, locales or organizations is entirely coincidental.

FREE FALL

Pegasus Books LLC
80 Broad Street, 5th Floor
New York, NY 10004

Copyright © 2013 by Chris Grabenstein

First Pegasus Books cloth edition 2013

Interior design by Maria Fernandez

Library of Congress Cataloging-in-Publication Data is available.

ISBN: 978-1-60598-475-9

10 9 8 7 6 5 4 3 2 1

Printed in the United States of America
Distributed by W. W. Norton & Company, Inc.

# 1

FOR A COP, THERE'S NOTHING WORSE THAN HEARING AN OLD friend say "I didn't do anything, Danny!" two seconds after you pull her out of a nearly lethal cat fight.

Of course, these days, that's just the icing on the cake. Or, as I like to say, the suds on the Bud.

Despite all the "Life Is Good" T-shirts on sale at the Shore To Please Souvenir Shoppe, life has not been so great lately down the Jersey shore in "sunny, funderful" Sea Haven.

First off, there was a hurricane (that turned into a super storm) named Sandy, which, until last October, was also one of my favorite Bruce Springsteen songs. All of Sea Haven was shut down for two full weeks. No one was allowed on or off our eighteen-mile-long barrier island, except, of course, the governor of New Jersey and the President of the United States.

Eight months later, our battered seaside resort has pulled back from the brink. It's early June and everybody's excited about the upcoming summer season.

Everybody except me.

Because of bummer number two: John Ceepak is no longer my partner.

Funny story.

See, late last August they made Ceepak the Chief of Police. By early October, he was tired of pushing paper, untangling paper clips, and wearing these "Buy One Get The Second At Half Price" suits his wife Rita found for him at the Men's Wearhouse. So, after pulling us all through Sandy (don't worry, some day I'll tell you that story, too), when things had more or less settled down in the new year, Ceepak initiated a search for his own replacement.

After interviewing dozens of candidates, the township council hired another new Chief of Police. An older guy named Roy Rossi. With the new boss on paper-shuffling duty, Ceepak and I were poised to become the SHPD's first team of full-time detectives.

But that never happened.

See, I forgot to mention last year's other big blast of hot air and swirling garbage: our mayoral election.

The guy we wanted to win didn't.

And the guy who got re-elected has never been very fond of Ceepak or me. About fifteen seconds after all the New York and Philadelphia TV stations declared that the Honorable (how they came up with that title for him, I'll never know) Hubert Sinclair had won re-election, the guy initiated budget cuts. Said we had to bring the deficit under control for the sake of our grandchildren. Tough choices had to be made.

That's what he said. What Mayor Sinclair *meant* was that people who ticked him off had to be made miserable.

Buh-bye SHPD detective bureau.

Ceepak is still chief of detectives. He just doesn't have anybody in his tribe. He is allocated "personnel" on an "as-needed" basis. So, mostly, I spend my shifts cruising the streets in a patrol car.

With my new partner.

Sal Santucci.

"You hungry?" Sal asks as we cruise down Ocean Avenue just after sunset.

We're heading toward the southernmost tip of the island where we'll make a U-Turn and head back up to the lighthouse on the northernmost tip. Down south is where the swanky people have always lived in their bajillion-dollar beachfront bungalows. The first homes rebuilt after the super storm. The kind of homes other people like to burglarize, especially during the first week of June, when the tourist season isn't in full swing and the island is still mostly empty.

"We ate an hour ago," I tell Santucci.

"I'm still hungry."

"Shift ends at eleven. Pick up something on the ride home."

"We should swing by Pizza My Heart. If you're wearing a uniform, they'll give you a free slice *and* a fountain drink."

"Which you don't take because it's against the rules."

Yes, in Ceepak's absence, I am the patrol car's Keeper of The Code.

"What rules?"

*The ones they told you about in that lecture you slept through at the police academy,* I want to say.

But I don't.

Because 24-year-old Salvatore Santucci is the late Dominic Santucci's nephew. I was there when his uncle—who was on the job with the SHPD for fifteen, maybe twenty years—was gunned down by a psycho killer just outside the Rolling Thunder roller coaster. So I cut Sal some slack. We all do.

"We're cops, Sal," I say. "We can't accept gifts."

My young partner (well, he's three years younger than me) slumps down in the passenger seat to pout and fidget with the tuning knob on his radio. "I don't want a freaking 'gift,'" he mumbles. "I want a slice. Sausage and peppers."

I ease the steering wheel to the left and we roll into Beach Crest Heights. I give the white-shirted guard in the gatehouse a two-finger salute off the tip of my cop cap. He waves his clipboard back at me. It's Kurt Steilberger. We went to high school together.

"A gift," I say to Santucci, "means any fee, commission, service, compensation, gratuity, or—"

The radio interrupts my Remedial Graft lecture.

"Unit A-twelve, what is your twenty?"

I grab the mic.

"We're in Beach Crest Heights. Over."

"We just received a nine-one-one call. Report of Assault. One-zero-two Roxbury Drive. The caller says his mother is fighting with his nurse."

"We're on it."

I jam down on the accelerator. Tires squeal. Engines roar. We thunder down the road. I feel like I'm in the middle of a Springsteen song.

We screech to a stop in the driveway made out of interlocking pavers fronting 102 Roxbury Drive. It's a brand-new, three-story, vinyl-sided mansion with bright white deck railings all over the place.

"Caller is Samuel Oppenheimer, age thirteen," reports the radio. "He is still on the line with nine-one-one."

"We are on scene," I say into the radio.

"Will advise nine-one-one."

"Have them tell Samuel to let us in the front door, if he can do so safely."

If not, I'll let Santucci kick at the lock. I'm betting he was paying attention when they taught him how to do that at the Academy.

I toss the radio mic to the floor and swing open the driver side door.

"I'll take the lead," I say.

"Let's roll!" shouts Santucci, sounding totally stoked.

Inside the house, we hear a scream. Female.

And then another, younger voice. Samuel.

"Stop it! The police are right outside!"

I race up the steps to the front porch. Bang on the door. Someone yanks it open on the other side.

Samuel Oppenheimer. He's in a wheelchair and clutching a cordless phone. He looks terrified.

"Over there!" he shouts, pointing to a sunken, white-on-white living room.

I see the back of a raven-haired lady in a purple tracksuit. She is throttling a kinky-haired, younger woman in yellow scrubs who is wildly swinging her arms and trying to kick her way free. But the older woman has her hands locked in a vice grip on the younger woman's throat, and that keeps the nurse far enough away that her slaps, scratches, and kicks don't land.

I move closer.

I can't see the younger woman's face. It's buried beneath a whirlwind of flailing curls.

"Break it up!" I shout.

"Knock it off!" adds Santucci.

I grab hold of the strangler's shoulder.

She snaps her head around. All sorts of chunky gold jewelry clatters on her neck and ears as she shoots me a dark and dangerous look. I half expect her to hiss.

But her brain finally kicks in and she realizes there is a uniformed police officer in her living room with his hand firmly attached to her clavicle.

Now her eyes go all wide and terrified.

She drops her chokehold.

The nurse gags and reflexively brings her hands up to her neck.

"Thank goodness you're here!" says the older woman.

I quickly scan her face. Her hair is jet black, her nose perfect, her skin taut and wrinkle-free. She looks like she wears makeup in her sleep.

"That vile creature attacked me!" she screeches in my face.

"You . . . attacked . . . *me*," gasps the other woman.

"I did no such thing."

"Ma'am?" I say. "I need you to move to the other side of the room."

"This is my home—"

"Now!"

Yeah. I sort of shouted it.

"Mom?" says the boy, up in the higher level in his wheelchair. "Please? Do like he says."

"You heard Officer Boyle," says Santucci. "Move it."

I look over to the nurse.

She's my age. Maybe twenty-seven, twenty-eight. A mountain of dark, curly hair. Olive skin. Chocolate brown eyes that aren't quite dark enough to hide her fear.

And, of course, I know her.

It's Christine Lemonopolous. One of my old girlfriend Katie Landry's best buds.

"Christine?" I say, arching up an eyebrow, hoping for a good explanation.

Her lips quiver into what she probably hoped might end up as a smile. It doesn't.

"Can you breathe?" I ask. "Is your airway clear?"

She nods.

"What's this all about?" I ask.

"I didn't do anything, Danny."

"Liar," snarls the other one.

"I swear on Katie's grave." Christine's voice is raw and raspy. "I didn't do anything!"

Like I said, there's nothing worse than hearing that from an old friend.

Especially when she drags the late, great love of your life into it.

# 2

It's a good thing the McMansion has so many rooms.

It's time to separate the combatants.

The lady of the house is fuming in one corner of the sunken living room. Christine stands in the other. The boy with the phone is parked near the blizzard colored sofa, shaking his head.

I know how he feels.

"Ma'am?" I say to the woman in the designer tracksuit. "Your name, please?"

"Shona Blumenfeld Oppenheimer. Widow of *Arthur* Oppenheimer."

She puts "Arthur" in italics when she says it. I guess I'm supposed to be impressed. I'm not sure why but, then again, I don't know that many impressive people.

"Mrs. Oppenheimer," I say, "I need you to wait in another room."

"Why?"

"He's separating the parties involved in the altercation," snaps Santucci, who, I guess, paid attention in cop class that day. "It's what we do when attempting to ascertain what happened in a dispute such as this one you two got goin' on here."

"You're going to take *her* statement before mine?" Mrs. Oppenheimer flaps a well-toned arm toward Christine.

"No, ma'am." I nod toward the boy. "We need to talk to your son first."

"I'm his mother. I should be there."

"No, ma'am. You should not."

"He's not well. I'm going to call my lawyer."

I give her a confused look. "Why?"

"To make sure everything is . . ." I can tell she's struggling to find the right word. "Legal!"

Found it.

"Don't worry, it will be," says Sal. "Officer Boyle here was trained by John Ceepak."

"Who?" says Mrs. Oppenheimer as she and Santucci finally move out of the living room.

"Biggest overgrown Boy Scout you could ever meet. Come on, I'll tell you all about him . . ."

I grin. Santucci actually handled that pretty well.

"Christine?" I say when they're out of the room.

"Yes, Danny?"

"Your neck okay?"

"It hurts."

"Do you want an ambulance?"

"No. I don't think it will swell up any more."

"How 'bout you wait in the kitchen? Maybe put some ice on it?"

"Good idea."

She leaves and I move into the upper living room. Take a seat in a very comfy, very white chair. The boy in the wheelchair is staring at the phone in his lap. Turning it over and over.

"You're Samuel Oppenheimer?"

"Yes, sir."

"You feeling good enough to talk?"

"Yes, sir."

"Great. So, you're the one who called nine-one-one?"

"Yeah."

"Good for you. Smart move."

Samuel looks up. We make eye contact. "Thanks," he says.

"So," I say with a shrug. "What happened?"

"They got into a fight, I guess. My mom's been sort of stressed lately."

"What do you mean?"

"She and my nurse, Christine, have been getting on each other's nerves. They used to be friendly. Not anymore."

"Christine, Ms. Lemonopolous, she's here a lot?"

"Yes, sir. She lives here."

Oh-kay. A live-in nurse? Not sure where this is going. Christine is curvy and cute. Don't know if she's, you know, dating anybody or even whose team she's playing on. So I just nod a little. Hope Samuel will give me more to work with. He does.

"Christine is just my home health aide. She doesn't really have a place of her own, I guess, and can't afford to find one because she quit her real job, so Mom let her stay here rent-free in exchange for helping me with my feeding tube and, you know, the seizures. She also does housecleaning, the laundry, and I guess you'd call it babysitting if Mom stays out late on a date. Stuff like that."

"So, how long has Christine been living here with you guys?"

"About a year, maybe. I had somebody else before, but I like Christine better."

I press on.

"So, what happened tonight?"

"I dunno. They both went totally ballistic. I was in my room. All of a sudden, I heard shouting. Then something crashed and glass shattered."

I look to the floor. See shards of clear and green glass, not to mention a broken-off wine goblet stem.

"I rolled out here as fast as I could," says Samuel, "and saw the two of them going at it. Christine was kicking at Mom. Mom was grabbing Christine's throat. I told Mom to stop. She told me to, you know, 'eff-off.'"

"That when you called nine-one-one?"

"Yeah. You guys got here fast."

"We caught a break. We were in the neighborhood. You okay staying here tonight?"

He gives me a look. "What do you mean?"

"You sure you'll be safe? If not, we've got places you could go . . ."

"Don't worry. My mom isn't going to strangle me, if that's what you mean."

"Okay. If you feel different, just call nine-one-one. Or, here." I hand him one of my business cards. "Call me. I'll come pick you up."

Samuel cracks a grin.

"Will you turn on those sirens again?"

I grin back. "Roger that."


Next up is Christine in the Kitchen with the Ice Pack.

We're not playing "Clue." She's administering first aid to her neck wounds.

A pair of purple bruises—what Ceepak would call ligature marks—have blossomed where Mrs. Oppenheimer's two hands used to be.

"Do you mind if I take a photo?" I say, gesturing toward her neck.

"No."

I pull out a small digital camera.

"Can you hold your chin up a little?" I say.

Christine does.

I snap some very unflattering photos of her bloated and bruised neck.

"So, what happened?"

"We had . . . a disagreement." Her voice sounds like she spent the night screaming at a Bon Jovi concert.

"About what?"

"Some issues. So, I tried to defuse the situation by walking out of the room. That's when *she* attacked me."

I don't react to that. "So, you live here? Take care of Samuel?"

"Yes. Part-time. He needs help with his G-I tube. And seizures. I'm basically on call all night long. Sleep in the guest room closest to Samuel's bedroom with a baby monitor. On weekends I clean the house and do the laundry. Stuff like that."

"You still do weekdays at Mainland Medical?"

Mainland Medical is the hospital on the far side of the causeway that operates our Regional Trauma Center. It's where the Medevac helicopter took Katie Landry when a sniper who was gunning for me shot her instead. Christine was one of Katie's emergency room nurses.

"No," says Christine, kind of softly. "I left Mainland a while ago."

"Really? What happened?"

"I'd rather not talk about it, Danny. Not right now. Okay?"

"Sure," I say. "Stay here. I need to talk to Mrs. Oppenheimer."

"She'll lie, Danny."

I nod and grin. "Thanks for the tip."

Mrs. Shona Oppenheimer and Officer Santucci are waiting for me out on one of the decks hanging off the back of the house.

11

"Mrs. Oppenheimer?" I say. "What happened here tonight?"

"I wanted to print out a new diet I'd found on line for my sister, but Christine was hogging the printer with paperwork related to her position with Dr. Rosen."

"Dr. Rosen?"

"Arnold Rosen, DDS. The retired dentist who lives in that big house up in Cedar Knoll Heights. It's still the nicest piece of shorefront property on the island. It sits atop a bit of a bluff above the dunes, so Sandy's storm surge didn't swamp it."

I nod. The folks in Cedar Knoll Heights were lucky.

"Dr. Rosen is ninety-four," Mrs. Oppenheimer continues. "Not drilling too many teeth these days."

Santucci chuckles. Guess these two had hit if off in my absence.

"Christine works at the dentist's home during the day, seven to seven. She works here nights."

"So," I say, "you two were fighting over the printer?"

"Hardly," says Mrs. Oppenheimer. "Apparently, some paper became jammed in the feeder, and Christine started using the most foul language imaginable in front of my very impressionable young son."

"Your son was in the room with the printer?" I say because that's not where the son said he was.

"No. He was in his room. But Christine was shouting so loudly, I'm sure he heard every word. That's when I calmly asked Christine to leave."

"But as I understand it, she lives here. Takes care of Samuel."

"That was always a temporary arrangement. I can find other pediatric home health aides. In fact, I already have."

"I can verify that," says Santucci. "She called the, uh . . ."

"AtlantiCare Agency. They're sending someone over right away."

"So, you're evicting Christine?" I say.

"You bet I am," says Mrs. Oppenheimer. "She was like a wild animal. Charged at me. Kicked me in the shin."

12

She rubs her leg so I know which one got whacked.

"I grabbed her by the neck to keep her at bay. But she kept swinging and trying to kick at me. I had to exert a great deal of effort to protect myself. I wouldn't be surprised if I bruised her neck something fierce."

I rub my face a little. "You know, Mrs. Oppenheimer, Ms. Lemonopolous told me a very different story . . ."

"Oh, I'm sure she did. But don't let those big brown eyes fool you, officer. That woman is a crazed monster."

# 3

So, basically, we're in a "she said/she said" situation.

Both sides give completely different versions of what happened and the one semi-independent witness, Mrs. Oppenheimer's son, can only tell us that he saw the two women whaling on each other in his living room.

So I ask all three parties to write up their statements—in separate rooms. Santucci and I will head back to the house (that's what we call the SHPD headquarters) and fill out a "review only" Case Report. In other words, there isn't enough evidence to request an arrest warrant or to charge anybody with anything. Just enough for me to hunt and peck through the paperwork.

Fortunately, Christine agrees to leave the Oppenheimer residence.

"Permanently," sneers Mrs. Oppenheimer before I separate the parties again.

"Do you have someplace safe you can go?" I ask Christine when her former employer is out of the room.

"Yes. I also work for Dr. Rosen. I'll be fine."

Santucci and I head back to the house and do our duty.

I type up our report with one finger on the computer. If I could text it with my thumbs, it would take a lot less time.

A little after eleven, I climb into my Jeep and head for home. On the way, I stop at Pizza My Heart and pick up a slice. With sausage and peppers.

I blame my heartburn on Santucci.

I'm sacked out and dreaming about driving a jumbo jet down the New Jersey Turnpike, looking for a rest stop with a parking lot big enough for a 747, when my cell starts singing Bruce Springsteen's "Land Of Hope And Dreams." That's not part of the dream. That's my ringtone for John Ceepak.

"Hey," I mumble.

"Sorry to wake you."

I squint. The blurry red digits tell me it's 2:57 A.M.

"That's okay. I had to get up to answer the phone anyway."

"We have a situation."

"Is everything okay with Rita? Your mom?"

"Affirmative. However, I was having difficulty falling asleep this evening so I went into the other room to monitor my police scanner."

Yes, some people drink a glass of warm milk or pop an Ambien. Ceepak? He chills with cop chatter.

"Do you remember Katie Landry's emergency room nurse friend Christine Lemonopolous?" he asks.

"Sure. In fact, she was involved in an incident a couple hours ago down in Beach Crest Heights. Santucci and I took statements."

"I heard her name come across the radio. Cam Boyce and Brad Hartman were working the night shift when nine-one-one received a complaint of a woman sleeping in her car outside a residential property in Cedar Knoll Heights. They investigated and identified the 'vagrant' as Christine Lemonopolous."

"Where are you now?"

"Eighteen-eighteen Beach Lane in the Heights."

"I'm on my way."

You may think it odd that Ceepak would run out of his house at two-thirty in the morning to make sure a woman he barely knows is okay.

Not me.

I've been working with the guy for a while now. This is what he does. He jumps in and helps first, asks questions later.

Before he came to Sea Haven, Ceepak was an MP over in Iraq, where he won just about every medal the Army gives out including several for rushing in and saving the lives of guys he didn't know— even when common sense (and my intestines) would've said run the other way.

Cedar Knoll Heights is, as the name suggests, a slightly elevated stretch of land overlooking the beach. That elevation? It saved the million-dollar homes lining Beach Lane in The Heights from Super Storm Sandy's full wrath and fury.

When I reach 1818, I see Ceepak's six-two silhouette standing ramrod straight beside a dinged-up VW bug. It's not Ceepak's ride. He drives a dinged-up Toyota.

The VW is parked in a crackled asphalt driveway leading up to a three-story mansion. The lawn is a tangle of sand, weeds, and sea grass.

"Thanks for joining me," says Ceepak.

I know I must look like crap, having crawled out of the rack with chin drool and bed hair, a problem Ceepak will never know. He's thirty-seven, been out of the Army for a few years, but still goes with the high-and-tight military cut.

Christine waves to me from behind the wheel of her VW.

I wave back.

I haven't seen Christine Lemonopolous in years. Now, we bump into each other twice in one night.

Ceepak motions for me to step out to the street with him.

He wants to discuss something "in private."

"So, you and Santucci sent Ms. Lemonopolous up here to Dr. Rosen's home?"

"Right. She told me Dr. Rosen would let her spend the night."

Ceepak cocks an eyebrow. "In the driveway?"

"No. She's one of his home health aides. I figured he had a spare room for her."

"Perhaps. But Ms. Lemonopolous never requested accommodations from Dr. Rosen. Not wishing to disturb his rest, she chose, instead, to spend the night in her vehicle. Neighbors complained. Boyce and Hartman swung by to arrest her for vagrancy."

"Now what?" I ask.

"I promised Cam and Brad that we would find a more appropriate venue for Christine to spend the night."

And Ceepak is a man of his word.

"Well, she can't go back to where she's been staying," I say. "There was an altercation. And she doesn't have a place of her own."

"So she informed me. Christine has hit hard times, Danny."

"You guys talked?"

Ceepak nods. "Apparently, she left her high-paying position in the trauma center at Mainland Medical."

"Did she say why?"

Ceepak shakes his head. "Nor did I ask. At this juncture, it is none of my business. I have no need to pry into her personal affairs."

Like I said earlier, it's been a rough year for a lot of folks in Sea Haven. Ceepak's wife, Rita, for instance, lost her catering business when all the big parties and beach bashes quit pitching their tents around town—even before Sandy blew into town. She's back waitressing at Morgan's Surf and Turf.

I glance at my watch. 3:22 A.M.

"Christine is due back here for her nursing shift at oh-seven-hundred hours," says Ceepak.

So, she could grab some more Z's—if we can find a place for her to crash for a few hours.

"I was hoping, Danny, that, given your numerous female friends, you might know someone who could take Christine in for the remainder of the night."

I go down a mental checklist. I do have a lot of gal pals. Kara Cerise. Barb Schlichting. Dawn Scovill. Heidi Noroozy. What can I say? It was a long, cold, lonely winter. But I don't know any of those ladies well enough to barge in on them at three-thirty in the morning with a stray cat.

And I can't have her stay at my place. It's tiny. Christine's a curvaceous hottie. Do the math.

Ceepak can't take Christine to his apartment, either. His adopted son, T.J., may be off at the Naval Academy in Annapolis (freeing up the fold-out sofa) but he and his wife (plus Barkley the dog) share a very cramped one-bedroom apartment over the Bagel Lagoon bake shop. Ceepak's mother moved to Sea Haven last winter, but she's in an "adults only" condo complex. And by adults, they mean people over the age of fifty-five without kids or grandkids.

"Should we take her to the house?" I suggest. "Let her bunk in one of the jail cells?"

"Probably not our best option," says Ceepak.

Finally, it hits me. "How 'bout Becca?"

Our mutual friend Becca Adkinson's family runs the Mussel Beach Motel. It's the first week of June. The summer season won't really start for another couple of weeks. They probably have a few vacant rooms.

"Excellent suggestion, Danny."

Yeah. I just hope Becca and her dad agree.

Oh, by the way, Becca's father, Mr. Adkinson? He's the guy who ran for mayor against Hubert H. Sinclair.

The guy who lost.

# 4

Becca says yes.

"I'll escort you over there," I tell Christine.

Hey, I'm wide-awake now. Besides, it's already Saturday. My day off.

Before Ceepak leaves, he tells me to "keep my calendar open" next week.

"I've asked Chief Rossi to assign you to a one-week stint with me starting Monday."

Finally. Good news. "What's up?"

"Annual SHPD pre-season ride inspections. As you know, there are many brand-new amusements on the boardwalk this summer."

True. After Sandy hit, almost all the rides on the boardwalk had to be replaced. You might remember our Mad Mouse roller coaster. Well, Sandy turned it into a water park ride. A photograph of its twisted steel carcass sitting out in the Atlantic Ocean was on the front page of newspapers everywhere in the days after the storm.

"Some of these new rides," Ceepak continues, "may, in my estimation, have criminal records."

"Huh?"

"Sinclair Enterprises has installed a 'Free Fall' on its pier. It is 'used equipment,' Danny, purchased from Fred's Fun Zone, a ragtag amusement park near Troy, Michigan where, according to my research, the Free Fall was responsible for one death and several injuries."

Ceepak. The guy does criminal background checks on amusement park rides.

"Plain clothes?" I say.

"Roger that," says Chief of Detectives Ceepak.

"Awesome."

Baggy shorts and a shirt loose enough to hide a holster. My kind of uniform.

"The rides really don't open till ten or eleven," says Ceepak.

"You want to grab breakfast at the Pancake Palace first? Say, nine-thirty?"

"That'll work. My mother and her senior citizen group are taking a bus trip to the boardwalk Monday. Want to make sure everything is up to snuff."

"You don't think they're going to ride the rides, do you?"

"Actually, with my mother, you never know."

True. Adele Ceepak is what they call a pistol. Or a firecracker. Something that sizzles and pops and does things you weren't expecting.

I escort Christine and her VW up to the Mussel Beach Motel.

Becca, who's bubbly and blonde, meets us out front in a pair of sloppy sweats.

"Saving another damsel in distress, Danny Boy?" she jokes with a yawn. That's her cute way of saying thanks one more time for what went down in the Fun House last summer. It's a long story. Remind me. I'll tell you sometime.

"You remember Katie's friend, Christine?" I say.

"Sure. Rough night, huh?"

Christine smiles. "Something like that."

"You still at the hospital?"

"No. I'm mostly working as a home health aide these days."

"Cool. Well, you must be tumblewacked. Come on. I put you on the first floor . . ."

"How much do we owe you?" I ask.

"It's on the house," says Becca. "Hey, it's what Katie would want."

Becca had been one of Katie Landry's best friends, too. A lot of people were. Katie had been like that.

"Thanks, Beck," I say. "I'll check in with you tomorrow, Christine."

I head toward my Jeep.

"Hey, Danny," calls Becca. "There's two beds in the room if you want to just crash here tonight instead of driving all the way back to your place."

"It'd be fine with me, Danny," adds Christine.

I think about it. For two seconds.

"Good night, Becca. See you tomorrow, Christine."

I don't look back. I just keep on walking.

Hey, it's what Ceepak would do.

# 5

I RACK UP A GOOD SEVEN HOURS OF SACK TIME AND CRAWL OUT of bed a little after eleven.

This is why they invented Saturdays.

I tidy up my apartment. Okay, I pick up the socks and boxer shorts off the floor and toss then into a plastic hamper I should probably replace because I think it used to be white. Now it's sort of grayish.

Hungry, I hop into my Jeep and head off in search of grilled Taylor Pork Roll, eggs, and cheese on a roll with salt and ketchup. It's a Jersey thing.

A little after one, I swing by the tired mansion on Beach Lane. 1818 looks even worse in the sunshine. It's not storm damage. It's time damage.

I'm in a clean polo shirt, shorts, and flip-flops. I also forgot to shave. Like I said, it's Saturday.

When I rap my knuckles on the screen door, Christine answers it. She's in a cheery smock decorated with kittens and puppies, loose fitting green scrub pants, and pink-and-white running shoes. She smiles when she sees it's me. I try not to wince when I notice how much make-up she had to trowel onto her neck to hide her ring of bruises.

"Hey," I say.

"Hey," she whispers back.

"You okay?" I ask, wondering why she is whispering.

"Yeah. Dr. Rosen's still asleep."

I guess when you're ninety-four, the rules about when you should wake up on Saturday are even looser.

"Thanks for setting me up with Becca last night."

"Sure. So, do you have some place to stay tonight?" I'm whispering now, too. Don't want to wake the old guy up.

"Yes. Dr. Rosen is letting me have the other guest bedroom."

"The other one?"

"The night nurse, Monae, already lives here. She's asleep right now, too, because she stays up all night, every night. Makes sure Dr. Rosen doesn't fall again. That's why he needs the twenty-four-hour awake care. He slipped and fell a while ago. Broke his hip on the terrazzo tile floor in the kitchen."

I flinch. Terrazzo is hard stuff. Falling on it would feel like whacking your leg with a bowling ball.

"He went to rehab, did PT. He's still not great on his feet, though. Balance issues. Neuropathy in his feet."

"Did you get everything out of Mrs. Oppenheimer's place?"

"Not yet. Monae's brother and sister are going to help me move the rest. I don't have much. Mostly clothes. Couple books."

"When do you plan to do this?"

"Tonight. Shona won't be home. She has big plans with the Rosens."

Okay. Now I'm confused. "Mrs. Oppenheimer's coming up here while you're down at her place?"

"I'm sorry. Dr. Rosen's son, David, is married to Judith who is Shona's sister. *Those* are the Rosens that Shona's seeing tonight; David and Judith."

"So, did Mrs. Oppenheimer help you land this job with her sister's father-in-law?"

She nods. I get the sense this is something else she just doesn't want to talk about right now.

"Well, I'm free tonight," I say. "If you guys need any help with the move."

"What?" Christine shoots me a sly and dimpled grin. "It's Saturday night, Danny Boyle. Don't you have a hot date?"

"Nope. Not tonight."

"Really?"

I hold up my hand like a Boy Scout. "Scout's honor."

"Good to know."

Yes, I believe Christine Lemonopolous, the lovely Greek goddess, is flirting with me. Not that I mind. Hey, it's Saturday. I'm off-duty. I have a pulse.


Feeling the need to blow off a little steam, I head over to the Sunnyside Playland Video Arcade.

Sunnyside Clyde, the small-time amusement park's mascot, greets me. Clyde is this big, baggy-panted surfer dude with a huge ray-rimmed sun for a head who always wears dark sunglasses. I never understood why. If you're supposed to be the sun, do you really need sunglasses? Why? In case you see yourself in a mirror?

Anyway, Sunnyside Clyde waves when he sees me because the guy sweating inside the giant foam rubber ball is another pal of mine, Josh Grabo.

"Hey, Danny," his voice is muffled by his bright orange padding.

"Hey, Josh."

"Clyde, dude. I'm on duty."

"Right. Sorry."

"You doing anything tonight?" he asks.

I shrug. "Not really."

"Bunch of us are having a kegger over at Mike Malenock's place. Wanna come?"

"Sounds like fun," I say, vaguely remembering when it really would've sounded that way. "But, well, I promised somebody I'd help them move their stuff tonight."

"Well, if you guys get thirsty when you're done with the move, come to the kegger. You goin' in to check out 'Urban Termination II?'"

"Thought I might."

"Don't worry, dude. I cruised by earlier. You're still the high score. All three top spots."

Josh and I knock knuckles. He's wearing these big Hamburger Helper-sized white gloves. It's like I'm hanging out with Mickey Mouse's slightly seedier New Jersey cousin.

The video arcade game Urban Termination II is one of the many ways I hone the cop skill that, not to brag, has made me somewhat legendary amongst the boys in blue up and down the Jersey Shore. I have, shall we say, a special talent.

I can shoot stuff real good.

Sometimes, when we're out at the firing range, Ceepak even calls me "Deadeye Danny." Says I could've qualified as a Sharp-shooter or Marksman if, you know, I had joined the Army first.

Inside Sunnyside Playland, I nail a bunch of bad guys with a purple plastic pistol and listen to the whoops and ba-ba-dings and the voice growling, "die sucker die" every time I blast a thug mugging a granny.

A crowd of kids gathers around me.

It's fun.

For a full fifteen minutes.

I collect the winning tickets that spool out of the machine when I top my top score and hand them off to one of my fans, who only needs "two hundred thousand more points" before he wins a Walkman. Yes, a Walkman. The prizes at Sunnyside Playland aren't what you might call contemporary.

Fun with a gun done, I grab an early dinner at The Dinky Dinghy, the seafood shack famous for its "Oo-La-La Lobster." I go with a Crispy Cape Codwich because you don't need to wear a bib when you eat it.

Then I head for home.

Christine Lemonopolous does not call. Guess she didn't need my help moving her belongings out of Mrs. Oppenheimer's McMansion.

I don't go to Josh and Mike's kegger, either. If I did, I might have to arrest myself for a D and D. That's drunk and disorderly.

And Ceepak would hear about it. Probably on his police scanner two seconds after it happened.

Instead, I just go to bed.

Sunday morning, I resist the urge to swing by Dr. Arnold Rosen's beach bungalow to check in with Christine again. Instead, I actually go to church, something I've started doing a little more often lately—even though my mom and dad aren't in town to make me. They moved to Arizona a few years ago. It's "a dry heat."

I guess I go to church because of The Job.

The deaths I have witnessed.

The deaths I have caused.

After church, I head home, have a couple beers, watch baseball, order a pizza.

I spend a couple more minutes thinking about Christine. Wondering why I never noticed how hot she was before. But then I remember I only ever saw Christine when she was with Katie and gawking at your girlfriend's girlfriends, saying stuff like, "Wow, check out Christine's hooters," would, basically, be stupid, not to mention rude.

I call my mom and dad in Arizona. My brother, Jeffrey, has moved out there, too. He's at their house, smoking Turkey Jalapeno Sausages over pecan logs. I'm told they do this sort of thing in Arizona.

"When are you moving out this way, Danny?" he asks.

*"How about never?"* I want to reply.

But I don't.

Instead, I give the answer I give every time we talk: "We'll see."

Eventually, after my brother tells me how awesome Arizona is and how I could make a ton of money managing his Berrylicious Frozen Yogurt franchise, we say good-bye.

I head to the fridge. Pound down my last beer.

Around nine, I fall asleep on my lumpy excuse for a sofa watching a movie starring Sylvester Stallone. Or Arnold Schwarzenegger. Maybe Bruce Willis.

Sometimes Sundays can do this to a guy.

Make you wonder what the heck you're doing with your life when you could be pumping Berrylicious Frozen Yogurt into swirl cones and starting a family.

So I'm very happy when the clock radio goes off at 6 A.M. and Cliff Skeete's DJ voice booms, "Rise and shine, people. It's Monday morning. Time to put your nose back to the grindstone."

And then, of course, he plays "Manic Monday" by the Bangles.

Me? I'm glad it's Monday.

That means it's Ceepak time.

# 6

I HEAD DOWN TO THE PANCAKE PALACE A LITTLE AFTER NINE.

When I was a teenager, I used to break dishes and glasses there on a regular basis.

I was a bus boy.

The restaurant is pretty crowded, especially for the first week of June. I see mostly locals and a few scattered families. Kids, whose school years ended earlier than everybody else's, are chowing down on stacks of chocolate chip flapjacks, which are, more or less, ginormous chocolate chip cookies swimming in mapley syrup. (By the way, mapley means it's not real maple syrup; if you want that, it costs extra.)

Some grownups go for the "eggs-traordinary omelets," but most of them seem to be gobbling up Belgian waffles topped with Whipped Cream and strawberries, the New York Cheese Cake Pancake, or the Heart Attack Stack: six pancakes with butter, bacon bits, and sausage crumbles sandwiched in between every layer.

It's like the T-shirt says, "My Diet Gets Two Weeks Off Every Summer, Too."

Ceepak is seated in his favorite sunny booth near the front windows. He'll probably order Bran Flakes topped with whatever fruit is in season this week. I'll have black coffee and a toasted bran muffin. Yes, Ceepak has even influenced my morning food choices. No more Hostess Sno-Balls or Honey Buns for me.

There's a father and son in the booth behind Ceepak. The dad is diddling with his Droid phone. The boy is fiddling with the paper from his milk straw. They look like they haven't made much eye contact since maybe Christmas morning.

"I need to go outside to make a very important call, Christopher," the dad says to the boy. "Stay here."

"Yes, Dad."

And the father abandons his son.

Man, the kid looks bored. And sad. Some vacation he's having.

Fortunately, Diana Santossio, who's been waitressing at the Pancake Palace since forever (she used to lead the applause, high-school cafeteria style, whenever I dropped my bus tray), comes over to the table and gives Christopher a small box of crayons.

"Here you go, hon," she says. "You can draw right on the table cloth."

"Really?"

"Yep. It's paper. You can even take it home when you're done eating."

"Cool."

"Have fun, hon."

Donna sashays away while Christopher happily scribbles on the white paper table topper. I slide into the booth across from Ceepak.

"Good morning, Danny. I ordered your coffee. Black, per usual."

"Thanks," I say, noticing that Ceepak has already organized the sweetener packets in their little filing rack: White, Brown, Blue,

Pink, Yellow. I'm also pretty certain the salt and pepper shakers have been inspected, their screw tops found to be properly secured.

"You have a good weekend?" I ask.

"Roger that. We took my mother over to the mainland. She needed a new toilet bowl brush. Target has an interesting and wide selection."

I nod. I'm used to Ceepak's wild and crazy weekend adventures, especially since his mom moved to town. Of all the good sons in the world, John Ceepak might just be the best. Probably because he has to be. His father, Mr. Joseph Ceepak, is the worst excuse for a dad I have ever met. Mr. and Mrs. Ceepak are divorced even though Mr. Ceepak refuses to believe it. Especially after Mrs. Ceepak unexpectedly inherited two point three million dollars from her spinster aunt. When Joe "Sixpack" Ceepak heard about that, he came sniffing around Sea Haven looking for his ex-wife, who, at the time, was living in a "secure location" somewhere in Ohio.

You might wonder why Ceepak still lives in his dumpy one-bedroom apartment since his mom has all that money. I did. Until Ceepak told me, "I have not received financial assistance from either of my parents since I was sixteen, Danny. I do not intend to start now. It is her money. She should spend it as she sees fit."

Ceepak's dad, who never met a pile of money he didn't want to mooch, has, so far, kept the promise he made to us when I saved his sorry life at the same roller coaster where Dominic Santucci lost his. He has stayed out of Sea Haven. But his son tells me we need to be "extra vigilant" and "stand guard" since neither of us would be surprised if Joe Sixpack returned to Sea Haven to harass his ex-wife.

"We hope for the best, Danny," Ceepak likes to say. "But we prepare for the worst."

Like making sure his mom lives in a condo complex with 24-hour security guards and has an armed escort (her son) whenever she goes toilet brush shopping at Target.

"So, how many rides do we need to check out?" I ask.

"All of them," says Ceepak with a grin. "Might take all week."

"Roger that," I say, because, okay, I've been hanging around Ceepak for way too long. Plus, I'm happy to hear we're going to be working together for a solid chunk of time.

My partner is dressed in his standard detective uniform. Khaki cargo pants, L.L. Bean Oxford cloth shirt, striped tie, and light-weight navy blue sport coat. He keeps his gold shield clipped to the front of his belt, his Glock in a small-of-the-back crossdraw holster hidden under the vent flaps of his jacket. His shoes? Sturdy black cop shoes except on the rainy days when he slips on his waterproof Army boots.

I don't get to play detective every day, so I wear my shield on a lanyard around my neck. I keep my Glock at my hip, cowboy style. But since I don't tuck in my blousy Hawaiian shirt, nobody sees it.

"What are you doing, Christopher?"

Phone call finished, Daddy Droid has returned to the booth next to ours. He looks furious.

"Drawing," mumbles his son.

"On the tablecloth?"

"It's paper."

"I don't care. You're making a mess."

"She said I could."

"Who?"

"The lady."

"What lady?" fumes the dad, grabbing up the kid's crayons as quickly as he can. "I don't see any 'lady.'"

The boy looks around the room. Can't find Donna. I'm guessing she's in the kitchen, loading up another tray with twenty plates of food.

"She's not here . . ."

"Because you made her up."

"No, she . . ."

"Don't lie to me, Christopher!"

Ceepak has heard enough. He slides out of the booth. Stands. He towers over Mr. Droid by at least a foot.

This should be fun.

# 7

"YOUR SON IS TELLING YOU THE TRUTH, SIR."

"What? Who are you?"

"John Ceepak. Chief of Detectives. Sea Haven Police Department."

"Excuse me," says the dad, "but this is a private, family matter."

I'm standing now, too. "Donna gave him the crayons."

The dad shakes his head like he's clearing out his ears. "What?"

"The waitress," says Ceepak. "Her name is Donna. She told your son that it would be perfectly fine for him to draw on the paper tablecloth. All the children do it."

"Some adults, too," I toss in because I know one who does. Me.

The boy is looking at Ceepak like Superman just dropped in to the Pancake Palace to protect him from the evil fiend known as Dad, The Crayon Snatcher.

"Well, who exactly gave some minimum wage waitress permission to tell my son what he can and cannot do in my absence?"

"You raise an interesting if somewhat moot point," says Ceepak. "Be that as it may, it does not mitigate the fact that you accused your son of a very serious offense: Lying."

"Is this what you cops do down here? Butt into private, family affairs?"

"We try not to," I say. "But sometimes, well, we just can't seem to avoid it."

See, I know something Poppa Bear doesn't: John Ceepak lives his life in strict compliance with the West Point honor code. He will not lie, cheat, or steal nor tolerate those who do. So, to accuse someone of lying, especially your own son, well, geeze-o, man, that is an accusation that should never be made lightly.

"Come on Christopher." The dad grabs the kid's wrist.

"But . . ."

"We'll pick up frozen waffles at the store."

"I wanted pancakes . . ."

"There's no need for you two to leave, sir," says Ceepak, picking up a napkin to dab at his lips.

"Well, I sure don't want to sit here eating breakfast with Big Brother's nose up my butt."

He means Ceepak and me. We are the police state. The big, bad butt-sniffers.

"Then you are in luck," says Ceepak. "My partner and I were just leaving. Danny?"

"I've got this one." I lay some bills on the table, enough to pay for everything we would've eaten if, you know, we had ever ordered anything besides coffee.

"Have a good day." Ceepak gives the father and son a crisp two-finger salute off his right brow.

Little Christopher salutes right back.

Super Man and I leave the building.

Yes. When you work with John Ceepak, sometimes you miss a meal.

# 8

"SORRY ABOUT THAT," SAYS CEEPAK AS WE HEAD TOWARD THE Boardwalk.

"No biggee. That poor kid needed somebody to stand up for him."

"Indeed he did."

It's not even noon yet, but I can already smell the Italian sausages, green peppers, and onions sizzling on a greasy grill somewhere up ahead. My stomach gurgles so loudly, it sounds like I swallowed a demonic alien.

"Perhaps we can grab a quick bite at one of the boardwalk eateries," suggests Ceepak.

"That'll work," I say. Curly fries, cheesesteaks, and funnel cakes—all part of a complete, nutritional breakfast.

We climb up the steep steps to Pier Two.

"There's a Jumbo Jimmy's cheesesteak place on the other side of Ye Olde Mill," I say.

Ye Olde Mill is probably the oldest ride in all of Sea Haven. Not even a hurricane could knock it out business. A water wheel churns up turquoise blue water to make a gently flowing current that sends small boats drifting *slooooowly* down a lazy stream that's maybe six inches deep.

Since the scenery is pretty lame—like department-store window displays done by lazy gnomes—and the lighting is extremely dim, guys and girls in their tiny two-seater boats don't really have much choice but to start cuddling and canoodling in what has been unofficially called The Tunnel Of Love since 1949.

"Does Jumbo Jimmy's serve fruit?" asks Ceepak when we pass the water wheel.

"I think so. They have those bananas dipped in chocolate. And candy apples."

"John? Daniel?"

It's Ceepak's mother. She's with a group of about a dozen other senior citizens, all of them dressed in plaids and sherbet colors. Some are wearing those visors with the see-through green windowpane in the brim. Each of them holds a string of three tickets, enough to ride Ye Olde Mill.

Looking at Adele Ceepak, you'd never know she's a multimillionaire. She's extremely short, maybe five feet tall, and likes to dress in polyester red, white, and blue outfits with big, brassy belt buckles. Her hair is cut pixie short and is dyed the same golden color as her glasses frames. Mrs. Ceepak also has the brightest, happiest smile of any sixty-something senior citizen I've ever met, especially considering all the dark crap she had to live through before she threw her bum of a husband out the back door with the rest of the trash.

That last bit? That's how Mrs. Ceepak describes her divorce after she's had a glass or two of Chianti, her favorite.

"Hello, Mom," says Ceepak. He leans way down and gives her a kiss on her cheek. The tall genes? Ceepak definitely didn't get them from his mom.

"What are you two boys doing on the boardwalk? Shouldn't you be at work?"

"We are," I say.

"Those are your work clothes? Daniel, you look like a beach bum."

"We're undercover," I whisper.

"Oh." Mrs. Ceepak does that locking your lips with a key thing my grandmother used to do.

"We're here to inspect a few of the rides up and down the boardwalk," explains her son.

"Are they unsafe?"

"We hope not. But if they are, rest assured, we will pull their papers."

"Good for you. How about this Ye Olde Mill? Hank says that's the ride we should all ride first. He even asked me to share a boat with him."

Ceepak arches an eyebrow. "Hank?"

Mrs. Ceepak gestures toward a tall guy with thick white hair and skinny, sinewy legs. He looks healthy, like he plays tennis or rides a bike.

"Hank's a very good dancer," says Mrs. Ceepak. "He calls the Bingo numbers at the Senior Center on Tuesday nights, too. He's something of a celebrity in certain circles."

Ceepak looks like he wants to go over to Hank and say, *"What are your intentions, young man?"* but he doesn't get the chance.

There's a scream. Maybe fifty feet up the pier. A young dude in an Abercrombie & Fitch top, baggy shorts, and high-top sneakers comes tearing up the boards, a jungle print purse flapping by his side.

"He stole my bag! Stop him! Help!"

The kid, who looks vaguely familiar, has his arms pumping and keeps chugging straight at us.

"Halt!" Ceepak shouts, raising his hand like a traffic cop.

When he was an MP over in Iraq, Ceepak used to stop entire tank convoys in downtown Baghdad with his booming voice and a single flick of the wrist.

Too bad the purse-snatcher isn't a tank.

He keeps coming.

"Police!" I holler.

Now the kid stops. Looks left, right, over his shoulder.

"Where, man?" he shouts like I'm on his side.

Ceepak sweeps open his sport coat, plucks that gold shield off his belt, and holds it out at arms length so the sun can flare off its bright and shiny face.

"Stay where you are, young man."

"You heard him," shouts Ceepak's mom. "Stay put."

The kid squints when the badge's reflection pings him in the eye.

He looks around again.

And makes an extremely dumb move.

He dashes toward the back end of the Ye Olde Mill ride. I see him grab hold of the picket fence bordering the unloading dock and hop over it. Two seconds after he disappears, we hear a series of thrashing splashes.

Yes, he is running up the lazy river into The Tunnel of Love.

"I'll follow after him," says Ceepak, because he goes running six days a week, even when he doesn't have to. "Lock down the ride, Danny. Go in the front. Block his means of egress."

"On it."

Ceepak takes off.

"Go, Johnny, go!" This from Mrs. Ceepak. "That's my son."

"He's a good runner," says Hank.

Adele gives that a flick of her wrist. "Aw, he's not even trying."

# 9

I LOOP BACK TO THE FRONT OF THE RIDE.

I flash my badge necklace to the kid sitting up in the operator platform near the bright yellow water wheel. It's churning up frothy waves the color of the cheap blue aftershave they sell at Drinnen's Drug Store.

"Shut down the water wheel," I shout. "Don't send in any boats."

"Dude," he says, sounding like I just woke him up. "There's already a boat in the tunnel . . ."

I think fast.

"Then keep the wheel churning."

Maybe the current will slow the thief down. Maybe the love boat will bumper-car him down the line to Ceepak.

Or maybe our bad guy has a gun.

"No," I say to the operator. "Shut it off."

"Dude?" says the kid, holding up both hands. "On or off?"

"Off!"

The kid shakes his head.

I think he's disappointed in my rapid-fire decision-making abilities.

"Whatever," he mumbles as he bops the red button that freezes the water wheel.

I jump off the loading dock into the shin-deep riverbed.

"Yo, dude!" The kid shouts. "You gotta be in a boat. Insurance rules. No walking in the river. Yo? Dude?"

I slosh forward and duck my head under the arched opening cut into the plywood scene of Bavaria or wherever.

The tunnel is pitch-dark. Nice if you're on a romantic ride with your girlfriend. Not so much when you're on foot.

If I were Ceepak, I'd whip out my pocket flashlight.

But I'm not.

So I use my iPhone. Flick on the flashlight app that uses the tiny camera light to approximate a ten-watt bulb. It's better than nothing.

I pass a scene of cutout elves in pointy caps painting toadstools. Girls probably think it's cute. Guys don't care. At this point, early in the ride, they're just nervous, wondering when they should make their first move.

Up ahead is another dark stretch.

And a gently rocking boat.

I slog up the shallow trough, glad I wore cargo shorts to work today. Until the water splashing up my legs soaks through the thigh pockets and turns them into drooping water balloons.

With the current switched off, I'm moving faster than the boat in front of me. As I get closer, I hear smooching. And moans. And a playful "Slow down, Kevin," giggled by a girl.

Whose voice I recognize. Heidi Noroozy. We dated. Once.

"Excuse me, guys," I say, when I reach the stern.

The startled lovers spring apart. Nearly capsize their boat.

"Danny?"

"Hey, Heidi."

"Uh, hi." She starts buttoning stuff.

"Hey, Kevin." I recognize her new man. Kevin Tipple. He works at Boardwalk Books. Guess he's on his morning break.

I find that, if I squeeze along the starboard side of the little red dinghy, I can actually creep my way downstream. When I reach the boat's bow, I turn around. "Stay here, you two. There could be trouble up ahead."

"Is this a new part of the ride?" asks Kevin. "Like when the robbers stop the train in Wild West World?"

I think Kevin spends a little too much time in the fiction section of his store.

"Just stay here."

Kevin and Heidi nod. Their eyes go so wide they could both play Bambi in one of the ride's cheesy scenes.

"Halt!" I hear Ceepak's voice ringing off the walls in the tunnel up ahead of me.

"Forget it, po-po," shouts the purse-snatcher, who sounds like he could definitely use an attitude adjustment.

I hurry down the river. Make my way up to the next painted display. Geese. Talking to Little Red Riding Hood, a wart-nosed witch, and Pepe Lepew. What the diorama's story is supposed to be, I haven't a clue. I guess the plywood jigsaw cutouts were on sale, maybe in one of those yards where they sell bent-over-gardeners-flashing-their-bloomers as lawn decorations.

I round a bend.

And here comes the kid in the A&F jersey, a lady's purse slung over his shoulder. The bag does not match his shiny basketball shorts.

"Stop," I say, flashing my iPhone light in his face. "We've got you surrounded."

(Ever since I became a cop, I've always wanted to say that.)

"Hands over your head," adds Ceepak, splashing up behind the kid with a Maglite locked in one fist, his other hand clasping his wrist to steady the light.

The kid squints. Stares at me hard.

He swings around to check out Ceepak then turns back to me. "Wassup, braw?"

Of course he looked familiar. It's Ben Sinclair. Our honorable mayor's dishonorable son. We've dealt with him before. Several times, actually.

"Why you two always be harassing me?" he whines. "I didn't do nothing wrong, dawg."

Ben Sinclair is not a gangsta rapper. He's a rich white kid who once tried to strap a big subwoofer to the back of his scooter so he could cruise around Sea Haven pretending to be ghetto.

"You were resisting arrest," says Ceepak.

"Cuffs?" I ask.

"That'll work," says Ceepak, sliding the purse off Ben's shoulder while I work the kid's hands behind his back.

"Yo! That be police brutality, po-po."

"No, Benjamin," says Ceepak. "Those be handcuffs."

I can't help but crack up. Ceepak made a funny.

The three of us wade down Ye Olde Mill stream.

Ceepak even starts whistling.

It's a Springsteen tune, of course. "Tunnel Of Love."

# 10

Mrs. Ceepak is waiting with the lady whose purse Ben snatched when we come out of Ye Olde Mill.

"See, dear?" she says. "I told you my son and his friend would get you your bag back. I'm so proud of you, Johnny. You, too, Daniel."

"Thanks," we both say. For an instant, I feel like Ceepak and I are two years old and we both just made a good boom-boom on our potty training seats.

The Murray brothers, Dylan and Jeremy, swing by the boardwalk in their patrol car to process Ben Sinclair.

"He'll be out in under an hour," mutters Jeremy.

"Forty-five minutes," seconds his brother.

"We appreciate you guys handling this," says Ceepak.

Dylan Murray smirks at my soaked shorts and Ceepak's soggy pants.

"So what's with you two? Your adult diapers leaking again?"

"Something like that," says Ceepak with a grin.

"We took a turn in the dunk booth," I say. "Over on Pier Two."

"Wish I had known," says Dylan. "Would've bought a dozen balls."

"Yeah, it would've taken you a dozen to finally hit the target."

Yes, this is what we do. We bust each other's chops. It makes knowing that the mayor's bratty kid is going to skate free, no matter what he did, a little easier to stomach.

Ceepak and I follow the Murrays back to the house in my Jeep and hit the locker room where, fortunately, we each have a dry pair of pants. And socks. When I take my wet ones off, my toes look like yogurt-covered raisins. They're curdled worse than cottage cheese.

We grab a quick bite at the Yellow Submarine, this sandwich shop on Ocean Avenue (where you can get Mean Mister Mustard and Glass Onions on anything), then head back to the boardwalk and Pier Two.

On the drive over, Ceepak fills me in on the Free Fall ride's criminal background.

"The Sea Haven operators are calling their ride 'The Stratos-FEAR.' In Michigan, it was known as 'Terminal Velocity,' a name that, unfortunately, it soon lived up to. A fourteen-year-old girl was killed after falling one hundred and forty feet from her seat as it plummeted down the drop tower at a rate of descent approaching fifty miles per hour."

"What happened?"

"According to witnesses, the girl pitched forward while the ride was in free fall. She landed face-down on the pavement at the base of the tower; died on the way to the hospital."

"Was there an investigation?"

"Quite an extensive one. Officials at the amusement park stated that the victim's seat should not have been occupied because it did not have a functioning restraint system."

"What? The seat belt was broken?"

"Actually, it was the shoulder restraint. She was sitting in an open-air car. The only thing holding her in was the padded chest harness over her head and shoulders. The victim's restraint did not lock properly. The force of the drop caused it to flip up. The final report faulted maintenance workers for failing to designate that particular seat as being 'out of service' on the day of the accident."

"That's it? Some guy forgot to tape a sign on the girl's seat?"

"Management at the Michigan amusement park also conceded that all the restraints on the ride should have been checked manually by ride operators before the cars were hoisted skyward."

*Well, duh,* I think.

In Sea Haven, high school and college kids get summer jobs on the boardwalk running the rides. There are always a few whose only job is to walk around and jiggle everybody's safety bars before they signal the operator to hit the GO button. Well, that's the way it's supposed to work, if the ride is owned and operated by people who care about safety and doing the right thing.

The "brand new" StratosFEAR Free Fall?

Not so much.

The owner is Sinclair Enterprises.

As in Mayor Hugh Sinclair.

And as we approach the recycled ride, I see that the mayor's son, Ben, is the guy sitting in the control booth, his hand poised over the big green GO button.

Apparently, his dad's lawyers were working extra-hard today. They got him sprung in record time.

# 11

LUCKILY, THERE IS A BRIGHT YELLOW CHAIN BLOCKING ACCESS to the StratosFEAR, so Ben can't really take anybody for a ride.

A sign reading "Opening Soon!" dangles off the barrier.

"We'll see about that," mumbles Ceepak as he unclasps the chain.

We enter the switchbacks where customers will patiently wait to have the crap scared out of them.

The base of the StratosFEAR is painted with white, wispy clouds filling a blue sky. A squared-off white tower, with criss-crossing diagonal support struts and trusses, rises 140 feet to a blinking lightning-bolt pole topper.

A fresh-faced guy, maybe thirty, wearing a bright blue polo shirt and khaki pants, an accordion file tucked under his arm, comes ambling around the base. He sees us. Gives us a friendly finger wave. Then turns to the mayor's son in his controller seat.

"Blast her off, Ben."

"Whatever."

Ben, who's also dressed in a bright blue polo shirt with a "StratosFEAR" logo embroidered where the polo pony usually gallops, slaps his chunky green button.

Twelve empty chairs—three on each side of a boxy blue car—slowly elevate up the tower. The shoulder restraints are in the down and locked position.

Ceepak and I crane our necks to watch the ride in action.

Not that there's much action to watch. Just that clump of chairs slowly climbing the tower.

"When the car finally reaches the top," says Professor Ceepak, "it will pause momentarily. And remember, Danny, a body at rest tends to stay at rest."

True. When I'm on the couch, I tend to stay on the couch.

"The cable holds the chairs, the chairs hold the riders. So when the mechanism suspending the car lets go, the chairs will fall but there will be a slight delay before your body feels it is also falling."

"So you think you're falling all on your own. That you're not even sitting in your seat."

Ceepak nods.

"What fun."

"Only if you enjoy experiencing vertical acceleration upwards of three G's."

The empty ride reaches the blinking lightning bolt. It pauses and just hangs up there for a second.

And then, BOOM!

If there were people riding the ride, they'd be screaming their heads off and kicking their dangling legs. Because the thing plunges 120 feet in eight seconds flat. Your stomach would be in your nose, which is why you should never eat funnel cakes right before riding this ride. There is a quick puff of white mist. The car slows. Impressively. Then it eases itself down to the loading platform.

"Pretty neat, huh, guys?" cries the over-caffeinated dude as he bounds over to greet us. He shoots out his hand to Ceepak. Ceepak shakes it.

"Detective Ceepak. We've been expecting you."

"This is my partner, Danny Boyle."

"Well, hey there, Danny. I'm Bob."

I knew that already. It says "Bob" on his plastic nametag.

Ceepak pulls a sheaf of paper out of his sport coat's inside pocket. "As you may know, Mr. . . ."

"Please, Detective—call me Bob."

"Very well. As you may know, Bob, this ride was formerly erected at a small amusement park in Troy, Michigan."

Bob clucks his tongue. "Tragic what happened. But that's ancient history. Water under the bridge."

*Guts on the ground*, I want to add, but don't.

"We've cleaned the ol' gal up. Given her a new paint job. Jazzed up the lights and sound effects. Added some additional safety devices."

Bob hands Ceepak the thick accordion file.

"Here's all our paperwork. The engineers' reports. Structural analysis. Maintenance reports. Everything the state requires for a passed-with-flying-colors pre-season, pre-operational inspection. As you'll see, Sinclair Enterprises is in full compliance with title five, chapter fourteen-A of the New Jersey Administrative Code as it pertains to Carnival and Amusement Rides."

Bob is rocking back on his heels, proud to be the smartest kid in the class.

*Ooh. He memorized a law book.*

Ceepak flips through the documents tucked into little slots inside the file holder. He skims and scans them. Lets Bob sweat some.

"Good work, Bob," Ceepak finally announces. "Everything seems to be in order."

"Thank you. Now, if you fellows are on the same page . . ."

"How did you score on section five-fourteen–A dash four point eight?" says Ceepak.

"Come again?"

"The section pertaining to training and certification of ride operators." Ceepak nudges his head toward the control booth where Ben Sinclair sits, thumbing a text message into his phone.

"I believe the State Inspector was fine with our setup. Should be a paper in there . . ."

"Is Benjamin your proposed ride operator?"

"Yes. And you guys can thank me later for finding a way to keep him off the streets this summer. I hear he had another run-in with the law this morning? Some kind of misunderstanding in the Olde Mill?"

"No, Bob," says Ceepak. "There was no misunderstanding. Benjamin Sinclair attempted to snatch a purse. He then resisted arrest. He should be sitting in a jail cell right now, contemplating the consequences of his actions, not operating a potentially dangerous ride."

"Whoa, ease up, detective. There's nothing 'dangerous' about this ride."

"Mr. and Mrs. Ryan would disagree."

"What? Who are they?"

"The parents of the fourteen-year-old girl who died on this Free Fall ride when it was called the 'Terminal Velocity' up in Michigan."

Ceepak lets that sink in as he pulls a laminated card out of another sport-coat pocket.

"Was Benjamin Sinclair trained by Sandusky Amusements, the manufacturer of this ride?"

"Huh?"

"Does he have a certification from the manufacturer, Sandusky Amusements, in a format prescribed by the New Jersey Department of Community Affairs?"

"They didn't really ask for anything like that . . ."

Ceepak turns to face the control booth.

"Mr. Sinclair?" he calls out.

Ben is so startled, he nearly drops his cell phone.

"What?" It's amazing how he can make one word have so much snarky attitude.

Ceepak glances down again at his laminated card. "What is the weight limitation on this ride?"

"Huh?"

"The weight limitation."

"You don't have to answer that, Benjamin," says Bob.

"Yes, he does," says Ceepak. "Mr. Sinclair? The manufacturer's suggested weight limitation?"

Sinclair shrugs. "I dunno. Two fatties and one dude with a big butt?"

Ceepak turns to face Bob again.

"You will not be opening your ride any time soon."

"Wait a minute . . . the State. . . ."

"We will inform the State of your failure to comply with five-fourteen-A dash four point eight."

"Do you know how much money . . ."

"I'm not interested in financial details. But, rest assured, Bob, this ride will remain closed until such time as you hire a certified operator who has been trained by the manufacturer to operate the ride in accordance with the manual and any supplemental safety bulletins, safety alerts, or other notices related to operational requirements."

Poor Bob. Ceepak memorized more of the rulebook than he did.

"Danny?"

"Sir?"

"We're done here."

We turn to leave.

"Sore losers!" mutters Bob.

We turn back around.

"I beg your pardon?" says Ceepak.

"I know what's going on here. You two are still upset about the election. First you haul Hugh's kid off to jail on a trumped-up charge. Now this crap about operator certificates? Face it, boys, you backed the wrong horse. Adkinson lost. Sinclair won. Get over it."

Ceepak simply smiles.

"Hire a certified operator, Bob."

"We will."

"Then it's all good."

And this time when we turn to leave, we turn and leave.

All the other rides we inspect during the week pass, even the ones owned by Sinclair Enterprises.

His other operators all know their height requirements and weight limitations. "Two fatties and one dude with a big butt" is never the correct answer.

After work on Friday, Ceepak invites me to join him at his mother's condo for dinner.

"If you have no other plans this evening."

I don't. So I do.

Ceepak's wife, Rita, is working the Friday night dinner rush at Morgan's Surf and Turf, so it'll just be Ceepak, Adele, and me.

Mrs. Ceepak lives in an Active Adult Retirement Community called The Oceanaire. You have to check in at the gatehouse and be announced before the guards will even let you drive along the winding road that snakes around The Oceanaire's clubhouse and meanders through its manicured landscape of 25 semi-identical cape-style homes.

Mrs. Ceepak is waiting for us on the front porch of her unit. It's brand-new; neat and tidy.

"You like spaghetti and meatballs, Daniel?" she says when we climb out of my Jeep.

"Yes, ma'am," I say.

"Good. I know John does. Come on in. Let's eat. And then you boys need to help me find a good lawyer."

# 12

"WHY EXACTLY DO YOU NEED A LAWYER, MOTHER?" CEEPAK asks as we pass around the wooden salad bowl that has its own wooden salad-tossing forks.

I wonder if I'll ever own the kind of stuff Mrs. Ceepak has in her snug and cozy little home. Silverware that actually matches. Serving bowls. Drinking glasses that aren't movie souvenirs from Burger King. A framed needlepoint sampler and Princess Diana plates hanging on the walls.

Do you get the complete home starter kit when you finally decide to grow up and settle down? Or do you just collect stuff along the way?

"The lawyer's not for me, John," says Mrs. Ceepak as she passes the breadbasket, which is actually a basket lined with a checkered cloth to keep the bread warm. "It's for a friend of mine's caregiver. A gentleman named Arnold Rosen."

"The one who lives on Beach Lane?"

"That's right. Do you know him? He's ninety-four. Comes with his nurse to our afternoon bingo games at the senior center."

"Is the nurse named Christine?" I ask.

"Yes! Do you boys know her, too?"

"Yes, ma'am. She's a friend of a friend."

"Danny knows just about everybody in Sea Haven," says Ceepak.

"Well, this Christine is very pretty, Daniel. Has those dark Mediterranean features. Big brown eyes. Nice figure, too. From what I've picked up at the bingo games, she's a single gal. You should ask her out on a date. Nothing too flashy. Maybe just coffee or a light lunch. Definitely not a movie. You don't really get to chat at the movies . . ."

Across the table, Ceepak is grinning at me.

I guess now that her son is all settled down, it's Adele Ceepak's mission to fix me up so I can start collecting matching salad bowls of my own.

"Something to think about," I mumble and pop a plum tomato into my mouth so I don't have to say anything else.

"Why, exactly, does Christine need a lawyer?" asks Ceepak.

"Oh, some nonsense about attacking a former employer."

Okay. I put down my salad fork. "Mrs. Shona Oppenheimer?"

"That's right. Do you know her, too, Daniel?"

"Not really. I was on duty last Friday night and caught a call to investigate an altercation at the Oppenheimer home between Mrs. Oppenheimer and Ms. Lemonopolous."

"Danny and his partner were the first on the scene," adds Ceepak.

"Then you know this is all a bunch of hooey. No way did a sweet girl like Christine Lemonopolous 'attack' this Mrs. Oppenheimer. But Mrs. Oppenheimer, whose late husband I hear was a big Wall Street muckety-muck, has a boatload of money and bamboozled some judge into issuing what they call a TRO against Christine."

"A TRO is a Temporary Restraining Order," explains Ceepak.

"Oh. So it's not permanent?"

"Not until there is a formal hearing, which must take place within ten days of the filing of the TRO."

Ceepak knows a thing or two about how restraining orders work in the state of New Jersey. He should. He had one issued against his drunken father the first time Joe "Sixpack" Ceepak stumbled into town.

"Well, I want Christine to have the best lawyer in the state of New Jersey," says Mrs. Ceepak. "Do you boys know any crackerjack criminal defense attorneys? Because that's what Dr. Rosen says Christine is going to need to beat this thing. He says Mrs. Oppenheimer is probably assuming that Christine won't have the financial means to defend herself so she can just steamroll right over the poor girl."

Ceepak leans back from his mountain of spaghetti and erects a two-handed tapping finger tent under his nose. This is what he does sometimes when he thinks.

I use the free time to spear a crouton.

"If I were in a similar predicament," Ceepak finally says, "I would want Harvey Nussbaum to defend me."

Ceepak's right. Nussbaum is a pit bull. I've seen his ads on a couple benches up and down Ocean Avenue. *"I Turn Wrongs Into Rights!"* is his slogan. His mascot is a snarling bulldog wearing one of those curly lawyer wigs the barristers wear over in England.

"Good," says his mother. "Let's hire this Harvey Nussbaum."

"Wait a second," I say. "You want to pay for Christine's lawyer?"

"Heavens, yes. Somebody has to! I'm sure she's earning little more than minimum wage working for Dr. Rosen. She can't afford a lawyer. The girl doesn't even have a home of her own. She's living in Arnie's house in a guest bedroom."

"Mother," says Ceepak, "an expert criminal defense attorney such as Harvey Nussbaum can cost upwards of three hundred dollars per billable hour."

"So? I'm rich, remember?"

"Yes, ma'am."

"Besides, this is what Aunt Jennifer would want me to do with all that money she left me. See that sampler on the wall?"

"Yes," I say. "I was admiring it earlier."

"Well, it originally belonged to Aunt Jennifer. Did you read what it says, Daniel?"

"No. I couldn't really make out the words . . ."

Mrs. Ceepak pushes back her chair.

"I'll get it, Mother," says her son.

"Thank you, dear."

Ceepak goes to the wall and carefully lifts the framed sampler off its hook.

"Read it," says his mom.

Ceepak's not much on making speeches (another reason he hated being Chief of Police so much). But he does what his mother tells him to.

He reads the needlepointed words:

> *"Do all the good you can,*
> *By all the means you can,*
> *In all the ways you can,*
> *In all the places you can,*
> *At all the times you can,*
> *To all the people you can,*
> *As long as ever you can."*

Okay. I think I finally know how Ceepak became Ceepak. He inherited it from his Great Aunt Jennifer.

"That's a quote from John Wesley," says Mrs. Ceepak. "He wasn't a Catholic but, still, it's a good prayer."

"Yes, ma'am," says Ceepak.

"So you'll call this Harvey Nussbaum for Christine?"

"Danny and I will pay Ms. Lemonopolous a visit tomorrow. We will advise her of your generous offer and see if that is how she would like to proceed."

"Good. Now eat your spaghetti before your meatballs get cold."

And, once again, Ceepak and I both do like his mother says.

# 13

IF I EVER NEEDLEPOINT A SAMPLER TO HANG ON MY WALL, I think it'll be these lyrics from Bruce Springsteen's "The Ghost Of Tom Joad":

> *Wherever there's somebody fightin' for a place to stand*
> *Or a decent job or a helpin' hand*
> *Wherever somebody's strugglin' to be free*
> *Look in their eyes Mom you'll see me.*

From the live version, of course—the one with Tom Morello from Rage Against The Machine wailing on the fuzz-box electric guitar solos; not Bruce's original acoustic version off the *Nebraska* album.

So, first thing Saturday morning, I text Christine to let her know Ceepak and I want to swing by and talk with her about the TRO, maybe even lend her a "helpin' hand."

"DO YOU GUYS NEED A COPY?" she texts back.

"COULDN'T HURT," I thumb to her.

"OK. C U IN A FEW."

I swing by the Bagel Lagoon to pick up Ceepak.

He's sitting with Rita and their dog, Barkley, at the bottom of the attached staircase that leads up to their apartment.

"Hey, Danny," says Rita.

"Hey."

Barkley doesn't bark. He slumps to the ground. And farts. Barkley is old.

Ceepak fans the air in front of his face. "Sorry about that."

"That's okay," I say. "All I smell are the onions and garlic coming out of the kitchen's exhaust fan."

Rita knuckle-punches Ceepak in his bulging arm muscle. "See? I told you not to let Barkley have a bite of your bagel."

"My bad," says Ceepak. He raises a brown paper sack. "Thought we'd take Christine and Dr. Rosen some fresh-baked bagels this morning."

"Sounds like a plan. They're expecting us."

"Then it's all good."

Ceepak kisses Rita.

"This won't take too long," he says when they finally break.

"Hurry home."

"Roger that."

And they kiss again. I look up and pretend like I'm fascinated by the Bagel Lagoon's gutter system or something. Ceepak and Rita? They don't need a Tunnel of Love. They smooch whenever and wherever they feel like smooching.

Even if Barkley cuts the cheese.

Which, of course, he does.

Onions and garlic, again.

With a hint of pumpernickel.

On the ride over to Dr. Rosen's house, Ceepak drifts into his super-serious analytical mode.

"You say Mrs. Oppenheimer was strangling Christine when you and Santucci entered her home?"

"That's what it looked like to me. The ligature bruises on Christine's neck were so bad, I made a photographic record for evidence—in case we ever needed it."

"Good crime-scene technique, Danny."

"Hey, don't forget, I was trained by the best."

Ceepak, of course, totally ignores the compliment.

"Mrs. Oppenheimer was strangling Christine," he muses, "yet she is the one requesting the restraining order? Curious."

"She probably wants to beat Christine to the punch; stop Christine from requesting a restraining order against *her*."

"It's a possibility, Danny."

I can tell that this case, if we can call it that, intrigues him. Ceepak's a lot like Sherlock Holmes. He's not happy unless his big brain is busy noodling out a solution to a puzzling problem.

A very pretty African-American woman, about the same age as Christine, greets us at the door.

She's wearing royal blue nurse's scrubs and toting a plastic pill organizer; a big one with 28 compartments. I'm guessing Dr. Rosen's on a lot of medications—maybe one for every year of his life.

"Are you Danny?" she asks.

"That's right. And this is my partner, John Ceepak."

"I'm Monae Dunn," she says with a smile. She has a good one. Her long, straight hair is pulled back with a headband the same bright blue as the rest of her uniform.

"Is Christine here?" asks Ceepak. Probably because he isn't busy admiring Monae's body like some people I know.

"No. She ran over to Kinko's, so I'm covering. Trying to get Dr. Rosen's medicines organized. You ever know anybody to need so many pills? I bet this blue one is to prevent him from having side effects from this green one." She sees Ceepak's brown paper bag. "Did you boys bring bagels?"

"Yes, ma'am," says Ceepak. "Fresh-baked."

"Uhm-hmm," she says knowingly. "Well don't just stand there letting them go all cold. Come on in. Arnie's on the phone with his son Michael. Michael lives in Hollywood. He's a gay."

Ceepak and I just nod.

"They're on speakerphone because Arnie refuses to put in his hearing aids when he knows company is coming."

We follow Ms. Dunn into the house, which looks like it hasn't been redecorated since 1960-something. Except for the walls. Those looks like an art museum dedicated to a single subject: the life and times of a blonde-haired, blue-eyed boy with a fantastic smile. There must be over two dozen framed photographs of the same shaggy-haired kid. Blowing out birthday candles. Playing baseball. Riding a BMX bike. At Disney World. Sea World. The Wizarding World of Harry Potter. LEGOLAND.

I have a feeling the blonde boy is Dr. Rosen's grandson, even though he's so good-looking that he could also be the kid who came with the picture frames.

We move into what I'm guessing used to be the dining room. Now there is a hospital bed set up where the table used to be—a look that doesn't really fit in with the whole New England seaside cottage style of the rest of the house. I notice a couple Dentist figurines set up on a sideboard. Most have to do with yanking teeth out of mouths with pliers.

Dr. Rosen is sitting in a wheelchair near the hospital bed and talking into a cordless phone.

"Arnie?" blurts Monae. "Visitors. Christine's police officer friends." She reaches for Ceepak's bagel bag. "Let me put those in the kitchen . . ."

She leaves and Dr. Rosen raises a hand to let us know he'll be with us shortly.

The former dentist looks a little weary and shrunken as he slumps forward in his wheelchair. He's wearing a navy blue Adidas jogging suit and Velcroed running shoes. His hair is white and neatly combed to the side. His upper lip sports a trim and very dignified mustache. There is an oxygen tank strapped into a hand trolley next to his wheelchair. Clear plastic tubing runs from the canister's regulator valve up to a thin nosepiece jammed up into his nostrils.

"Michael?" Dr. Rosen says to the phone. "I have visitors. Exalted members of the local constabulary."

He shoots us a wink. And I can tell, the guy might be ninety-four, but he's still sharp, with it, and kind of funny.

"Okay, Dad," says the voice on the speakerphone. "But seriously, call the guys at Best Buy. They'll come over and install it for you."

My eyes drift over to an adjoining room where I see the unopened cardboard carton for a Panasonic TC-P55ST50—their 3-D, high-def TV with a 55-inch-wide plasma screen. I also see unopened Amazon and Barnes and Noble boxes stacked on the couch. And on the floor.

"It's a very generous gift, Michael," says Dr. Rosen. "But . . ."

"No buts. I gave Best Buy my credit card number. They'll hook up the satellite dish, too."

Okay. Now I'm drooling like Homer Simpson in a doughnut factory.

"But," says son Michael on the speakerphone, "the guys from Best Buy can't do your exercises for you. Did Monae set up the recumbent bike?"

"Yes, Michael. She and Christine put it in my bedroom."

"Good. It's a Monark. Excellent for rehab patients."

"Michael?"

"Yeah?"

"The girls did a Google on the bike. Did it really cost you twenty-six hundred dollars?"

"I don't know. I'll have to ask my accountant. I just told my people to get you the best low-impact exercise machine on the market because your doctors want you exercising."

"But twenty-six hundred dollars . . ."

"Call it an early Father's Day gift. Oh, here's another one: I'm flying home to New Jersey next weekend!"

The expression on Dr. Rosen's face?

I don't think he's looking forward to his son's visit.

# 14

DR. ROSEN LOOKS UP FROM THE PHONE WITH AN EMBARRASSED smile, then raises his hand to let us know he won't be on the phone very much longer.

"Well, that's terrific, Michael. It'll be great to see you again."

"We wrapped our final episode last night. Thought it might be fun to spend some time with you. Whip those gals of yours into shape."

"Hiya, Michael!" This from Monae, who has come back into the dining room with a raisin bagel slathered with peanut butter.

"Hiya, sweetheart. You taking good care of my pops?"

"*Your* pops? Sorry, Michael. Christine and me? We're adopting him."

Michael laughs. Dr. Rosen laughs. Ceepak and I smile. It's a regular Hallmark moment.

"And Dad?" says Michael. "Andrew and I have some exciting news to share with you."

"Oh, really? What is it?"

"Uh, uh, uh. No cheating. I need to tell you this news in person."

"Very well. Will Andrew be coming with you?"

There is a long pause.

"No, Dad. Andrew is busy."

"Oh, I'm sorry to hear that. Well, give him my best. I'm sorry we won't get the chance to see him this trip, but I understand—professional commitments come first."

"Yes, Dad."

Okay, I'm not a voice analysis expert, but Michael Rosen doesn't sound as happy as he did two minutes ago.

"Love you, son," says Dr. Rosen.

"See you next Friday," says Michael. And then he must jab a button on his phone because we're hearing nothing but dial tone.

Dr. Rosen holds out the telephone. Monae takes it.

"It's this button here, sir. The red one with the little phone picture on it. That turns it off."

"Thank you, Monae." Dr. Rosen wheels a couple inches closer to Ceepak and me. "So sorry to keep you fellows waiting. That was my youngest son, Michael. A very important television producer out in Hollywood. Very successful. Six Emmy Awards. Several other professional citations. You're Adele Ceepak's son John, right?"

"Yes, sir."

"She's shown me photographs. And let me just say, she is *extremely* proud of you."

"And I of her, sir."

"Attaboy. Good for you. Monae?"

"Yes, Arnie?"

"Have you offered our guests a glass of lemonade or, perhaps, a Stewart's root beer?"

She turns to us. "You want a root beer or lemonade?"

"No, thank you," says Ceepak.

I hold up my hand. "I'm good."

"You want a bagel, Arnie?"

"We have bagels?"

"The policemen brought 'em. They're warm."

"Yes, dear. A bagel would be nice."

Monae leaves again. She has a sassy way of walking out a door. Reminds me of the motion of the ocean.

"So, gentlemen," says Dr. Rosen, "you are conversant with Christine's unfortunate situation, I take it?"

"Yes, sir," I say.

"However," says Ceepak, "to be clear, we are here this morning only as concerned individuals. We are not operating in our official law-enforcement capacities."

"Of course, of course." Dr. Rosen shakes his head. "I can't believe Judge Guarnery signed the TRO. He used to be a patient of mine. Worst overbite I ever saw."

"Well, sir, the TRO is only the first step in the process. Even when a Temporary Restraining Order is issued under a judge's signature, there must be a hearing on the complaint within ten days."

"And do you gentlemen have any suggestions as to how Christine can best prepare for this hearing?"

"It might be advisable for her lawyer to subpoena the police report for the incident in question. Request any and all available evidence gathered at the scene."

I grin. Ceepak's hinting at those neck photos I took.

Dr. Rosen sighs. "Her lawyer. Unfortunately, young Miss Lemonopolous is not in a financial position to retain competent counsel. She simply can't match Mrs. Oppenheimer's monetary resources. And I can't loan her the money, as I can't be seen as taking her side in this matter—not if I wish to keep the peace with my daughter-in-law, Judith."

"Who's Mrs. Oppenheimer's sister," I say.

"Ah. I see you are aware of my predicament. I do, of course, have several friends at temple who are lawyers, highly respected members of the bar. I myself work with Steven Robins, a senior partner at Bernhardt, Hutchens, and Catherman. However, as I stated, I can't really assist Christine without incurring the justified wrath of my son's wife, Judith."

"We're thinking about hiring Harvey Nussbaum," says Ceepak.

Dr. Rosen nods. "An excellent if prohibitively expensive idea."

"My mother has offered to pay Ms. Lemonopolous's legal bills."

"Really? That's extremely generous. But if I may, why would she be willing to do such a thing?"

I almost say *Because of this antique needlepoint thing her dead aunt gave her,"* but I don't.

"Because," says Ceepak, "what Mrs. Oppenheimer is attempting to do offends my mother's innate sense of justice. Mrs. Oppenheimer has to know that if this restraining order sticks, if Christine cannot have it expunged from her record, it will be impossible for her to ever return to her former job at Mainland Medical."

"You are correct," says Dr. Rosen. "If Christine loses this fight, her career and, quite possibly, her life will be ruined. It is a mitzvah, what your mother is doing."

According to my friend, Joe Getzler, a mitzvah is a good deed done from religious duty. And according to Joe, it doesn't matter which religion, either.

The front door opens.

Christine, smiling brightly, comes into the dining room.

"Ah, Christine!" says Dr. Rosen. "Good news. It seems, my dear, that you have found your guardian angel!"

# 15

Turns out that the law offices of Harvey Nussbaum and Associates are open Saturdays for "your convenience."

In the afternoon, Monae Dunn and her sister Revae, who dropped by for a visit, agree to keep an eye on Dr. Rosen so Christine can go with Ceepak and me to meet her lawyer.

Harvey Nussbaum's offices are on the second floor of a strip mall on Sea Breeze Drive. The place is sleek and modern, except for the big stuffed bulldog that's propped on top of the receptionist's counter. It's decked out in a black barrister gown and curly white wig.

The walls are decorated with framed newspaper clippings trumpeting Nussbaum's victories. A former prosecutor, he handled the defense of a New Jersey mayor accused of extorting bribes from a milk broker to help that broker win a school district contract. The mayor got off. The milk broker went to jail. The milk broker did not hire Harvey Nussbaum.

On the other hand, Nussbaum also helped free a prisoner serving a life sentence in the New Jersey State Prison, who had been wrongly convicted of murder based on the evidence of a jailhouse snitch. Nussbaum used new DNA technology, not available at the time of the original trial, and set him free.

Like his slogan says, Harvey Nussbaum takes Wrongs and tries to turn them into Rights. Provided, of course, somebody pays him the right amount of money.

"So, which one of you two gentlemen is Ceepak?"

A short, wiry guy in funky designer glasses flits into the reception area like a hummingbird flapping a sheet of paper. With curly hair, a very high forehead (okay, he's practically bald), Harvey Nussbaum looks to be about sixty-something. He's wearing a tweed sport coat, a checked dress shirt, a red silk tie, creased blue jeans, and snazzy black shoes that probably cost more than all the shoes I have ever owned combined.

"I'm Ceepak."

"You're the one paying for my services?"

"Actually, my mother, Adele Ceepak, will be assuming the financial responsibility for Ms. Lemonopolous' defense."

"She here?"

"No, sir. However, if there is documentation requiring a signature . . ."

Nussbaum flaps a sheet of paper down on the receptionist's counter. "This documentation. I will also need a check for three thousand dollars as my nonrefundable engagement fee before I do any more work on Ms. Lemonopolous' behalf. I've already put in three hours since you called."

"I have my mother's Power of Attorney." Ceepak reaches into his back pocket. "As well as a blank check she provided me."

"Fine, fine, whatever. Sign here. And here."

Nussbaum pulls a cheap pen out of the pocket of his expensive shirt. Clicks it a couple times before handing it off to Ceepak, who signs where the little sticky flags tell him to sign.

"Okay. Good. Come into my office. Ms. Lemonopolous?"

"Yes, sir?"

"We're gonna make this Oppenheimer woman pay for what she did to you. When I'm done with her, she'll make the Boston Strangler look like a choir boy."

"Oh, I don't want to hurt Shona . . ."

"Don't worry. You won't have to. I'll do it for you. Come on."

And we follow the pit bull into his den.

"Okay, let's see what we've got," says Nussbaum, flipping through a file folder when we're all seated around his desk.

I notice our chairs are kind of short. His, behind the desk, looks like it might be on an elevated platform.

Nussbaum takes a photo out of the file. I recognize the shot. It's one I took of Christine's bruised and battered neck.

"I called the SHPD right after you people called me. Demanded that they send me the police report of the incident in question, ASAP. They were quite cooperative."

"As I'm sure you will always find them to be," says Ceepak.

"Right, right. You two are cops, correct?"

"Yes, sir."

"In fact," I say, "I wrote up that police report."

Nussbaum flips to the front page of the Case Report.

"You're Boyle? The OIC? Officer in Charge?"

"If I need to leave the room because of any conflict of interest . . ."

Nussbaum holds up his hand. "Not yet. We're gonna be subpoenaing you . . . for the hearing . . ."

"Yes, sir."

"Of course, I have to wonder why you didn't arrest Mrs. Oppenheimer for assault and battery when you saw those ligature marks on Ms. Lemonopolous's neck. Why you checked 'Review Only' down here instead of 'Arrest Warrant.'"

"She claimed self-defense," says Ceepak, jumping to my defense.

"Come on, boys, don't piss on my boot and tell me it's raining. You two have been around the block. You both know your Forensics one-oh-one. So, Officer In Charge Boyle, since when are strangulation marks a sign of self-defense?"

I clear my throat. Nervously. "Mrs. Oppenheimer claimed that she had to hold Christine by the neck to stave off her kicks and punches."

"What? She couldn't do what most people do when someone's whaling on them?" The lawyer holds up both his arms to block his face and body. "How come she didn't pull a rope-a-dope like Muhammad Ali against George Foreman? Nineteen-seventy-four. The Rumble In The Jungle?"

Okay. I'm feeling pretty dumb. Like maybe I should've slapped the cuffs on Mrs. Oppenheimer and dragged her off to jail when we caught that 911 call.

"Is any of this relevant at this juncture?" asks Ceepak.

"Officer Boyle's incredible SNAFU on the night of the inciting incident?" Nussbaum shrugs. "Nah. You were in a she said/she said situation. The only independent witness was a scared kid, the son of the Sea Haven Strangler. I probably would've done the same thing. Break 'em up, send them to separate corners, call it a night. But now that Oppenheimer is coming after Ms. Lemonopolous with the full fury of the law instead of her two fists, now we fight back."

I nod. "Yes, sir."

"Okay, Christine. Why'd Mrs. Oppenheimer want to wring your neck?"

Christine takes a moment. Smooths out her pants legs. "We had a disagreement."

"Yeah, yeah. And you tried to 'defuse the situation by walking out of the room.' I read your statement. Nice. Very sweet."

He makes a "gimme, gimme" gesture with one hand.

"I need more."

"Well," says Christine, "I don't want to cause Shona any trouble . . ."

"What?" Nussbaum is livid. "This Oppenheimer woman and her high-priced attorney are trying to screw you for life and you don't want to cause her 'any trouble'? They got a judge to issue this exparte order, meaning the restraining order is already in effect, because you were going to cause 'irreparable injury, loss, or damage' between the time the thing was filed and a hearing. They're saying just seeing this sheet of paper would make you attack her again."

"Still . . ."

"Grow up, Ms. Lemonopolous. Otherwise I'm giving Mrs. Ceepak back her retainer check. I can't win this thing with one hand tied behind my back."

Christine closes her eyes. "Okay. But this is pretty horrible."

# 16

CHRISTINE IS READY TO TALK.

"Shona Oppenheimer wanted me to, more or less, spy on my other home health care client, Dr. Arnold Rosen."

"The dentist?" says Nussbaum. "Why?"

"Shona's sister, Judith, is married to Dr. Rosen's oldest son, David."

"And?" He does the gimme-gimme gesture again.

"Shona told Judith to recommend me for the position at her father-in-law's house."

"Why?" The lawyer scribbles something on his legal pad.

"They wanted me in Dr. Rosen's house so I could find out stuff."

Nussbaum looks like he's about to turn purple again. "Stuff?"

"Dr. Rosen is a very private man," Christine explains. "He won't allow family members to accompany him when he visits his doctors. He also refuses to sign the HIPAA forms that would give medical professionals permission to talk to his children about . . . anything."

"Does he let you go into the exam rooms with him?"

"Yes. But only because I'm an RN. And I have to leave if, you know, the doctor puts on a glove and asks Dr. Rosen to . . ."

Marty give her another spin of his hand. TMI—Too Much Information. Time to move on.

"Judith, that's Shona's sister . . ."

"Yeah, I got that bit." Nussbaum circles what he had written earlier on the legal pad.

"Judith was worried about her father-in-law's medical condition. I could understand. I mean, if my parents were ninety-four, I'd want to know everything I could about their health."

"But Dr. Rosen didn't want his kids knowing diddly?"

"That's right. And since he used to be a dentist, he reminded me of my own oath as a nurse. Our code of ethics."

Ceepak's eyes light up the way they do whenever somebody else mentions their Code.

"Enlighten me," says Nussbaum.

"Some people call it the Florence Nightingale Pledge. We all stood up and recited it when I graduated from nursing school. I solemnly swore to 'hold in confidence all personal matters committed to my keeping and family affairs coming to my knowledge in the practice of my calling.'"

Now Ceepak is nodding like a happy bobble-headed doll.

"So, long story short," says Nussbaum, "you didn't do what you were hired to do in Dr. Rosen's house?"

"Not according to Judith. So, she kept pressuring her sister. Nagging Shona to have me write up reports about Dr. Rosen's doctor visits. To Xerox any medical records I could find. To feed Judith information."

"What kind of information?"

"Anything having to do with his health. Physical and—" Christine hesitates. "Mental."

"What?" says Nussbaum. "You think they wanted him declared mentally incompetent? That way they could ship him off to a nursing home or the nuthouse so they could move into his mansion?"

"Sorry, Mr. Nussbaum," Christine says with a frown. "I know you're trying to help me, but I don't think it would be appropriate for me to speculate about family affairs that came to my knowledge while engaged in the performance of my professional duties."

"Agreed," says Ceepak, who is a stickler about obeying the whole code even when it would be easier to chuck the parts that work against you.

"Okay, okay," says the lawyer. "Fine. Not important. So why did Shona strangle you that night?"

Christine takes in a steadying breath. "I had just caught her rummaging around in my shoulder bag, looking for medical information about Dr. Rosen, I guess."

"Did she find anything?"

"Of course not. We keep all those kinds of documents at Dr. Rosen's house in a locked filing cabinet."

"So all you were doing the night of the altercation was protecting your patient's right to privacy?"

"Yes, sir."

"Okay. That's good. That's excellent. By the way, how is Arnie doing?"

"Very well. Especially for someone in his nineties."

"Tell him I said hello."

"I take it you know Dr. Rosen?" says Ceepak.

Nussbaum smiles. Points to his teeth.

"In this town, who doesn't? I mean, if you're a certain age. For years, Dr. Rosen was *the* dentist in Sea Haven. Capped four of my molars. Even his root canals were painless." Nussbaum flips through more papers. "This TRO. Who signed this thing, again?"

"Judge Ken Guarnery," says Ceepak.

"What a putz. My guess? Mrs. Oppenheimer's late husband, 'Slick Opie' Oppenheimer, handled the judge's investment portfolio back when Guarnery was just a schmuck lawyer, which he was, believe you me. I wouldn't be surprised if the dearly departed Arthur Oppenheimer bankrolled Kenny Boy's first run for the bench. My gut tells me the judge owed Mrs. Oppenheimer, big time. Why else would the yutz sign this thing? Okay. Now you two boys in blue need to leave. My client and I have to talk. In private."

After Christine finishes up with her lawyer, we shuttle her back to Beach Lane.

"Do you need to be anywhere right now?" Ceepak asks, once Christine is back inside the house with Dr. Rosen.

"Nope," I say.

Yes, it's Saturday, around 5 P.M. and, once again, I have no date. Maybe, once this restraining order dealio is done, I should follow up on Mrs. Ceepak's advice. Ask Christine out.

"Rita is working the Early Bird dinner shift at Morgan's Surf and Turf," says Ceepak, explaining why he isn't rushing home. "I'd like to swing by the boardwalk. Check out the Free Fall. Make certain they are obeying our shutdown order."

So we head back to Pier Two.

When we walk up to the towering ride, it's still idle.

But there is a new sign dangling off that chain barrier: "Opening next weekend!"

Bob, the manager guy, comes strolling over when he sees us checking out the ride.

"Howdy, guys. Been meaning to call you two. We've hired an operator who fulfills all your requirements. He's a carnie from up north. He'll be here next weekend."

"Has he been trained and certified by the manufacturer?"

"Yep. Trained at their factory in Sandusky, Ohio. He faxed us a copy of his license and the factory certification."

"We'll need a copy of it."

"Sure. I'll fax it over first thing Monday. You'll get a kick out of it, too."

"How so?"

"Guy has the same last name as you."

"Come again?"

"Our new operator. His name is Joseph Ceepak. Any relation?"

Ceepak's face goes ghostly white.

"Yes. He is my father."

# 17

CEEPAK SPENDS EVERY FREE HOUR THE NEXT WEEK PREPARING for "the imminent invasion" of Joseph Ceepak.

"I knew this day would come the moment Mother made the decision to move to Sea Haven. The money she inherited is simply too tempting a target for my father to ignore."

True. With Adele's millions, Joe "Six Pack" Ceepak could buy his own beer distributorship.

The last time his father was in town, Ceepak had an Emergency Restraining Order issued to keep his father away from his immediate family—him, his wife Rita, and his adopted son T.J. Mrs. Adele Ceepak was never listed on that order because she wasn't even in New Jersey at the time. Plus, as Honest Abe Ceepak reminds me, there never was a judicial hearing to turn his ERO into an FRO, a Final Restraining Order.

"Sadly," he says when we discuss it over a beer one night, "due to my lack of follow-through on the matter, my father has every right to seek gainful employment here in Sea Haven."

"But he promised us," I say. "When you saved his sorry life after that nutjob shot him. He said he'd never darken your door again. He gave us his solemn word he'd leave your mother alone."

"So he did, Danny," says Ceepak grimly. "So he did."

I guess Ceepak knows that every vow his father has ever made to him was nothing but hot, boozy air.

Meanwhile, I'm served a subpoena to appear in Judge Ken Guarney's courtroom on Friday morning at 8:30 A.M. to give testimony in the matter of Shona Oppenheimer v. Christine Lemonopolous.

Thursday night, a little after 8 P.M., I swing by the Rosen house to see how Christine is holding up.

The first thing I notice in the driveway is a brand-new electric wheelchair with a reinforced metal frame and big balloon tires like on a dune buggy.

"Nice, hunh?" says Monae Dunn, as she comes out to the porch. "Michael sent it. You are looking at a ten-thousand-dollar motorized beach wheelchair."

"Seriously? It looks like a moon rover."

"Uhm-hmm. You need tires that size on account of all the sand. And you steer it with that joystick thing right there. Michael wants to go 'walking on the beach' with his father to tell him his and Andrew's 'big news.' He's flying in from Hollywood first thing tomorrow morning. Taking the redeye."

"Michael bought that high-def TV for his dad, too, right?"

"Uhm-hmm. And the satellite dish. And the exercise bike. He even sent a box of those Omaha steaks last week. Michael is *extremely* generous. But, between you and me, I think it's because he feels so guilty."

"About what?"

"Not being here like his brother."

"Maybe," I say because I find it helps to be noncommittal when listening to gossip. "Is Christine around?"

"Uhm-hmm." She nods toward the door.

I head inside. I walk even though I'm half-tempted to test out Dr. Rosen's brand-new moon rover, see if those balloon tires could haul me up the steps like an ATV.


Dr. Rosen is in his regular wheelchair, spooning a bowl of thick soup out of a bowl resting on a table attached to its armrests. Christine is sitting beside him with a cloth napkin, ready to mop up any spills.

"Ah, Officer Boyle!" Dr. Rosen says when he sees me. "To what do we owe the pleasure of your company?"

"I just wanted to see how Christine was holding up. Tomorrow's the big day."

"I'm good, Danny," she says. "Thanks."

"By the way, sir—I like your new wheelchair out front."

Dr. Rosen shakes his head. "I told Monae to put that thing in the garage. Frivolous waste of money. But that, I'm afraid, is my youngest son, Michael. Never very frugal or practical. You'll see."

I just nod.

Hey, I have my own family crap to deal with. I don't need any extra from the Rosens. So, I change the subject.

"Is that your grandson?" I ask, gesturing at the closest jumbo sized portrait of the shaggy-haired boy.

"Indeed. That's Little Arnie."

"They named him after you?"

"Yes, Officer Boyle. He is my living legacy. Quite a smile, don't you think? All natural. Didn't even need braces or a retainer like his father did when he was a boy."

"Good-looking kid."

"Quite the athlete-scholar, as well. I suspect he has the smarts to get into my old alma mater, U Penn Dental School." Dr. Rosen shakes his head, remembering something unpleasant. "His father, on the other hand, did not."

"Well, like I said, I, uh, just wanted to drop by and wish Christine good luck. Can't really do it tomorrow when I'm in uniform, in court . . ."

"Officer Boyle," says Dr. Rosen, "I wonder if you might convey a message to your friend, Detective Ceepak?"

"Sure."

"Kindly inform him that what his mother has done, rushing in to assist Christine, a woman she barely knows, has inspired me."

"She'll be happy to hear it, sir."

"In fact, I hope to, one day, replicate her generosity with some spontaneous act of kindness of my own."

"Yes, sir."

"Now then, are *you* prepared for tomorrow, Officer Boyle?"

"I think so. My job in court is pretty easy. I just have to recite the facts as I recall them."

"Take care, Officer Boyle. I have received top-secret intelligence from the enemy camp: according to Judith, her sister has engaged a young gun by the name of Stan Trybulski to plead her case to the court."

"I'm not worried. Christine has Harvey Nussbaum."

"Indeed she does. However, Mr. Trybulski, who is perhaps half Mr. Nussbaum's age, already commands *four* hundred dollars per billable hour."

# 18

FRIDAY MORNING, I'M IN COURT, FEELING LIKE A MARINATED pork butt because I'm just waiting to be grilled by Stan Trybulski, Shona Oppenheimer's high-priced young attorney.

I appear to be the only witness waiting to testify. I don't see Shona's son, Samuel, or anybody else.

Harvey Nussbaum and Christine Lemonopolous are seated at the defendant's table. He's in a snazzy suit with a bright red handkerchief tucked into the chest pocket. Christine is wearing her nurse's scrubs.

Shona Oppenheimer and her attorney, whose suit looks even more expensive than Harvey's, are at the plaintiff's table. Judge Ken Guarnery is perched up on the bench, looking very imposing in his black robes.

The Plaintiff gets to go first.

"Your honor," says Trybulski. "My client, Mrs. Shona Blumenfeld Oppenheimer, a well respected member of this community . . ."

The judge actually nods and smiles at Shona Oppenheimer. She smiles back. It's like they're at a champagne reception raising money for Judge Guarnery's next political campaign.

Christine doesn't stand a chance.

". . . Mrs. Oppenheimer not only employed the defendant, Christine Lemonopolous, as a home health aide to care for her son, she also provided Ms. Lemonopolous with room and board, making her a de facto member of the Oppenheimer household."

Nussbaum looks like he's about to object, but he doesn't.

"On the evening of June 7th, Ms. Lemonopolous attacked Mrs. Oppenheimer."

This time, Nussbaum pops up. "Objection. Does the plaintiff have any proof to substantiate her assertion?"

"Of course, your honor," says Trybulski. "It is all spelled out, right there in the Restraining Order form as specified . . ."

"That's not proof. That's just her side of the story."

"We also have the police report."

Harvey flips open a file folder on the table in front of him. "You mean this police report? The one with the photographs?"

"The photographs are irrelevant," says Trybulski. "The responding officers failed to document Mrs. Oppenheimer's shin injuries and limited their intake of evidence to dramatized depictions of Ms. Lemonopolous's bruised neck."

"Well, that's what I would have done, too," says Harvey. "If I was a cop and saw someone getting strangled . . ."

"Enough," says the judge. "Objection overruled. The defendant will be given ample opportunity to present evidence supporting her version of events later in this proceeding."

"Yes, your honor. And I promise, when it's our turn, we won't just do a read-aloud of some form we filled out."

"Harvey?"

"I'm just saying, your honor." He sits back down.

The judge turns to the plaintiff's table. Smiles again. "Please proceed, counselor."

"Thank you, your honor. Now, as you know, what is most important in a hearing such as this, is establishing that my client is in immediate need of the protection that would be provided by the permanent restraining order."

Here the lawyer turns to her client.

"Mrs. Oppenheimer, can you tell us why you fear further violence from Ms. Lemonopolous?"

"Certainly," says Shona, sitting up straight in her chair, just like they probably rehearsed it. "Because Christine is a ticking time bomb. She has what they call 'PTSD.' Post Traumatic Stress Disease."

"Do you mean Post Traumatic Stress Disorder?" coaches her lawyer.

"Yes. Christine is extremely prone to angry outbursts and crazy flashbacks."

Harvey stands. "Objection, your honor."

Judge Guarnery gets a squeamish look on his face and says, oh so politely, "Mrs. Oppenheimer, this is a very serious accusation. Do you have evidence to substantiate your claim?"

"Sure. I talked to a doctor friend and he told me . . ."

"Hearsay, your honor," says Harvey, tossing up both his arms.

"Yes. I'm afraid we can't admit hearsay evidence, Shona. Objection sustained."

"Your honor," says Trybulski, her lawyer, "those with PTSD engage in self-destructive behavior such as alcohol abuse and . . ."

"Whoa," says Harvey. "Again with the PTSD?"

"Did you have difficulty understanding my ruling, Mr. Trybulski?" asks the judge, sounding like a kindly old uncle. "If so, I would be happy to elucidate . . ."

"No, that's okay," says Trybulski. "Allow me to rephrase."

"Kindly do."

"My client desperately needs the protection this restraining order will provide because she is currently living her life in constant fear of what Ms. Lemonopolous might do next. Need I remind you: Ms. Lemonopolous is a highly trained medical professional. She understands the pharmacology of drugs. She knows how to hurt people. She is a menace to my client."

Trybulski strides to his chair. Sits down.

"Is that it?" asks the judge.

"Yes, your honor. For now."

"Would the defense care to cross-examine the plaintiff?"

"Well, let's see," Harvey says sarcastically. "They presented *so much* evidence. Where to start? Oh, how about the police report. Nothing much in there. She said one thing, my client said another. The plaintiff's son couldn't tell who started what. Oh, right. The pictures. But you can look at those yourself, your honor."

"I already have."

"So, okay, this PTSD thing."

"You don't have to go there, Mr. Nussbaum. I have already stricken Ms. Oppenheimer's unsubstantiated remarks from the record."

"Thanks. But let's say, hypothetically, an emergency-room nurse *did* wind up with Post Traumatic Stress Disorder right after her best friend in the world was horribly murdered. Let's say, for the sake of argument, that this same hypothetical nurse realized what was happening to her and went to her employers to ask for a long-term leave of absence.

"Furthermore, let's say the folks at, oh, let's call the hypothetical hospital Mainland Medical, thought so highly of this young trauma nurse that they helped her find a in-house treatment program, which everyone agreed would be kept strictly confidential, thereby putting it under the protection of the federal government's HIPAA Privacy Rules.

"How could anybody but the hypothetical nurse and her hypothetical doctors even know about this hypothetical incident?

Unless, of course, somebody, let's say another hypothetical doctor, maybe a hypothetical plastic surgeon, whose favorite customer was a hypothetical woman named Mrs. Oppenheimer, violated the young nurse's privacy rights as stipulated under the Health Insurance Portability and Accountability Act of 1996."

Harvey stops.

The courtroom is stone cold quiet.

"I'm just sayin', your honor," he adds with a shrug. "Hypothetically."

I never take the stand.

Judge Guarnery has no choice but to toss out the temporary restraining order. He totally expunges its existence from Christine's record. He even suggests that Mrs. Oppenheimer "have a little chat" with her "hypothetical" plastic surgeon friend and advise him to obtain legal counsel, as he could be brought up on charges for his "flagrant violation" of HIPAA regulations.

I guess the whole PTSD deal was one of the things Christine and Harvey Nussbaum chatted about last Saturday after Ceepak and I left the room. Ceepak could relate. When he first came home from the horror show over in Iraq, my partner had been prone to nightmares. Especially when he was awake and someone set off fireworks, like an M-80 tossed into a dumpster.

The second we're outside the courtroom, Christine jumps into my arms to give me a big hug. Full disclosure? She does, indeed, have a great bod.

"Where's Mr. Ceepak and his mom? I want to thank them, too!"

"Um, they're both kind of busy. The Free Fall opens tomorrow."

"Huh?"

Christine is confused. Can't blame her. What I just said makes absolutely no sense.

Unless, of course, you know that skeevy Joe Ceepak is coming to town.

# 19

Saturday morning, Ceepak and I are off duty but both of us are carrying our sidearms.

We meet in the parking lot that fronts Pier Two, home of the StratosFEAR Free Fall.

"Thank you for doing this with me, Danny," says Ceepak.

"No problem." Ceepak doesn't trust himself to stay calm, cool, and in control when confronting his horrible excuse for a father for the first time in nearly a year. Today, being restrained and dispassionate will be *my* job.

It's about 10:30 A.M.

The rides usually open around eleven. Ceepak figures his father, a Sandusky Amusements certified ride operator, will already be on the job, going through his pre-flight checklist.

We walk up the pier, which resembles a carnival midway thirty minutes before they let the suckers in. Blinking signs are flickering to life. Baskets of Oreos and Snickers bars dripping pancake batter are being dunked into bubbling vats of French fryer oil. Fluffy stuffed animals are being hung on pegs—prizes not too many basketball shooters, frog bog boppers, softball-into-a-basket tossers, or balloon poppers will actually take home.

Up ahead, I see the NASA-blue StratosFEAR car rising up its bright white tower. It slips behind the electronic sign spelling out S-t-r-a-t-o-s-FEAR that rings the ride. It creeps, like an extremely slow elevator on a high-rise crane tower, toward the top. Fortunately, the seats are all empty.

When we reach the ride entrance, the car comes sliding down like a shot. The brakes slam on. Fog puffs out. The car glides to the bottom.

"Looking good, Joe!" we hear Bob the manager holler.

"Thanks, Bob."

And there, sitting in the control booth, is none other than Joseph Ceepak.

I almost don't recognize him. His wild tangle of greasy hair is neatly trimmed, parted, and combed to one side. His face is shaved clean of the salt-and-pepper stubble I remember. Instead of a sloppy Hawaiian shirt with food stains dribbled down the front, he's wearing a clean and pressed polo shirt and crisp khaki shorts.

"Johnny?" he says when he sees us staring up at him. "Boyle? Hey, great to see you two." He squirms around on his stool. "Hey, Bob? Is it okay if I take my five-minute break a little early?"

"Sure, Joe!" Bob calls back. Then he gives us a cheery wave, the kind suburban guys give each other when they're out mowing their lawns.

Joe Ceepak flicks some switches and hurries down to greet us.

His son's jaw joint is doing that popping in and out thing it does near his ear whenever he's trying not to explode.

"My goodness, Johnny. Good to see you, son. Been too long. You too, Boyle. I would've called you, but, well, I just got into town last night. They're putting me up in a motel till I can find an apartment. Had to punch in bright and early this morning."

And then he stands there, hands on hips, smiling proudly at his son.

Whose eyes are narrowing into slits tighter than window blinds yanked all the way up.

"Why are you here?" Ceepak finally says.

"Didn't they tell you, Johnny? I'm a factory-trained and certified operator. See, the plant that manufactures these American steel rides is located up in Sandusky, not too far from where I was living after, you know, last summer when, well, I would've died if it wasn't for my jarhead son!"

He actually says the word "jarhead" with some affection. Usually, he sneers it at his son. Says stuff like "you effing jarhead moron."

Not today. In fact, I have never seen Mr. Ceepak smile so much. And his teeth aren't the color of brown deli mustard anymore, either.

"You and Boyle here saved my life, Johnny. I'll never forget that. Cross my heart and hope to spit."

"Please forgive me, sir, if I doubt your sincerity."

"Hey, I don't blame you, Johnny. Goodness, I'd doubt it, too. The way I've behaved? Despicable. Heck, I wasn't much of a dad—to you or Billy. But trust me, Johnny, a man can change. What did Jesus say? 'There will be more joy in heaven over one sinner who repents than over ninety-nine righteous persons who need no repentance.' Well, let me tell you, boys: right now Jesus and his friends are having one heck of a hosanna hollerin' hootenanny up there in heaven. Come on, son. Rejoice with Jesus. What once was lost now is found."

"How goes the family reunion?" Manager Bob has ambled over to join us. He's doing that smile and heel-rocking thing again.

"Peachy," I say, so Ceepak doesn't have to speak.

"Apparently," says Ceepak, sounding extremely skeptical, "my father is a new man."

"That I am, Johnny boy. Be sure to tell your mother. Hey, maybe the three of us can get together for dinner some night soon. You can come too, Boyle. My treat."

"That, sir," says Ceepak, "is never going to happen."

His father keeps grinning like an idiot. "How's Adele doing? I bet she misses me."

"No, sir. She does not."

"I read about her in the newspaper this morning. They're calling her Sea Haven's newest Guardian Angel."

"Is that your mom?" says Bob. "The one who hired a lawyer to defend that cute nurse who doesn't have a pot to piss in? Awesome!"

"Adele's my wife . . ."

Ceepak holds up his very strong right hand to signal his father to stop right there. "*Ex*-wife . . ."

"Okay. Sure. Say, this gal, Christine Lemondrops, the one your mom bailed out, she a friend of yours, Johnny?" He asks it with just a hint of his old lechery.

"She's *our* friend," I say. "And her last name is Lemonopolous."

"Good. That's nice, Boyle. You need a gal pal. Johnny here is already hitched and settled down. Speaking of which, when can you and the missus swing by the motel to say hey?"

"How about never, sir?" says Ceepak. "Will never work?"

"Ouch," says Bob, with a goofy giggle.

But Mr. Ceepak keeps on smiling like those brainwashed people in cults, right before they chug a jug of the Kool Ade.

"Careful, Johnny," he says. "'Judge not, that ye be not judged.' Matthew. Chapter seven. Verse one."

"You would do well to memorize the remainder of that chapter, sir."

"Excuse me?"

"Verse 15: 'Beware of the false prophets, who come to you in sheep's clothing, but inwardly are ravenous wolves.'"

"Oh–kay," says Bob, laughing nervously. "We better postpone Bible study till church tomorrow morning and get back at it. We open in fifteen, Joe."

"Right. And Bob?"

"Yes, Joe?"

"Thanks again. For giving me this opportunity."

Bob claps old man Ceepak on the back. "Are you kidding? We're the ones who should be thanking you. Heck, if you hadn't answered our ad, your son here would've kept the StratosFEAR shut down all summer long."

Bob chuckles. Joe chuckles.

Ceepak and me? We're not in a chuckling kind of mood.

# 20

WE GRAB A COLD SODA (WHAT CEEPAK STILL CALLS A POP) AT a pizza stand twenty feet away from the StratosFEAR.

I'm thirsty, so I gulp mine down. Ceepak, on the other hand, sips maybe two drops.

Both of us watch Mr. Ceepak hoist a couple carloads of squealing riders up the tower and drop them. At first, they scream and kick their feet. Then they laugh. It's good old-fashioned fun.

But I'm thinking one of the nearby T-shirt shops ought to start selling clean underpants, too.

"I don't trust him or his supposed transformation," Ceepak finally says.

Hey, I can't blame the guy.

Years ago, Joseph Ceepak murdered his youngest son, William Philip Ceepak—my Ceepak's little brother. The sneaky bastard made Billy's death look like a suicide. And he got away with it. For years. Even when Ceepak and I were able to have a prosecuting attorney up in Ohio re-open the case, the slimy worm wiggled off the hook.

So, I'm with Ceepak. I'm not buying this whole Bible-thumping, born-again Christian act. Joseph Ceepak is not a lost sheep. He's a wolf who went to a pop-up Halloween shop and asked for the Little Bo Peep costume.

"He's here for Mother's money," says Ceepak, his eyes focused on the Free Fall. Not the ride; the control booth.

"Maybe we should request a fresh Emergency Restraining Order."

"Trust me, Danny: I have already put in the paperwork."

We might've stayed there all day, nursing our Cokes, keeping an eye on Joe Ceepak, waiting for him to slip out of his sheep costume, do something stupid enough for us to arrest him, but my cell phone chirps.

It's Christine Lemonopolous.

She's sobbing.

"Christine?" I say. "What's wrong?"

"He's dead, Danny. Dr. Rosen. He died this morning."

# 21

Ceepak and I head over to the Rosen house on Beach Lane.

"They want Christine out of the house," I say, relaying the rest of our conversation. "Today. Like right now."

"Sad," Ceepak says.

"Yeah. Where's she gonna go?"

"Actually, Danny, I was thinking about the late Arnold Rosen."

Oh. Right. The dead guy. Guess he's worse off than even Christine.

And then neither of us says anything else on the fifteen-minute drive down Beach Lane from the boardwalk. Death will do that to you, get you thinking. About Ceepak's baby brother, Bill. My only real girlfriend, Katie Landry. My buddy Mook. Dominic Santucci.

And the two men I've personally sent to their graves.

When the Grim Reaper is riding with you, he always hogs the mental radio.

We park and climb out of my Jeep just as two gentlemen in black suits carry a rubberized body bag out the front door.

Ceepak stops walking and bows his head.

I do the same.

And then I hear Ceepak start muttering a prayer: "God full of mercy who dwells on high, grant perfect rest to the soul of Arnold Rosen."

When Ceepak was over in Iraq, he saw a lot of guys die. Christians. Jews. Muslims. I'm guessing he memorized the right things to say for every religion when nothing you can say seems right.

We wait for the funeral home attendants to do their job and drive away in their black vehicle with the black-tinted windows. I make a sign of the cross. Sorry. It's a nun-inflicted reflex.

Making our way toward the front porch, I notice that brand-new dune buggy wheelchair still sitting in the driveway. Guess Dr. Rosen never got to try it. Guess Monae never hid it in the garage like she was supposed to.

Inside the house, we see three mourners clustered around Dr. Rosen's empty hospital bed: two men, one woman.

The woman has long, white-blonde hair and is dressed in a canary yellow tennis outfit that's a little too short and hugs her body a little too tightly—especially since she has a whole lot of body to hug. I'm guessing this blonde is Shona Oppenheimer's sister, Judith, even though Shona has jet-black hair.

Judith only has jet-black eyebrows.

And unlike super-skinny Shona, Judith has bulges and lumps swelling up in places where woman don't usually have what Ceepak calls "protuberances." Even her face is sort of bloated. Her cheeks and jowls crowd out her eyes, nose, and mouth so much it's hard to tell if she and her sister have similar facial features.

Standing next to Judith is a beanpole-ish, balding man sporting a scraggly goatee. He's wearing shorts, sandals, and a faded pink polo shirt. He also looks a little nebbishy, a Yiddish word that my buddy Joe Getzler taught me (along with schmuck, putz, and bupkes). It basically means he looks "pitifully timid." I'm guessing he's David

Rosen because the other guy, standing across the bed from Judith, looks totally Hollywood and has to be the rich son, Michael, from LA-LA land.

Michael is wearing black jeans, black cowboy boots, and an open-collar black shirt that looks like it probably cost several hundred dollars at some black clothes boutique in Beverly Hills. His hair and beard are so neatly trimmed they appear to be the exact same length. That takes work. Or money.

"Oh, hello," says Judith, very sweetly. When she smiles, she looks like one of those puffy marshmallow clouds on a TV weather map. "May we help you gentlemen?"

"Sorry to intrude," says Ceepak. "I'm Detective John Ceepak with the Sea Haven Police. This is my partner Danny Boyle. Please pardon our intrusion and know that we are sorry for your loss. Dr. Rosen was good man."

Judith blinks her piggy little eyes. Repeatedly.

"Did you know my father-in-law?" she finally asks.

"Only briefly," says Ceepak. "But he had a very stellar reputation among the long-term residents of Sea Haven."

"He certainly did," says the guy with the close-cropped hair and beard. "I'm Michael. Do you know my big brother David?"

"No," says Ceepak, stepping forward and extending his hand. "I don't believe I've had the pleasure." He shakes David's hand and then turns to Michael to shake his, too.

Like always, I follow along and do what Ceepak just did.

"Again," says Ceepak, "our condolences on your loss."

"Gosh, detectives," says Judith, "I don't mean to be rude but, may I ask: Why are you gentlemen here?"

"My dad was ninety-four years old," says David with a goofy grin. "Surely you don't suspect foul play in his death."

"Of course not," says Ceepak.

"Of course not," echoes Judith, with a soft smile. She has a very sweet and gentle presence. Reminds me a little of this movie from the 1960s they used to show us at Holy Innocents Elementary. Debbie Reynolds in *The Singing Nun*. I half expect her to break into song: *"Dominique, nique, nique."*

Then I remember the Rosens are Jewish.

"We're here," says Ceepak, "to assist Ms. Lemonopolous."

"Christine?" says Michael.

"Yes. We understand she needs to vacate the premises."

"We'd appreciate it," says David, kind of brusquely. "Her services, as you might imagine, are no longer required now that Dad has passed. Monae has already moved out of her room."

*Yeah,* I think, *because Monae can probably move in with her brother or sister.* Christine cannot.

"We've already contacted the rabbi," says Judith. "The temple is making arrangements for Dad's funeral."

"Which," adds David, "needs to happen right away."

"Jewish tradition," adds Michael.

Ceepak nods. Me, too. I went through a lot of this when Joe Getzler's grandfather died a couple years ago.

"We'll be sitting shiva at our home," says Judith. "Just makes everything easier."

"Plus," says David, "we need to clean this place up. Get it ready to put on the market. Can't have anyone camping out in the guest rooms. It'll slow things down. Christine has got to go."

"Understandable," says Ceepak. "Where is Christine now?"

"We asked her to take a walk on the beach," says Judith. "The three of us needed to discuss some family matters. In private."

"For instance," says Michael, "we need to decide who gets to take home *all* of these lovely photographs of my nephew, Little Arnie."

"Dad liked them," says David.

"Oh, I'm sure he did." Michael gestures toward a photograph of the blonde boy poised like a quarterback about to heave a pass. "This is my personal fave. Such the little athlete. Guess he must take after Judith's side of the family."

Judith smiles and blinks some more.

David's eyes drop, like he needs to examine his sandal straps.

Michael grins like he's holding the hot cards in a high-stakes poker game.

Geeze-o, man.

This is one weird, freaky family.

# 22

FINALLY, JUDITH BREAKS THE LONG, AWKWARD SILENCE.

"Our emotions are little raw right now, officers," she calmly explains.

"Understandable," says Ceepak. "We'll wait outside for Christine."

"Do you have some place for her to stay tonight?" asks Michael, the only one who seems the least bit concerned about the displaced help.

"We'll work something out," I say.

Mentally, I'm already speed-dialing Becca. But it's the middle of June now. Schools are letting out. The Fourth of July and a horde of tourists are coming fast. The "NO" signs are popping up in front of the "VACANCY" lights on hotels up and down the island.

Ceepak and I head out the back door.

We walk across a weather-beaten deck filled with graying teak furniture plus a rusty Weber kettle grill with antique cobwebs glued to its legs. We're on a bit of a bluff overlooking the ocean maybe fifty feet in front of us. This is an impressive piece of property. Somebody's about to inherit an awesome beach house.

"Perhaps you should give Christine a call," Ceepak suggests after we both scan the shoreline, looking for her.

I pull out my cell phone. "So where do we take her this time? The Mussel Beach Motel is probably booked up for the rest of the summer."

"Roger that," mumbles Ceepak. I can tell he's perplexed, too.

"And now she doesn't have any kind of job. No way can she pay rent, unless she goes back to the emergency room."

"She may not be ready for a return to the ER at this juncture," says Ceepak, who, like I said, understands Christine's PTSD better than anybody. Working in a trauma center, faced with life-and-death decisions every time the double doors swing open? That's probably not what her doctors and psychiatrists are ordering for Christine right now.

"Well," I say, "maybe she has some savings. But this is the start of the peak tourist season. Rents will be jacked up till Labor Day. If she had any family in the area, she never would've had to spend the night in Dr. Rosen's driveway . . ."

"Could she stay at your apartment, Danny?"

Wow. First Ceepak's mom wants me to date Christine. Now her son wants her to move in with me?

"You, of course, could stay with Rita and me," he continues. "T.J.'s sofa bed is still available."

Okay, this is tough.

I mean I like Ceepak and his wife, Rita. Living with them would be okay. I guess. Unless Ceepak makes me get up every morning and run three miles before we all do military-style jumping jacks.

On the other hand, it's baseball season. I love my own plasma screen TV—even though it's only half as big as the one Michael bought for his father. I also like how close my refrigerator is to my couch. You don't even need to stand up to grab a beer.

But then I see Christine's mop of dark, curly hair bouncing up over the dunes. Soon I see her. She's not in a bathing suit or anything but she looks good.

And sad.

No, crushed is more like it.

She's probably been wandering up and down the beach wondering the same stuff Ceepak and I have been wondering about. Now that Dr. Rosen is gone, what's going to happen to her?

"Yeah," I say. "Your place sounds like a plan."

"Just for the time being," says Ceepak. "We'll figure something out."

"It's all good," I say. Then I smile at Christine as she makes her way over the dunes.

"Hey, guys." She sniffles back a tear. "Can you believe it? They say it was probably a heart attack. I think it was my fault . . ."

"What? Come on, Christine. He was ninety-four years old . . ."

"But the restraining order mess. Me and Shona going to court. Judith getting all upset. I think it sent his blood pressure shooting through the roof . . ."

"Christine?" says Ceepak, using the firm, deep voice he sometimes uses with me. "You did not kill Dr. Rosen. Old age did."

"I don't know . . ."

That's when Ceepak's phone blares an obscure Springsteen song called "The Wish," a tribute the Boss wrote about his mom. That means the caller is Ceepak's mother.

I know this because I showed him how to program in different ringtones to ID callers once his family on the island grew beyond just Rita. If he wants me to put in a ringtone for his dad, I think I'll go with Meatloaf's "Bat Out Of Hell."

Ceepak jabs the speakerphone button.

Probably so Christine can say "thank you" to his mom in person.

"Hello, Mom. I have you on speakerphone. I'm here with Danny and Christine, the young nurse you helped so much."

Mrs. Ceepak doesn't say anything.

"Mom?"

"Are you at Arnold Rosen's house?"

"Yes, Mom. He passed away this morning."

"I know. One of my bingo friends just called . . ."

"He was ninety-four, Mother. He lived a good long life."

Again silence.

"Mom?"

"Arnie called me late last night, John. He was worried. Told me he was 'surrounded by assassins'! John?"

"Yes, Mother?"

"Do something. Please? I feel it in my bones: One of those assassins murdered Arnold Rosen."

# 23

CHRISTINE AND I ARE STANDING THERE, STUNNED, STARING AT Ceepak, who is staring at his silent cell phone.

He looks stunned, too.

"That can't be right," says Christine. "Why would anybody want to kill Dr. Rosen?"

"Not knowing, can't say," mumbles Ceepak, who, it seems, has slipped into his analytical automaton mode. He thumbs a speed dial number.

"What's up?" I ask.

"Calling Chief Rossi."

The new guy. Great. The Chief of Detectives has to call the Chief of Police and tell him what his mommy just said. I don't envy Ceepak on this call.

"Roy? John Ceepak. Sorry to be bothering you on the weekend. I see. Yes, sir. Things do get busy around town in the summer. Yes, sir. It's all good. Sir, I need to call in a favor but I wanted to run it by

103

you first. I'd like to contact Dr. Rebecca Kurth, the county medical examiner. Arnold Rosen passed away this morning. That's right. Ninety-four, sir. Well, there is some suspicion of foul play . . ."

Here, Ceepak takes a long pause.

"My mother talked to Dr. Rosen last night. In their conversation, Dr. Rosen expressed a fear that someone was out to kill him. Yes, sir. My mother. No, sir. She does not typically get involved in our homicide investigations. In this instance, however, she was friendly with the deceased. Bingo, sir. Yes, sir. At the Senior Center."

Ceepak is using a thumb and finger to massage the bridge of his nose while the Chief unloads on him in his ear.

"Well, sir, we have, in the past, done favors for Dr. Kurth. I don't think this will, as you suggest, 'ruin our relationship' with the county medical examiner's office. Yes, sir, you have my word. If Dr. Kurth, as you say, 'laughs in my face,' I will let the matter drop. Thank you, Chief."

Ceepak thumbs the OFF button.

"You guys are really going to investigate Dr. Rosen's death?" says Christine with a nervous titter. "He was ninety-four."

"Indeed," says Ceepak. "However, he was not on Hospice Care, therefore an investigation into the cause of his death may be warranted."

"It's up to Dr. Kurth?" I say.

"Roger that." Then he turns to Christine. "How was Dr. Rosen this morning when you came on duty?"

"Tired, I guess. He didn't want to wake up and eat breakfast or take his morning pills. Finally, after a little cajoling, I got him out of bed, escorted him to the bathroom, helped him clean up, brought him back to bed. He still wouldn't take his pills. Wanted to sleep some more."

"So you let him?"

She nods.

"And where did you place his morning pills?"

"Back in the kitchen with the pill organizer."

"What happened next?"

"I had to go to my room."

"Why?"

"Around 8 A.M., David and Judith showed up. They're still mad at me about what happened in the courtroom with Judith's sister. So Monae agreed to cover for me."

"When did you give Dr. Rosen his pills?"

"I guess it was around eight thirty, after David and Judith finally left. Monae knocked on my door. Told me they were gone; that I was back on duty. I finally got Dr. Rosen to drink a can of Ensure—because he needed something in his stomach before he took his medicines. I had his morning pills all set in a paper cup, but he wanted to talk first."

"About what?"

"Family stuff."

"Christine?" says Ceepak.

"Yes, sir?"

"Your patient is deceased. The possibility that he might've been murdered has been raised. Your obligation is to the truth now, not your patient."

"So you're saying I'm free to discuss 'family affairs' that came to my knowledge during the practice of my calling?"

Yep, it's code versus code.

And if I'm following the ethical logic, here, our need to learn the truth in the pursuit of justice outweighs Christine's obligation to keep mum about the dead man's family.

# 24

CHRISTINE TAKES A MOMENT BUT WINDS UP ON THE SAME PAGE as Ceepak.

"The reason Dr. Rosen was so tired this morning was because, last night, Monae drove him to The Trattoria, a restaurant on Ocean Avenue."

The Trattoria is one of Sea Haven's swankiest dining spots. They charge so much, they only have like ten tables and a back room for "private affairs."

"Michael Rosen had booked the restaurant's private room so he could share what he called 'exciting news' with his father and brother. Judith and Little Arnie weren't invited. When Dr. Rosen arrived at the restaurant, Michael told Monae to 'order anything she wanted' in the front dining room while the Rosens had their dinner."

"Did Monae mention anything about this dinner when you relieved her this morning?"

"A little. And then, seeing how tired and upset Dr. Rosen was, I have a feeling that, whatever Michael's big news was, it didn't go over very well."

"So, after you talked about the dinner and he drank his Ensure, you gave Dr. Rosen his pills?"

"That's right. And he drifted back to sleep." Christine's voice catches. "He never woke up. A few minutes later, I was in the kitchen, making tea, when I heard his bed rattling. I thought maybe he was trying to get up and go to the bathroom. I looked in on him. He seemed to be resting peacefully. So, I went ahead and fixed my tea. When I was done, I went back out and . . ."

"He was dead," Ceepak says, so she doesn't have to. "Thank you, Christine. I know it's difficult to relive those final moments but your recollection could prove important. Why don't you go finish packing your belongings into your car?"

"But where am I going? The motel again?"

"Afraid not," I say, fishing my key ring out of my pocket. "Too many tourists in town. You're going to stay at my place until we come up with something better."

Christine looks either confused or interested. One of those.

"I'm going to bunk with the Ceepaks," I add quickly. "Do you know the Sea Village Apartment Complex?"

"Sure. It used to be a motel, right?"

Christine is correct. But the motel owners realized they wouldn't have to work so hard sanitizing toilets for people's protection if they charged by the month instead of the week.

"I'm in one-eleven. There's a parking spot right outside the door. Sorry about the bed. I forgot to make it this morning. Oh, you might want to pick up some toilet paper, too. I was running a little low."

Christine surprises me with another hug.

"Thank you, Danny."

She scurries off into the house.

"So," I say, "should we call Dr. Kurth?"

"Roger that," says Ceepak, shifting back into Robocop mode. "The rattling of his bed prior to his death adds fuel to my mother's suspicions. It could have been death throes, the sudden, violent movements those dying often make immediately prior to their passing . . ."

"Or?"

"It could've been a convulsion, Danny. From cyanide poisoning."

And so we call Dr. Kurth.

Ceepak has her office, home, and cell numbers.

Yes, over the past few years, we've kept the county medical examiner's office kind of busy.

We finally reach her on her cell. At her daughter's soccer game. Ceepak puts her on speakerphone.

"Sorry to disturb you, Rebecca."

"What's up, John?"

"We need a quick autopsy."

There is an awkward pause.

So Ceepak continues. "Arnold Rosen passed away this morning."

"The dentist?"

"Yes, ma'am."

"Wasn't he like a hundred years old?"

"Ninety-four."

"And you want me to do an autopsy on a ninety-four year old dentist because . . . ?"

"Suspicions have been aroused regarding the circumstances of his death."

So far, so good. Ceepak hasn't had to say, *"Because my mommy told me."*

"I don't know, John . . ."

"You could limit the toxicology screen."

"To what?"

"Cyanide poisoning."

"Seriously? Who would want to poison a ninety-four-year-old man?"

"Dr. Kurth?"

"Yes, John?"

"If you find the poison, I promise you, Danny and I will move heaven and earth to find the answer to that question."

Another pause.

Maybe a sigh.

Hard to tell on a cell phone.

"Dr. Rosen is Jewish, correct?" says Dr. Kurth.

"Roger that."

"Okay. They're going to want to hold his funeral ASAP. If we're doing this, we need to do it today."

Yet another pause. So I pipe up. "Are we doing it?"

"Yes," says Dr. Kurth. "Where's the body?"

Ceepak looks at me. I shrug. The hearse we saw earlier didn't have anything like "Fred's Funeral Home" decals plastered all over it.

"We'll get back to you with that information," says Ceepak.

"Hurry. My other daughter's birthday is today. We're doing a cookout and ball bounce."

"Thank you, Rebecca."

"You boys owe me one."

"Roger that," I say while Ceepak nods.

He thumbs off the phone.

We both look back at the beach house.

Now it's Ceepak's turn to sigh.

Because he knows we have to walk back inside and say, *"Excuse us, where is your father's dead body? We'd like to pump his stomach."*

Should be fun.

# 25

HEADING BACK INTO THE BEACH HOUSE THROUGH THE BACK door, we hear a lady screaming her head off.

Judith.

"Severance pay? Are you insane, Michael?"

"She worked for Dad for six months . . ."

"Christine gets nothing," says David. "Zip. Nada."

"She humiliated my sister in open court . . ."

Ceepak clears his throat. Loudly.

We're cops. We don't get to eavesdrop without announcing our presence.

"Excuse us," he says when we step into the room where the Rosen family stands arguing around their late father's empty hospital bed.

Judith beams us her singing nun smile again, squeezes her chubby pink thighs together to squelch her rage.

"We have arranged alternate housing for Ms. Lemonopolous," Ceepak announces.

"Thank you," gushes Michael. "I was a little worried. Does she need money? Because I could lend her . . ."

"Oh no, Michael," says Judith, sweeter than corn syrup. "You don't need to do that. It's a kind and generous offer, but Dad paid Miss Christine a very substantial salary. I'm sure she'll be fine without the family's continued assistance." Judith, who really shouldn't wear miniskirts, locks her focus on Ceepak. "Do you officers need something else? We have so many preparations to attend to. Our rabbi, Dr. Bronstein, is on his way over to help us make the necessary arrangements."

"Yes, ma'am," says Ceepak. "Where is Dr. Rosen's body?"

"Excuse me?"

"Which funeral home will you be using?"

"Grossman & Mehringer. Why?"

"The county medical examiner, at our request, is going to perform a post mortem toxicology screening."

"What?" this from Michael. "An autopsy?"

Guess he produces cop shows out in Hollywood.

"You're joking right?"

"No, sir. We want to eliminate even the slightest possibility that your father was poisoned."

"Poisoned?" says Judith, her smile slipping dangerously close to a sneer. "Dad was ninety-four years old. He passed away in his sleep. Please, officers, allow him to die with a modicum of dignity."

"Besides," says David, "doesn't this 'county medical examiner' have more important duties to attend to? It's Saturday. They'll get time and a half. That's why Dad's property taxes are so high."

Michael stays mum.

"What if we don't approve of this autopsy?" says Judith. "Surely, as his family, we have a say in this matter."

"Actually," says Ceepak, "in the state of New Jersey the medical examiner autopsy, unlike a hospital autopsy, does not require permission from the next of kin. It is done under statutory authority. Also, it will not delay your funeral arrangements as . . ."

There is a knock at the front door.

"That's probably Rabbi Bronstein," says David. "I'll let him in."

David practically runs to the front door. Judith blinks and smiles some more.

"Hello, Rabbi," David says out in the entryway. "Thank you for coming so quickly."

"Of course, David. How are you holding up?"

"Okay. I mean we expected this, but . . . still . . ."

David leads Dr. Bronstein into the dining room.

"He was your father," says the rabbi, a gentle-looking man in a dark suit and yarmulke. "Your grief is understandable. But grief is an ancient and universal power that helps us humans mend our broken hearts. Hello, Judith. Michael. My condolences on your loss."

"Thank you, Rabbi," says Judith, brushing at her blonde hair. "I wonder if you could help us with an unfortunate situation . . ."

She gestures toward Ceepak and me.

We're her unfortunate situation.

"Hello, Rabbi Bronstein," says Ceepak.

"John. Always good to see you."

"These police officers want to do an autopsy," says Judith, jutting out her plus-size hip and resting a hand on it.

"Is this true, John?"

"Yes, sir. We'd like to eliminate any doubt as to the cause of Dr. Rosen's death. However, to do so, we will need access to his corpse."

"Of course. Have you alerted the morticians at Grossman & Mehringer? They may have already begun their embalming procedures."

"Rabbi?" Judith sounds, well, mortified.

The Rabbi shrugs. "What Detective Ceepak and the police are asking is reasonable, Judith. And I, of course, harbor no religious objection to the procedure. Go, John. Do this thing."

"Thank you, Rabbi."

"Shalom. Might I call you later?"

"Of course. Do you still have my cell number?"

"Yes." Bronstein taps his suit coat pocket. "It's in my phone. From February."

"I look forward to talking to you." Ceepak turns to face the Rosen family. "Again our condolences on your loss. And rest assured, the medical examiner will treat your father's remains with the utmost respect and dignity."

I take that as our cue to hurry out the front door.

So we do.

When we're in my Jeep, I ask Ceepak, "So where to?"

"My mother's. I want to ask her for the full details of her conversation with Dr. Rosen."

I crank the ignition and we take off. I have one of those swirling gumball-machine lights in my glove compartment that I could slap on the hood of my Jeep (it plugs into the cigarette lighter) but I figure running over to see Ceepak's mom isn't really a lights-and-sirens type event.

"So," I say, "what happened back in February?"

"Some local skinheads spray-painted swastikas on the front doors of B'nai Jeshurun."

"And you cracked the case?"

"Roger that. One of the boys left his full handprint on a can of black spray paint he had tossed into the bushes not far from the temple doors. I ran it through the system. Made a match."

"How come I never heard about this?"

"We opened and closed the case in under twelve hours. I believe you had the night off."

"But I never saw the swastikas."

"The two boys—who, by the way, confessed immediately, when I noted the incriminating black paint caked under their finger-nails—agreed to scrub the doors clean before I escorted them over to the Ocean County Juvenile Detention Center."

Of course they did. Ceepak can be very convincing.

While I drive, Ceepak works his phone. He keeps all his conversations on speakerphone so I can stay up to speed.

The morticians at Grossman & Mehringer are instructed not to touch Dr. Rosen's body and to expect Dr. Kurth's imminent arrival. The Funeral Home agrees to cooperate and "help in any way possible." They've worked with Dr. Kurth before.

The next call goes to Dr. Kurth. She'll make her examination, take her fluid samples, and get the body back to the funeral home "before sundown."

She promises us results ASAP.

"Not that we're going to find anything except what he ate for breakfast."

Ceepak thanks Dr. Kurth.

Five minutes later, we pull up to the Oceanaire condo complex's guard shack.

"Hey, Detective Ceepak," says the young guy with the clipboard on guard duty. "Here to see your mom?"

"Roger that. And, Bruce?"

"Sir?"

"Be extra vigilant. As anticipated, my father has returned to Sea Haven."

"Don't worry, sir." He taps a sheet of paper taped to the top of his small desk. "We have the protocol and procedures right here. We are ready to rock and roll."

"Excellent. Keep up the good work."

"You got it, man."

The gate rises.

"That's Bruce Southworth," says Ceepak as we cruise into the condo complex. "He has the potential to be a fine law-enforcement officer some day."

"Good to know."

Ceepak's phone chirrups. It's his standard ringtone, not one of the ones I programmed in for him.

He jabs the speakerphone button.

"Hello?"

"John?"

"Rabbi Bronstein."

"Yes. Might I speak freely?"

"Certainly, sir. I'm here with my partner, detective Boyle."

Wow, that's right. This, for the time being, anyway, is a murder investigation. That means I'm a detective again.

"The young man who was with you at the house?"

"That's right."

"Then he should hear what I am about to say, too."

"What's wrong, rabbi?"

"I didn't want to mention this in front of his children but, late last night, just after midnight, Arnold Rosen called me."

"And?"

"He told me he was 'surrounded by assassins.' This autopsy you're doing? I feel it could prove a wise and prudent move."

# 26

MRS. CEEPAK OFFERS US COFFEE IN CHINA CUPS WITH SAUCERS.

I don't have any saucers, just coffee mugs. This is why there are numerous brown rings staining most of my furniture.

Hope Christine can deal.

Mrs. Ceepak also has an assortment of Pepperidge Farm cookies. And they're not in the box or the bag. They're on a glass tray sculpted to look like a flat flower.

"We wanted to ask you about your conversation last night with Dr. Rosen," says Ceepak.

"Fine, dear. Would you like a Mint Milano, first?"

"No, Mom. Thanks."

"How about a Brussels?"

"No, thank you."

"A Tahiti? They have that coconut you like."

Ceepak takes a cookie and crunches it. I guess he's lost this battle before.

I pick up a dainty cookie, myself, and almost extend my pinky finger while I nibble around its edges. Almost. Mrs. Ceepak is crunching a Mint Milano. And since we all know it's rude to talk with your mouth full of food, the only sound in the room is that of crisp cookies being ground to bits by multiple molars.

Ceepak finishes his cookie, dusts off his hands.

"Mom, in your conversation last night with Dr. Rosen, what else did he say?"

"Oh, John, he was so sad. Felt like his whole family was against him. His two boys, his daughter-in-law."

"Were those the assassins he feared?"

"I suppose. Apparently, David and Judith were furious because, just last week, Arnie visited his lawyer and made a few changes to his will."

Okay. Maybe I've seen watched too many "48 Hours Mystery" shows and old episodes of *Columbo*. But "Last Minute Changing Of The Will" is always a prime murder motivator—either to stop the changes or reap the rewards.

"What changes did he make?"

"I'm not sure, John. Arnie didn't go into specifics. Just said that, when he told David and Judith what he'd done, they both blew up. 'You're jeopardizing your only grandson's future,' they said. His other boy, Michael, the one from Hollywood, he didn't seem to mind, but Michael has money of his own. Do you think the changes Arnie made to his will is the reason someone murdered him?"

"First, Mom, we don't know yet whether he was murdered or not . . ."

"I do."

"You do? How?"

"Female intuition."

Oh-kay. Too bad the Supreme Court won't let us arrest people on the grounds of "my mother said so" anymore.

"Second," Ceepak continues, "we'd have to know the particulars of the will alterations or amendments to see who would benefit, who would lose."

Mrs. Ceepak puts down her cup and saucer. "Then it's all my fault."

"Come again?"

"Arnold told me that what I did with Christine, paying for her defense attorney, inspired him to help those less fortunate. He said he wanted some portion of his last will and testament to be a mitzvah. To do some good."

"Perhaps he bequeathed a generous donation to a favorite charity," says Ceepak.

"Which would funnel money away from his kids and grandson," I say.

"You see?" says Mrs. Ceepak. "It *is* my fault."

Ceepak reaches over and places a gentle hand on his mother's knee.

"Mom, if the autopsy indicates foul play, rest assured, justice will be served."

Mrs. Ceepak puts down her tiny cookie.

"I liked Arnie Rosen, John. Felt sorry for him, too. He could get so angry over the smallest slights. One time, a gal at the senior center brought him sweet tea when he wanted it unsweetened. He blew up. Called the gal all sorts of horrible names." She sighs. "Growing old, you lose control over so much of your life. That can change people. Make them moody. One minute you're sweet, the next you're yelling at a gal at the senior center. Other times, after bingo, Arnie and I would just sit and talk. He is a very intelligent man. Quite the vocabulary. He taught me when to use 'who' and when to use 'whom.' I told him about Billy."

Ceepak puts down his cookie.

"How your father always teased him about being a sissy boy. How that horrible priest took advantage of him. How Billy died."

I put down my half-eaten cookie, too.

"That's when Arnie told me about his son. Michael. The one who lives in Hollywood."

"We met Michael at Dr. Rosen's house today," says Ceepak.

"Nice boy?"

"Seems like it. Of course, we only had the briefest encounter . . ."

"Arnie didn't like the fact that his son was 'blatantly and openly gay.' Those are his words. Blatantly and openly." Mrs. Ceepak shakes her head. "I tried to tell him that your son is your son and you love him no matter what. Arnie didn't want to hear it. Between us, I think that's why the boy moved so far away. He knew he wasn't welcome at home."

That's when Ceepak's other cell phone jangles like an alarm clock.

It's his work phone. He always carries two; doesn't want to blur the line, he says, between his professional and personal life.

While Ceepak tugs the thing off his belt, I'm wondering if Dr. Kurth already has our test results. If so, it'd be a new Indoor Forensics record.

"This is Ceepak, go."

Yeah. That's how Ceepak answers his work phone.

"Roger that. Call nine-one-one. We're on our way." He clips the phone back to his belt. "Danny?" He reaches behind his back, just to make sure his Glock is still in that cross draw holster. I stand up and tap my hip under my shirttail to do the same.

"What's up?" I ask.

"Gatehouse."

"Got you."

We're kind of talking in code. No sense scaring Ceepak's mom by letting her know her ex-husband has come a'callin'.

# 27

WE HOP IN MY JEEP.

"Is it your dad?" I say.

"Negative. His emissary."

I think emissary means messenger and not a building full of foreign diplomats. I'll look it up later. Right now, I slap the swirling red light on the hood of my ride. When he sees us coming, Mr. Ceepak's "emissary" will know he or she just stepped into a pile of serious trouble.

We break The Oceanaire's posted 15 mph speed limit and whip around the roads snaking back to the gatehouse.

Bruce Southworth, the young security guard, is out of his hut, his clipboard clutched in his hand, like he'll use the thing as a weapon if he has to.

Young Benjamin Sinclair, decked out in his sloppy StratosFEAR uniform khakis and polo shirt, is straddling the seat of his motor scooter, holding a bunch of flowers wrapped in a cone of clear cellophane. One of the bouquets they sell at the Acme grocery store near the dairy department.

"Yo," Ben says to Southworth. "Open the freaking gate, dude. Sun's wilting the flowers, big time."

"Mrs. Ceepak does not wish to receive anything from anyone associated with her ex-husband," says Southworth, professionally and politely.

"Roger that," says Ceepak, as we roll out of my Jeep and march over to the guardhouse.

"Yo!" says Sinclair. "Help me out here, po-po. Tell this clip-board monkey fool to step off and get out of my grill. I just be delivering flowers from your old man. They're for your old lady."

"She doesn't want them," I say because Ceepak is too busy trying to figure out what the heck Ben just said.

"For real, dawg? Dag. My pops only be sending my moms flowers after she catches him bangin' some skanky beach babe."

"Mrs. Ceepak does not want flowers from her ex-husband," I say.

"Aw, come on. Let me in. I promised Joe Cool I'd make the drop, dawg."

"The grounds of The Oceanaire are considered private property," says guardhouse Bruce. "Access to the area beyond this gate is only granted to our residents and their invited guests."

I'm impressed. The kid's good.

In the distance, I hear the wail of police sirens.

He also knows how to dial 911.

Ben hears the approaching cop car, too. He tugs down on the strap of his motorcycle helmet. If he wasn't wearing one, I'd arrest him on the spot for violating the State of New Jersey's Mandatory Helmet Law.

"Go home, Ben," I say as the sirens move closer.

"Can't, Holmes. I'm OTJ. On the job."

"Then go back to the boardwalk."

"A'ight, a'ight."

"Ben?"

"Yo?"

"Why do you talk like that? You go to Pine Barrens. It's a prep school."

Ben doesn't answer, but he does drop his fake ghetto gangsta act.

"What am I supposed to do with these stupid flowers? Give 'em to the other cops when they get here?"

Ceepak steps forward. Snatches the bouquet out of Ben's hand. I feel sorry for the roses. From the sound of crinkling plastic, I think Ceepak is strangling their stems.

"My mother," he says, quite calmly, "is an avid gardener. She keeps a compost bin. These will make a excellent contribution to her pile of vegetable peelings and kitchen scraps."

"She still in Unit Three?" asks Ben with an ugly little smirk.

Ceepak glares at him, hard.

"Yeah," says Ben. "Mr. Joe Cool knows *exactly* where his old lady lives, dude. Deal with it."

Ben putters off on his scooter.

Ceepak and I wait for the on-duty guys to arrive. We fill them in on what went down.

"We'll cruise up this way a little more often," says Julie Whitaker, one of the officers in the patrol car. "Keep an eye on things."

"Appreciate that," says Ceepak.

He gives Julie a two-finger salute. She snaps one right back.

When Julie and her partner drive away, Ceepak and I head back to Unit Three.

It's time to talk to Ceepak's mom about installing a home security system.

Something other than her son.

# 28

WE TELL MRS. CEEPAK ABOUT HER HUSBAND'S PRESENCE ON the island then try to persuade her to install a burglar alarm (and maybe a machine-gun nest up on the roof).

She thinks a home security system would be a "silly waste of money. That's why we have the nice young guards in the gatehouse."

So Ceepak and I decide we'll try, once more, to persuade his skeevy dad to leave the poor woman (who just happens to be filthy rich) alone.

We have to wait through ten drops of the StratosFEAR ride till Mr. Ceepak gets his 3 P.M. break.

"Roses have always been her favorite," says Mr. Ceepak. "I used to bring her a single rose every time I took her out on a date."

Why do I think the young Joe Ceepak used to pluck those roses off a neighbor's bush ten seconds before knocking on Adele's front door?

The three of us are squeezed inside a cramped, glassed-in building. The free fall ride's control shack. Outside, the walls are painted sky blue with wispy clouds. There's even a sign labeling this tiny booth "Mission Control."

Inside, the walls are sheets of bare plywood and two-by-fours. Windows ring the upper third of the hexagonical hut, turning it into a hothouse reeking of vomit.

"Sorry about the stench, boys," says Mr. Ceepak, who sits on a stool near a metal box of chunky control buttons and knobs. A mop handle leans against the wall. Its stringy head is soaking in a murky bucket near Joe Ceepak's feet.

"Couple college kids got tanked on beer before riding the ride. Blew chunks like puke geysers when they landed. Vomit splattered everywhere. I had Ben mop it up before sending him over to Adele's. Good kid, that Ben. Hard worker. Type of boy that would make any father proud."

Mr. Ceepak takes a swig from a quart jug of warm orange juice. I might be the next to hurl.

"You know, Johnny, I would've delivered those flowers myself but, like you told Bob and the guys at Sinclair Enterprises, this ride can only stay open if there's a factory-trained and certified operator running things in the control booth. For now, that's me. They got me working twelve-hour shifts, seven days a week. Not that I mind. The pay is decent. The overtime is even better. And son, not that you care—I need the cash."

"Sir," says Ceepak, "I will only say this one more time: stay away from my mother and her money."

"Her money? Who said anything about her money?"

"I know why you are here."

"Well, you should. From what Bob tells me, you're the one who told them they had to hire me. And for that, I am eternally grateful . . ."

"For the record," says Ceepak, "I never instructed Sinclair Enterprises to specifically hire *you.*"

"Geeze, Johnny. Why do you always have to be such a hard case? Maybe you should talk to a cop shrink. Work on your anger-management issues. Does this town seriously have some kind of law against people surprising their wives with flowers?"

"She is not your wife."

"Says who?"

"The State of Ohio and an ecclesial tribunal of the Catholic Church, which granted her an annulment."

"In defiance of God's holy word? No church can do that, son. Even if they have a Pope."

"Sorry, sir. They did."

"'I hate divorce, says the Lord God of Israel.' Malachi. Two-sixteen. That's from the Bible."

"Stay away from her. Or you will be arrested."

That's from Ceepak's personal bible.

Mr. Ceepak shakes his head. "I fear for your immortal soul, son. Helping Adele defy God's Holy Word? 'A wife is bound to her husband as long as he lives!' That's from the Bible, too."

"So is that guy with boils all over his butt," I say, remembering the Book of Job from my stint in Catholic High School.

Mr. Ceepak has a confused look on his face again; the one he used to get when he was tanked all the time.

Someone raps knuckles on the glass windows.

Bob.

He raises his arm. Taps his wristwatch. Shoots me and Ceepak a wink and a smile.

"Duty calls, boys," says Mr. Ceepak, gesturing toward the squalid little shack's flimsy door to let us know it is time for us to go. "And Johnny, as you probably know, only certified operators are allowed inside the control booth while the ride is running. So, I gotta ask you boys to leave. Now." He gulps down another chug from his warm orange juice jug.

Ceepak puts his hand on the door. "Stay away from my mother."

"Yeah, yeah. I heard you the first time."

Ceepak and I walk out of the booth. Manager Bob follows after us.

"Your dad sure has one heck of a work ethic, Detective Ceepak. And don't worry. The guys in HR have another factory-trained and certified operator all lined up. Fellow by the name of Shaun McKinnon. Should be on the job Monday. Coming down from Ohio. We'll be able to give your pop a couple nights off. Maybe you two can catch up and smooth things over."

"That, Bob, is never going to happen."

As we walk around the StratosFEAR, I see why Mr. Sinclair was so eager to open his new ride: There is a line, maybe a hundred people long, snaking through the switchbacks and down the pier.

Behind me, I hear a chorus of high-pitched squeals and screams as the open-air chairs whoosh down the girder tower at breakneck speed.

"Awesome," I hear a couple kids on line say in breathless anticipation of their own plunge.

And guess who's at the end of the line?

Judith Rosen and her son, Little Arnie. Thirteen or maybe fourteen, he's wearing a Philadelphia Phillies baseball cap (sideways) on his boy band blonde head. Fortunately, Mrs. Rosen isn't wearing a miniskirt today, just tight jeggings and an unfortunate tank top. It looks like she's smuggling neck pillows around her waist.

"Good afternoon, Mrs. Rosen," says Ceepak when he sees her.

"Good afternoon, detective. Little Arnie was growing restless at home."

"Understandable," says Ceepak.

"So, have you heard anything?"

"From the M.E., you mean?"

"Yes. The, uh, tests you wanted done."

Both Ceepak and Judith are trying very hard not to use words like "medical examiner," "autopsy," and "toxin screening" in front of the late Arnold Rosen's only grandson.

"No, ma'am," says Ceepak. "These things sometimes take days."

"I see. David, of course, works for Sinclair Enterprises," Judith continues. "So, we're lucky. We get free tickets for all the rides; discount coupons for the restaurants and car washes. Comes in handy. Just about the only decent perk they give him . . ."

"Well, enjoy your day as best you can," says Ceepak. "And again, our condolences on your loss."

"Thank you," says Judith. "Officer Boyle?"

Yikes. I'm sort of surprised she remembers my name.

"Yes, ma'am?" I say.

"I understand you've met my sister, Shona? You've even been to her house?"

Oh. I get it now. We're still talking in code but she's letting me know that she knows I was the OIC the night her nephew called 911.

"Quick question." She still sounds as Midwestern sweet as sugar-frosted corn flakes. "Why did you side with Christine Lemonopolous?"

"Excuse me?"

"Why did you only photograph her injuries? Why not my sister's?"

"I, uh . . ."

"Mrs. Rosen," says Ceepak, "if you have queries about police procedure, past or present, might I suggest that you come to our offices to have them answered?"

"Of course. I just think you made a bad call, Officer Boyle. So be careful. Keep an eye on Ms. Lemonopolous. That girl has an extremely short fuse. I'm certain it's only a matter of time before she hurts or injures someone else."

# 29

I HEAD BACK TO MY APARTMENT TO GRAB SOME CLOTHES AND toiletries for my temporary move to Ceepak's place.

I also want to check up on Christine. See how she's doing. Keep an eye on that short fuse of hers. Wouldn't want my apartment to blow up while's she's using it. I'd never get back my damage deposit.

The Sea Village Apartment Complex sits halfway between what you might call "downtown" Sea Haven and the southern tip of the island where the rich folks like Shona Oppenheimer live.

I park my Jeep and head to Room 111. I fish in my cargo shorts for the keys before remembering, duh, I gave them to Christine.

So I knock on the door.

"Danny?"

Christine's voice would probably be muffled more if my front door weren't the cheapest kind they sell at Home Depot.

"Yeah."

"Just a second."

I hear a chain slide. Knobs turn.

She's using locks I forgot I even had.

"Hey!" she says when the door swings open.

Her curly hair is damp. Her face is scrubbed clean. She's dressed in a cute, chocolate colored blouse and is working one of my threadbare towels into her left ear. I hope the towel was actually clean and didn't just pass my early morning sniff test.

"Come on in," Christine says, her voice cheery and a little nervous. Yes, this is weird. We haven't even been on a date but it's like we're doing the whole "Honey, I'm home" bit from some ancient sitcom.

"I just need to grab a few things," I say.

"Sure. Make yourself at home."

I glance around the room. I love what Christine has done with the place.

Well, mostly, she's lit a fancy vanilla-scented candle to cover up the smell of my gym clothes (I really should wash that stuff more often). She's also draped a couple colorful scarves over the window and put some flowers in an empty pickle jar on my kitchenette table. Looks nice.

"I hope you don't mind," she says. "I added a few girly-girl touches."

"No problem. Just need to grab some clothes and my shaving stuff."

"Sure." She moves left. I go right. The room is so tiny we have to dance around each other to maneuver.

"I can't thank you enough, Danny."

"No worries."

I sidle past her. Open some drawers. Try to ignore the bras and Victoria Secret type items lying dangerously close to my boxer shorts.

Christine watches me pack. Smiles.

"I can see why Katie was so crazy about you."

Lump in throat time again. "She was?"

"Totally. 'Danny, Danny, Danny.' It's all she ever talked about."

"Really?"

"Cross my heart." When she says that, she makes the accompanying gesture. Across her chest. What I'm saying is Christine is, basically, pointing at her boobs. Not that she had to. I was already there.

"So, you hungry?" I ask.

"Starving."

"You want to go grab a bite?"

She hesitates. "I should probably eat in for a while. I'm a gal on a budget, Danny. My savings can't last forever and I've lost two jobs this month . . ."

"My treat."

"No. You've done enough."

"Come on. Nothing fancy. The Dinky Dinghy."

"The shrimp place?"

"I'm a regular."

Christine goes to my desk, flips through the glossy pages of a "See Sea Haven" tourist magazine she must've picked up when she stopped off to buy toilet paper.

"They might have a coupon in here. Everybody else does. Score! Twenty percent off!"

# 30

THE DINKY DINGHY ADVERTISES ITSELF AS "FINE DINING WITHOUT the atmosphere."

It's basically a squat, flat-roof building that could double as a dry cleaner's. Bright, shrimp-pink poles hold up signs advertising clams, shrimp, lobster, and chowda. It's mostly a fresh fish market that does a brisk takeout business but has five or six picnic tables out front in the gravel lawn for people like Christine and me.

We take a table two away from one occupied by a tourist family on their first day of vacation (you can tell by the farmer tan lines and SHNJ tee-shirts). They're happily digging into a seafood feast, what the Dinky Dinghy calls "The Works": fried shrimp, fried scallops, crab cakes (sort of fried), fried flounder filets, fried clam strips, a bucket of fries, and a quart of coleslaw. I don't think the coleslaw is fried but I bet they're working on that.

"This looks amazing," Christine says, sitting down with her blackened salmon sandwich, garden salad, and bottle of Vitamin

Water Zero. I went with the "Scrumptious Scampi." Lots of garlic. If I know my breath stinks, I won't be so tempted to kiss Christine when our non-date dinner date is done. I'm drinking a Stewart's Orange 'N Cream. We came in my car. I am the designated driver.

"You want a beer or some wine with dinner?" I ask.

Neptune's Nog, a package store, is right across the street, on the other side of Ocean Avenue.

"No, thanks."

"You sure?"

"Yes. Thank you. Some of the meds I take . . . well, it's best if I don't drink."

"Cool," I say, even though I probably should've thought of something better.

Christine pushes her tray a few inches away. Gets this serious look on her face.

"It was right after Katie died," she says. "My whole life went into a kind of free fall."

"You don't have to talk about it if you don't want to."

"I do, Danny. You and Ceepak and Ceepak's mom have done so much for me. Besides, talking is good."

"Okay."

"It started right after Katie died. I just couldn't do my job any more. Every time the ER doors swung open, I saw Katie, covered with blood, lying on the gurney. It could be a guy who'd been in a motorcycle wreck, but I'd see Katie. I started making mistakes. Little things. But even little mistakes can kill someone who's already in a trauma situation."

"So you quit?"

Christine nods. "They called it a long-term leave of absence. Set me up with a program. The hospital was very helpful."

"Because you're a very good nurse. They don't want to lose you."

That earns a small smile. "Well, you're very sweet to say so." She shakes her head. "I thought PTSD was just something soldiers earned in war zones. I didn't think it could happen to me. But I had never had someone that close to me die before."

I wish I could say the same.

"So how's it going?" I ask. "Now?"

"Better. I feel like I could, maybe, go back to the hospital. Maybe not the trauma unit, right away . . ."

"That's a good idea. Maybe you could work someplace, I don't know, happier. Maybe the maternity ward."

Christine laughs. "Screaming babies? Anxious new mothers? Nothing stressful about that . . ."

I'm laughing now, too. "Guess you're right. Anyway, I think it's great that you still want to be a nurse. Someday. Somewhere."

"I don't know what else I'd do, Danny. My mom always said I was born to be a nurse."

Funny. Mine always says I was born to be a pain in her patootie.

"And Shona Oppenheimer knew all about this . . . situation?"

"It was supposed to be kept super-confidential."

"But somebody told Shona."

"One of her plastic surgeons. The lady who gives her the Botox shots." Christine taps her forehead. "Dr. McWrinkles works at the hospital sometimes, too. I guess she knew somebody who knew somebody who was in the mood to gossip . . ."

"Ohmigod," I hear a woman shout.

"He should've chewed it more!" growls a man.

I whip around. It's the family. The mom and dad are up off their picnic benches, hovering behind a kid, maybe ten, who keeps coughing.

"He's choking!" screams the mom.

"I'm okay, mom," gasps the boy. "It's just stuck."

Christine is up and over to their picnic table two seconds before I am.

"Can you breathe?" she asks the boy.

He nods.

"I'm a nurse," she says, calmly taking the little boy's wrist in her hand.

"I'm a cop," I add. "I'll call nine-one-one."

"Hang on, Danny," says Christine. She looks at her watch, checks the boy's pulse. "His vitals are good."

A waitress—a pal of mine named Ansley Parker—comes running out of the seafood shop.

"Do we need to do the Heimlich, Danny?" she asks.

Guess Ansley's been studying that poster every restaurant has hanging on a wall for so long, she's ready to jump into action and pump the kid's abdomen with her fist.

"Hold up," I say.

"Does it feel like it's stuck?" Christine asks the boy.

"Yes," the boy answers, proving that his airway is clear. He taps his sternum. "Right here. I can't cough it up."

"Danny?"

"Yeah?"

"Pour some water on my hand, please."

"Oh-kay."

I grab a bottle of Poland Spring someone at the table had been drinking. Do as I was told.

"Okay, hon," Christine says to the kid, "we need to upchuck that chunk of food. You willing to give it a shot?"

The kid smiles.

"You've thrown up before?"

"When I had the stomach flu," he says, his voice a little hoarse. "Yeah."

"Good. This will be just like that." Christine looks to the parents.

"What are you going to do?" asks the mom.

"Stimulate his gag reflex."

The dad raises his eyebrows and makes the classic "gag me now" gesture: two fingers to his open mouth with the tongue lolling out.

"Right," says Christine.

"Okay," says the mom.

Christine turns to the boy. "You ready to do this thing, buddy?"

The kid nods.

Christine places her (sort of) clean fingers into the boy's mouth.

He gags.

Up comes an explosion of brown, chunky mush.

And one white hunk of scallop.

Christine's cute chocolate brown top? It is now slimed with dribbling tan slop.

"Thank you!" gushes the boy, breathing deep just to prove that he can do it without coughing.

"Thank goodness you were here," says the mom.

"You're lucky to have her as a girlfriend," the dad says to me, shaking my hand, like I did something to be congratulated for.

I think all three of them want to hug Christine.

But they hesitate.

No sense in everybody's top getting ruined by all that regurgitated chum.

# 31

WE TAKE TURNS SHUFFLING IN AND OUT OF MY APARTMENT
to gather up our dirty clothes and head to the nearest 24-hour
laundromat.

Christine, of course, needs to peel off her soaked blouse and
change into something clean.

I wait in the parking lot until she comes out of unit 111 in
a new outfit, toting a canvas sack like Mrs. Claus. Then I dash
in to grab my stinky gym clothes, socks, and whatever else is
tossed in the corner of the closet or tucked under the bed. I stuff
it all into a brown grocery sack because I'm all about re-using
and re-cycling.

Once again, we take my car. I'm a little worried about how
Christine is going to scrape up gas money without a job.

It's dark out. Moths are dive-bombing into the halogen
streetlamps up and down the avenue. Christine is wearing what I
think they still call a halter top. As in, *"Halt! Don't go there, Danny."*

If you were familiar with my romantic history, you'd know I don't have the best long-term luck with the ladies. My girlfriends either end up as sniper targets or turn into psycho-freak bunny-boilers. It's never a simple boy-meets-girl-and-they-hop-into-a-fast-car Springsteen song for me.

During the spin cycle, Christine tells me how scary things were at the late Arnold Rosen's house this morning, right before Ceepak and I showed up.

"That Judith told me to get out of the house or she'd finish what her sister started."

"You're kidding?"

Christine shakes her curly head. "I know she comes off all sweet and nicey-nice but trust me, Danny, she can be a real witch."

"Good to know," I say, even though I'm not sure Christine is what they call a reliable source. I'm guessing that, whenever she sees Judith Rosen, she also sees Shona Oppenheimer. Coming at her, arms outstretched like a zombie, hands ready to crush her windpipe.

And of course, Judith keeps insisting that Christine is the evil one.

After we transfer our sopping wet clothes to the dryers, Christine tells me more.

"We were friendly at first," she says. "Shona and me. So, when I lost my day job with Mrs. Crabtree, Shona suggested I take the job at her sister's father-in-law's house."

"Who's Mrs. Crabtree?"

"Mauna Faye Crabtree. Sweet little old lady. Eighty-eight years old. I was with her for three months before she passed away."

I nod. I figure burying your clients is just part of the whole home health aide deal.

"I was so grateful to have more work," Christine continues. "I really didn't have any kind of problem when they asked me to keep an eye on Dr. Rosen's medical condition. I thought Judith and David were just looking out for a stubborn old man who wouldn't reveal anything about his health conditions to his family. But then, they started asking me to do weird stuff."

"Like what."

"Find his will. Keep tabs on anything Michael Rosen said or wrote to his dad. Smuggle out medical records."

"Did you do any of this stuff?"

Thankfully, Christine shakes her head.

"No. Dr. Rosen was my patient, not Judith or David. My loyalty was to him, not them."

"Which isn't what David and Judith wanted to hear?"

"Not at all. So Judith nagged her sister. Told Shona to get on my case. Push me harder. Search my shoulder bag."

"Which takes us to the night I caught the nine-one-one call."

"Yeah."

"So, what do you think David and Judith were really after?"

Christine shrugs.

"Do you think Harvey Nussbaum was right?" I say. "Did they want Dr. Rosen's beach house?"

Another shrug. "Only one thing I know for sure about the Rosen family. Little Arnie was Dr. Rosen's favorite. He called his grandson his 'living legacy'—the heir to the 'Rosen bloodline.' He even hoped Little Arnie would grow up and become a dentist and restore 'our family's good name at U Penn.'"

"He certainly has the smile for it," I say, remembering all those photographs hanging on the walls of Dr. Rosen's home.

"No doubt about it. He's a good-looking kid. Nice face."

Christine doesn't add any commentary.

Like how Little Arnie is lucky he didn't end up with his father's face, which sort of resembles the bongo-thumping chimpanzee with the beatnik beard from one of those monkey-of-the-month calendars.

"I guess now that Dr. Rosen is dead," says Christine, "the two brothers will split everything. David will get his half of the house, Michael his."

When our clothes come out of the dryers, Christine goes to this tall, flat table in the back of the laundromat and starts folding her things, even her undergarments. For me, this is a novel concept. Usually, I just stuff everything back into the brown paper bag I brought it in and go with the rumpled look.

Tonight, however, I pretend like I always fold my clothes and match up my socks. After watching Christine in action for a minute or two, I even figure out how to do it. Sort of.

And then I drive Christine home to my place, which is now, temporarily, her place.

"You want to come in?" she asks.

That vanilla scent from those candles in my apartment? It's on her skin and in her hair, too. Her chocolate brown eyes are wide and eager. I can feel heat radiating off her body. As the windows start fogging up, I feel like I'm sitting in a cozy sauna with a warm batch of Nestle Toll House cookies.

"Ceepak's probably waiting up for me," I say. My voice cracks the way it did back in sixth grade on the word "me."

"Well, maybe one day, Danny Boyle, you'll let me show you how much I appreciate all that you've done for me."

"Okay," I say, making sure it comes out deep and low. "Some day."

"Promise?"

"Cross my heart."

Christine leans in and kisses me. On the cheek. The move jostles everything her halter-top was supposed to be halting.

But somehow, I keep my hands firmly gripped on the steering wheel.

# 32

I NEED A BEER.

I'm not sure Ceepak has any in his fridge. At least not the real stuff. Ever since his time in Iraq, he's big on Near Beer—stuff like O'Doul's and Coors Non-Alcoholic.

So I pull into the parking lot for Neptune's Nog Discount Liquor Outlet.

It's another flat-roofed building the size of a small supermarket with every kind of beer neon glowing in its front wall of windows. Bud. Miller. Corona. Sam Adams. Blue Moon.

Inside the store you'll find aisles lined with shelves crowded by battalions of wine and liquor bottles, not to mention rack after rack of salty snacks. You'll also see towering stacks of beer packaged in what they call suitcases—24-can cartons with a handy handle for toting down to the beach or up to your motel room.

I pull into the parking lot next to a dinged-up Ford F-150 pickup and douse the headlights so the moths will leave my Jeep alone and go attack the fluorescent tube lights giving the package store its ghoulish green glow.

The instant I climb out of my Jeep, I see Ben Sinclair and a few of his young suburban gangsta buddies leaning against the booze mart's grocery cart return corral.

They have their hands stuffed into the front of their hoodies or the pockets of jeans hanging halfway down their butt so they can show off their plaid Ralph Lauren boxer shorts.

They're waiting.

For somebody in the store, judging by the way one of the kids keeps craning his neck and going up on tippy toe.

By kids, I mean neither Ben nor any of his crew are over twenty-one, the minimum legal drinking age.

I know who they're waiting for.

The same guy me and my underage buds used to wait for outside a package store on a warm June night down the Jersey Shore: an older dude to go inside to buy us our brewskis for a small handling fee.

I hang near my Jeep. Wait to see who Ben's dude is. Ours was a wino we called Clint The Splint because he always seemed to have one limb or another in a plaster cast. He'd go into Fritzie's package store and get us anything we wanted for five bucks. Cigarettes. Boone's Farm. Malt Duck. Colt 45. Slim Jims. Hey, we had to eat something.

I hear sleigh bells tinkle. The front door swishes open.

And out comes Mr. Joseph "Sixpack" Ceepak.

# 33

I'M WONDERING WHAT BIBLE VERSE MR. CEEPAK'S GOING TO quote when I bust him for buying alcohol for minors.

Whistling merrily, he strides out the sliding door and into the harsh glare of those overhead fluorescents. He's still in his StratosFEAR uniform and wears a cocky grin on his face. One arm is wrapped around a grocery sack full of jingling glass bottles. His other is toting what looks like a filing-cabinet-sized carton of Budweiser. Maybe they're doing 48-packs now.

Ben and the boys over by the cart corral give off a couple "Boo-yahs" and swarm like a wolf pack toward Mr. Ceepak.

"You get the Mike's and vodka, too?" asks Ben.

Mr. Ceepak is about to answer when he sees me step out of the shadows.

"Good evening, Officer Boyle," he says.

I nudge my head toward his groceries. "That all for you, sir?"

Now Ben and his pals try to act casual but their worried eyes betray them. They're probably wondering if the old fart Ben hired is going to rip them off for a hundred bucks worth of booze plus whatever handling fee he charges.

"Yeah," says Mr. Ceepak. "This is all mine."

One of the kids is about to say something when Ben elbows him in the ribs.

"Setting up housekeeping," says Mr. Ceepak. "Excuse me. Need to load up my truck." He gestures toward the dirt splattered workhorse parked next to my Jeep.

"I thought you put down the bottle when you picked up the bible, sir?"

"The two are not mutually exclusive, Officer Boyle. Ecclesiastes nine tells us to 'Seize life! Eat bread with gusto; drink wine with a robust heart. Oh yes, God takes pleasure in your pleasure!'"

"So, you're just out here pleasuring God, huh?"

"Doin' my best, Boyle. Doin' my best."

"Hey, as long as you don't drink and drive, I have no problem with you buying enough beer, hard lemonade, and vodka for, oh, I don't know . . ."

I make a show of counting heads in Ben's bunch.

". . . five guys. Just so long as you're not going into liquor stores up and down the island buying booze for kids."

"What?" Mr. Ceepak wheezes out a laugh. Coughs up a nasty wad of sputum. Puts down his cargo so he can jab another cigarette in his mouth to keep his shriveled lungs' mucus mines working. "Why would I do something dumb like that?"

"I don't know." I turn to Ben. "Back in the day, we'd find a wino to do our shopping for like five bucks."

"It's ten now," says Ben's dumbest friend before Ben can elbow him again.

Mr. Ceepak laughs his chesty chuckle. Torches his smoke with a butane lighter that's decorated with a bikini babe.

"Not a bad idea, Boyle. Not bad at all. Ten bucks a pop, huh? Interesting idea. I could use a little extra walking-around money."

"I thought you were making double, triple overtime sending that chair lift up and down on the boardwalk."

"Oh, Ben's daddy pays me good. I ain't complaining." He smacks down a wet drag on his cigarette. "But let's be honest, here. No matter how hard I work, how many hours I put in, I'll never make a million bucks."

Ben Sinclair eyeballs the paper sack and giant cardboard beer carton sitting on the ground. He can't resist. Makes the slightest move for it.

"Whoa," I say. "Are you trying to steal Mr. Ceepak's daily recommended intake of adult beverage?"

"It's ours, dude!" bellows the dumb one.

I scratch the back of my head. "It's yours? Mr. Ceepak says it's his. I don't know. This is a difficult situation. Maybe I better call the cops. Have them come up here and help us figure this thing out. Oh, wait. I *am* a cop . . ."

"Go home, boys," snarls Mr. Ceepak. "We'll talk tomorrow, Ben."

"B-b-but . . ."

"Beat it. Now."

The dumb one puts on his tough guy act. "Yo, old man. You owe us . . ."

"I don't owe you crap, kid." Mr. Ceepak finger-flicks the glowing butt of his cigarette at the boy. "Get lost. All of you. Unless you want Boyle here to arrest your pimply butts."

"Come on, Ethan," says Ben.

Muttering and mumbling, the young men shuffle off into the darkness.

Mr. Ceepak pops a fresh cigarette into his lips.

"You know, Boyle," he says, sending the cancer stick wiggling up and down, "the last time I was in the can, my cellmate was a CPA."

"Huh. I guess you really do meet the most interesting people in jail."

"Oh, you do, Boyle. You do. This guy, Richard Michael Johnson, he was sharp. Swindled the bank he worked for out of a million bucks just by rounding down numbers on his computer. Nobody noticed. Not until he got greedy. Anyway, he told me all a man really needs is one million dollars to be beer and pretzels rich for the rest of his life."

"What's 'beer and pretzels' rich?"

"Less than Wine and Cheese. Nowhere near Caviar and Champagne. I get my hands on a million bucks, Boyle, I'm a happy camper. I go back to my trailer park in Ohio, drink beer and eat pretzels all day long."

"What about protein?"

"What?"

"That's a lot of carbs, sir. Beer. Pretzels. Where's the beef? Maybe you should go to Mickey Dee's and order off the Dollar Menu. You could get a McChicken . . ."

"Cute, Boyle," says Mr. Ceepak, bending down to pick up his groceries, that flicking cigarette perfectly balanced in his lips. "You're still a wise ass, huh?"

"It's what I do best, sir."

"Yeah, well, do me a favor. Tell Johnny I'm not greedy. Adele cleared two point three million when her whacky old aunt kicked the bucket. By rights, we should've split that payday fifty-fifty. But like I said, I'm not greedy. All I want are my beer and my pretzels. One million bucks, Boyle. That's all it costs for you boys to never, ever see me again."

"I thought all we had to do was save your sorry life at the Rolling Thunder roller coaster."

"That was nothing special. You two are cops. It's your job. You had to save me or they'd dock your pay."

"Look, sir," I say, because it's getting late and I'm getting tired of the same-old, same-old with Joe Sixpack. "Your ex-wife is not going to give you a dime. End of story."

"She should. It's all over the bible. 'Wives be submissive to your husbands!'"

"Right. I'll tell Adele you said that."

"That's okay. I'll swing by some day and tell her myself. After all, you and Johnny can't guard her 24/7 now, can you?"

# 34

I HEAD INTO THE STORE, GRAB A SIX-PACK OF SAM ADAMS Summer Ale for me, a sixer of Coors Non-Alcoholic for Ceepak.

Tempted as I am to pop one for the ride home, I don't.

It's a little after eleven when I crunch into the gravel parking lot behind The Bagel Lagoon.

I carry my sack of packaged goods up the outside steel staircase to Ceepak's apartment on the top floor. Using the spare key Ceepak gave me, I let myself in.

The small one-bedroom apartment is dark. Barkley is too old and deaf to do any kind of watchdog duties any more. He just rolls over and cuts the cheese when I come in the door. Twenty-two-hundred hours is the typical lights-out time for Ceepak and Rita. That's 10 P.M. in the Eastern Non-Military Time Zone.

There's a clamshell night-light softly glowing near the fold-out sofa bed, which is made up with sheets and a wool army blanket tucked in so tight you could bounce a dime off it like they always do during inspection in Army movies.

I take the beers to the kitchen area, tuck both six-packs into the fridge, and then pull out a frosty bottle of Sam Adams.

"Mind if I have one of those?"

Ceepak. The guy's stealthy. Even in his bedroom slippers.

"I picked up some of the Coors for you."

"Think I'll go with the real deal tonight. If you have one to spare."

"Definitely."

I hand him a bottle. We grab seats at the linoleum topped kitchen table.

"How's Christine?"

Realizing that *"hot as hell and ready to get busy"* isn't the kind of information Ceepak is typically interested in, I say, "Hanging in."

He nods. "Good."

"I ran into your dad," I say. "At the liquor store. Neptune's Nog, down on Ocean."

"And?"

"The born-again act is just that—an act. He hasn't changed a bit. He just has a new price."

"Which is?"

"One million dollars. Your mother gives him a cut of her inheritance, he promises to leave town."

"Is that so?"

"Yeah. He even has bible verses to back up his claims."

"I'm sure he does. But Danny?"

"Yeah?"

"It's never going to happen."

"Roger that," I say.

We clink bottles, something guys usually only do in beer commercials.

Then we drink and think in silence.

Until it's time for our second beer.

Then we drink and think some more.

# 35

ARNOLD ROSEN'S FUNERAL TAKES PLACE EARLY SUNDAY MORNING at the Grossman & Mehringer funeral home's memorial chapel.

Ceepak, Rita, Ceepak's mom, and I go to pay our last respects.

Grossman & Mehringer's is located on Sea Breeze Drive, just about a block from the Salty Dog Deli, which, I'm told, caters a lot of the post-funeral receptions for those utilizing the services of the funeral home. Probably because the owner, Saul, makes the best Reuben sandwiches in the state, even though Saul once told me they're not kosher.

"It's corned beef, Swiss cheese, and sauerkraut on toasted rye bread," he said. "The combination of Swiss cheese, a milk product, with corned beef, a meat product, violates the rules for kosher food."

"So if you eat one, you're going to hell?"

"No. Because Jews don't believe in hell."

And then he told me that a forgiving and compassionate God would never create such a thing as Hell to punish souls for all eternity.

"Except maybe Hitler."

Saul's a very interesting guy. Makes good sandwiches, too.

Ceepak and I pick up our disposable yarmulkes in the lobby and head into the funeral chapel. Stained-glass windows filled with jagged geometric shapes filter and color the beams of morning sunshine streaming into the room.

I notice Christine sitting all alone in the last row of chairs. I think about going over to sit with her, but she warns me off with a subtle shake of her head.

"Oops. It's Sunday," I hear Mrs. Ceepak whisper to her son. "Does this count as going to church?"

"I don't believe so, mother. However, I am not that conversant with all the rules and regulations of the modern day Roman Catholic church."

"Well, Jesus was Jewish before he became Catholic, so I say it counts."

Monae Dunn is sitting on the left-hand side of the chapel with Michael and another African-American woman who looks like she might be Monae's sister, Revae. They're both in very nice, very black church dresses. Michael is wearing a nicely tailored black suit. I'm sort of curious as to how he knew to pack it for his weekend trip home.

Judith, David, and Little Arnie Rosen are seated on the right. Shona Oppenheimer and her son, Samuel, are right behind Judith, Arnie, and David. Shona leans forward to give her sister a gentle shoulder massage and all I can think of are those same hands throttling Christine Lemonopolous' neck.

Guess that's why Christine picked a seat six rows away.

Mrs. Ceepak leaves our row to go sit with that handsome gent Hank (the good dancer) and a few of Dr. Rosen's other "bingo buddies" from the senior center.

Other than that, the golden, padded chairs are pretty much empty. Not exactly a sold-out crowd.

I guess when you live to be 94 you lose a lot of friends and family along the way.

I'm glad Dr. Rosen's coffin lid is closed.

Whenever you can see the body in an open casket at a funeral it looks, to me anyway, like the guy who the show is all about got so bored with the whole thing he had to lie down and grab a quick nap. I have to figure that a casket, lined with those soft silken pillows, is the most comfortable seat anybody ever gets in church. Too bad you can't really enjoy it.

Rabbi Bronstein leads the service.

It's actually very moving. The rabbi tears black ribbons and hands them to family members to pin on their clothes to symbolize their loss. Psalms are recited, including some that Mr. Ceepak hasn't quoted at us yet. Rabbi Bronstein gives an eloquent eulogy for "this good and honorable man" Arnold Rosen. He even tells a small joke. "Arnold once told me he was named Dentist of the Year, back in the late 1970's. When I asked him what the award was, he said, 'Nothing much. Just a little plaque.'"

Everybody smiled. Well, everybody I could see.

Later, the whole congregation (except me) recites a memorial prayer. In Hebrew. Fortunately, there is a translation in the slender programs printed up for the event. Everybody's asking God to shelter the soul of the deceased "under the wings of His Divine presence."

The casket is then wheeled out of the funeral chapel while all the mourners, me included, recite the 23rd Psalm and follow the coffin up the center aisle.

I don't see Christine. She must've slipped out early.

We don't go with the family to the cemetery. Instead, we all head down the block to the Salty Dog Deli and order Reuben sandwiches or corned beefs on rye.

"It's what Arnie would've wanted," says Adele, deconstructing her towering six-inch-thick sandwich and rebuilding it into something that might actually fit in her mouth.

All of our sandwiches are stacked so high with sliced meat, vegetarians everywhere are weeping.

Neither Ceepak nor I mention a thing about her ex-husband's recent million-dollar request to Mrs. Ceepak. However, Ceepak does, once again, lobby hard for his mother to reconsider the installation of a home security system.

"I don't need a burglar alarm, John," she says. "Joe doesn't scare me. Not anymore."

"I'm worried, mother," says Ceepak.

"Me, too," adds Rita. "Your ex is a mess."

I raise my hand to add my vote. I can't speak because my mouth is full of ten pounds of pastrami.

"Well, you're all very sweet. But like I said, we have the security guards at the front gate."

"He could grow desperate, mother," says Ceepak. "Purchase a weapon."

"Can he do that?" says Rita. "I know he didn't serve much time in prison, but he *is* a convicted felon."

"Under federal law," says Ceepak, "those with felony convictions do, indeed, forfeit their right to bear arms. However, due in part to an overhaul of federal gun laws orchestrated by the National Rifle Association, every year, thousands of felons across the country have those rights reinstated, often with little or no review."

"Well, don't tell your father," jokes Mrs. Ceepak. "He might try the same thing."

The waitress brings Styrofoam cartons to our table so we can all box up the second half of our sandwiches and take them home. I'll probably be eating pastrami till Wednesday.

"Where are they sitting shiva?" asks Rita, probably to steer the conversation away from scary stories about Old Man Ceepak getting a gun.

According to my buddy Joe Getzler, "shiva" means seven in Hebrew. Traditionally, the mourning family receives guests and accepts condolences for a week. "Reform families only do it for three days," Joe told me. "Sometimes, if people have to travel, it only lasts a day."

I have a hunch that Arnie Rosen will be given short-shrift-shiva.

"The family will be accepting calls at David and Judith's house," says Ceepak.

"Should we go?" asks his mother. "Arnie was such a good man."

That's when Ceepak's cell phone chirrups.

"Work?" says his mother who, I guess, has memorized her son's different ringtones. "On a Sunday?"

"Apparently so," says Ceepak, squinting so he can read the caller ID window. "Dr. Kurth," he mumbles.

The medical examiner.

I'm glad the lid is down on my Styrofoam box. There's something slightly sickening about hearing gory medical details while staring at a juicy mound of meat.

"This is Ceepak. Yes, ma'am. I see. Well, be sure to thank them for the quick turnaround. We weren't expecting your answer until much later in the week. Any indication as to where it came from? Very well. Yes, ma'am. I will, indeed, tell her."

Ceepak closes up his phone.

"Danny?"

"Yeah?"

"You'll be with me again this week."

"More rides to inspect?"

He shakes his head. "Mom?

"Yes?"

"The county medical examiner said to tell you that you were correct. Arnold Rosen was murdered. Potassium cyanide."

Adele brings her hand to her lips. "Oh, my. Poor man."

"Dr. Kurth hypothesizes that the poison was given to Dr. Rosen with his morning medications. That someone poured a lethal dose of cyanide into a gel cap and slipped the tainted capsule into Dr. Rosen's pillbox."

"He was taking so many meds," I mumble. "It'd be so easy to do . . ."

"Roger that. Ladies? We need to take you home and then Danny and I need to pay a visit to the Rosens."

We're not going there to sit shiva.

We're going there to officially open our murder investigation.

# 36

WE DROP OFF CEEPAK'S MOM AND WIFE AND THEN SWING BY
the house to pick up Chief of Detectives Ceepak's new undercover
vehicle: an unmarked Ford Taurus Interceptor.

The sleek black beauty's bright white and red LED emergency
lights are hidden all over the car: behind the thick black grill up
front, along the black rim of the trunk in the back, across the top
of the tinted-black windshield. Called The Undercover Stealth,
the brand new Ford rides on 22-inch Forgiato black wheels and
Nitto tires, also black. To tell you the truth, Ceepak's new ride
looks extremely sinister.

Remember those budget cuts I was telling you about? They did
not affect the purchase order for the new Ceepakmobile. I'm pretty
sure one of Mayor Sinclair's biggest political contributors runs our
local Ford dealership.

We climb into the rolling stealth bomber, savor that new cop-car
scent, then cruise over to David and Judith's apartment at 315-B

Tuna Street (yes, some streets in the center of Sea Haven are named after fish).

"This murder investigation will be different than any we have undertaken in the past," Ceepak remarks as he pilots the incredibly smooth-riding vehicle up Ocean Avenue.

"Yeah," I say. "None of our other victims were ninety-four years old."

"True. This is also the first time we know exactly how the murder was done. We already have our weapon: a small capsule filled with potassium cyanide powder."

That's right. In the past, we've had to spend a lot of time on forensics and bullet trajectories and crime-scene analysis to figure out exactly how the deed was done. This time, we already know the How. We just need the Who and the Why.

"Guess there's no need to call Bill Botzong," I say.

Botzong is the head of the New Jersey State Police's Major Crimes Unit. He and his crew of crime-scene technicians do all that snazzy stuff they do on the CSI TV shows for police departments, like ours, that can't afford a high-tech lab full of gizmos and gadgets.

"Actually, Danny, we will, once again, be soliciting Bill's assistance. Hopefully, he and his team can help us track down the source of the potassium cyanide, a chemical with a wide variety of industrial uses."

Ceepak. The guy probably started doing his cyanide homework the day he asked Chief Rossi for permission to go to Dr. Kurth for a toxicology screening on a 94-year-old's corpse.

He fills me in with more cyanide details. How it can be distilled from the kernels of certain nuts such as almonds. How its bluish hue is why cyanide and cyan (blue) toner cartridges are word-root cousins.

"A lethal dose can be as low as one point five milligrams per kilogram of body weight."

And Dr. Rosen didn't weigh very much.

It'd be easy to hide a lethal dose of cyanide inside something the size of an Extra Strength Tylenol capsule, which, Ceepak reminds me, was done, by someone who's still at large, in the Chicago area—way back in 1982. That's why pain reliever bottles are so hard to open these days—even with your teeth, especially when you have a hangover. And why you now see "caplets" or "gel caps" instead of "capsules" on the shelves at CVS.

"Doing a quick Google search," Ceepak continues, "I found several sources of ninety-eight percent pure cyanide, available in powder, crystals, or briquette form."

"No way."

"It's a quite common chemical compound, Danny. One frequently used by jewelers to clean tarnish from gold and silver."

"So, which one of our suspects owns a jewelry store?"

Ceepak actually chuckles. "If only it were that simple."

Yeah.

But if it were, they wouldn't give you a super dude detective car.

"Well," I say, as Ceepak makes the right turn onto Tuna Street, "I guess we know that Christine was the one who gave Dr. Rosen his final and fatal pills."

"True. However, someone else could have very easily put the poisoned pill into Dr. Rosen's medical organizer without Christine knowing it."

"The first time I met Monae, the night nurse, she was filling up the tiny compartments in Dr. Rosen's weekly box with pills and capsules."

Ceepak nods. "Ms. Dunn is definitely on our short list, Danny."

Oh-kay. I didn't even know we had a list of suspects, let alone a short one.

"Who else?" I ask.

157

"Dr. Rosen's family, of course: Michael, David, and Judith. And then, I'm afraid, we must take a hard look at Christine Lemonopolous."

Ceepak's list?

They could be the assassins Dr. Rosen was so worried about.

# 37

315-B Tuna Street, David and Judith Rosen's home, is actually the upstairs apartment in a classic two-story, vinyl-sided beach house.

We climb up the back steps to an outdoor deck. Ceepak raps his knuckles on the regular door in the center, not the sliding glass patio doors down near the charcoal grill; those take you into a dining room with a card table covered with a red-white-and-blue paper tablecloth from the Party Store. While we wait, I study the roofline. I have a feeling the Rosens' bedroom ceilings are pretty steep—the way they would be if you lived in an attic.

David Rosen opens the door. He's still wearing the white shirt and suit pants he wore to the funeral, but he's taken off his tie, unbuttoned his top button, and untucked his shirttails. He's also gripping a twelve-ounce can of Milwaukee's Best Premium beer—always the cheapest brand in every package store.

"Detective Ceepak. Boyle. Come on in."

He leads us into the kitchenette of his tiny home. I notice a guitar propped up in a corner.

"Again," says Ceepak, "condolences on your loss."

"Thank you. And thank you for attending the services. I wanted to play my guitar at the funeral. Maybe do my slow hand version of 'Stairway To Heaven.' Judith wouldn't let me. Hey, who was that little old lady who came with you?"

"My mother. She knew your father from the Sea Haven Senior Center. Thought very highly of him."

"Huh. Small world."

David yanks open the refrigerator. Looks around for something to eat. Doesn't find anything to his liking. Closes the door.

"Hey, do you or your mom know a guy named Joseph Ceepak? 'Ceepak' is such an unusual name, it kind of stuck with me."

"He is my father."

"Really?" David smiles and nods like a kid who just guessed what was inside his birthday surprise bag. "Okay. I thought there might be a connection. He's working for us. Sinclair Enterprises."

"So I have heard."

"I head up the HR Department. That's Human Resources. Anyway, the other day, Friday I think, we get some mail, a *Guns And Ammo* magazine or something, that's been forwarded to Joseph Ceepak, c/o Sinclair Enterprises, 1500 Ocean Avenue, Sea Haven, New Jersey. That's our address . . ."

"David?" this from Judith out in the living room. "What are you doing in the kitchen?"

"Just a second," says David, eager to finish his story. "Every year, it's the same thing. We hire so many seasonal employees, I end up playing mailman from early June to just after Labor Day."

"Fascinating," says Ceepak even though David is boring me to death.

"So, is your dad still at the Smugglers Cove Motel, or has he moved in with you and your mom?"

Now Judith, dressed in her black funeral dress, clutching a clear plastic cup filled with white wine, comes into the kitchen.

"David? Why are you bringing this up, now?"

"I still have Mr. Ceepak's magazine. I'd like to make sure I forward it to the right location . . ."

Judith rolls her piggy eyes. "Honestly, David. You can be such a child."

And she walks away.

"It's my job, Jude. Okay? My job?"

"Right," she snaps back. "You're the head of human resources for the mayor's far-flung empire of tourist traps. That's why he pays you *soooo* much money . . ."

"We've been number one in revenues on the island, four years running."

Judith ignores her husband as we all follow her into the living room.

"Do we have any wine that's not in a box?" Judith says to the walls. "This tastes like crap."

"No," counters David, "it tastes like crap we can afford."

"I brought some Pinot Grigio," says Michael, sort of sprawled on the couch. I think he's half-tanked. "It's in the fridge."

Judith returns to the kitchen.

"Have you gentlemen come to sit shiva with us?" asks Michael. "Because you're in luck! My loving partner Andrew just FedExed us a *fabulous* Kosher sympathy basket." He gestures to a wicker basket overflowing with shiny goodies: snack packages, bags of dried fruit, shrink-wrapped baked goods. "There's apple cake, rugelach, Brazilian cashews, hummus, pretzel thins . . ."

"Actually," says Ceepak, "we have some news."

"About what?" says Judith, coming back from the kitchen with a fresh cup of white wine and the bottle she poured it from. "Your father's magazine subscriptions?"

"Oh, leave my big brother alone," says Michael with flick of his wrist and, I swear, a snarky little giggle. "Cease fire. At least for today. The poor boy just buried his daddy."

Why do I think there's a half-empty pitcher of cosmopolitans in that refrigerator, too?

"What's the big news, Detective Ceepak?" asks Judith, her snout twitching between her rubbery, blubbery cheeks.

"Is Ceepak a Polish name?" asks David, taking a big swig of bargain basement beer. I notice he's wearing a Bart Simpson wristwatch. Not your typical funeral accessory.

"David?" Michael says it this time. "Honestly. Keep it up, and I'm calling off my truce."

"What? I'm just interested. 'Ceepak' isn't a name you hear all that often . . ."

Man, this "sitting shiva" is turning out to be worse than some booze-soaked Irish wakes I've been to.

Ceepak moves to the center of the room.

Everyone stops drinking and/or giggling when he does.

They usually do.

"We heard from Dr. Rebecca Kurth, the County Medical Examiner."

"You're kidding me," says David, setting his beer can down on a nearby table.

"Coaster," says Judith.

David finds one. "You guys really went ahead and wasted our taxpayer dollars doing an autopsy on a ninety-four-year-old man?"

"Unbelievable," mutters his wife.

"This is why Dad's property taxes are through the roof."

"When did you become so right-wing, David?" snips Michael.

"When he realized you liberals were bankrupting this country's future," says Judith.

"Your father," says Ceepak, cutting off the family feud, "was, as we feared, poisoned."

"What?" says David. "No way. That's impossible."

"To the contrary. Dr. Kurth found the evidence to be persuasive and conclusive. Someone slipped a cyanide capsule into your father's medicines."

"Christine," mutters Judith. "I knew it. I told you."

She glares at me. Hard.

"I hope you're happy, Officer Boyle. Seems your hot little girlfriend is also a cold-blooded murderer."

# 38

"Christine?" says Michael. "You're insane, Judith. Why on earth would that sweet little nurse kill Dad-ums?"

"Because she's psychotic."

"Oh, come on . . ."

"Why did she attack my sister?"

"The woman is sick," says David, swilling the dregs out of the bottom of his beer can.

Judith turns on him. "Shona? My sister?"

"No. I meant Christine. She has that STD. We never should've let Dad hire her."

"Um, excuse me," says Michael. "I believe you two were the ones who recommended Ms. Lemonopolous for the job. You even persuaded Dad to terminate that first gal, what was her name? Kaufman?"

"Kochman," says Judith. "Joy Kochman."

"At the time we suggested that Christine take over for Joy," says David, "we didn't know she was a crazy person."

"Did you at least check her references?" asks Michael.

"We didn't have time," says David defensively. "Joy Kochman had to go."

"Why?"

"She became a problem, okay? You weren't here, Michael . . ."

"And you were." Michael rolls his eyes like he's heard that a million times.

"Michael's right, David," says Judith. "We should've done a thorough background check. Especially since her last patient, Mrs. Crabtree, also ended up dead."

*Well, duh,* I feel like saying.

The lady was old. That's what happens. But I don't say a word. Neither does Ceepak. Sometimes eavesdropping on one of these family squabbles can give you all sorts of useful information.

"Oh, my," says Michael with a mock gasp and a fluttering Southern Belle hand over his heart. "Her previous patient died, too? Is Christine Lemonopolous a serial killer? An Angel of Death like that nurse over in England who killed four patients? We based an episode of 'Crime And Punishment' on him. Best ratings of the season."

"Well, now you can do a new show," snips Judith, refilling her wine. "All about a nurse who gets away with murder because she has friends in the police department who'll do anything to protect her no matter how many clients she attacks or elderly invalids she bumps off."

And now Ceepak has heard enough.

"We are sorry to bring you this news while you are in mourning."

Michael gestures toward the gift basket again. "You sure you don't want apple cake?"

"No, thank you," says Ceepak.

I shake my head. "I'm good."

"However," says Ceepak, "we must request that none of you leave Sea Haven for the next several days as we attempt to ascertain who it was that murdered Dr. Rosen."

"What?" says Judith. "Surely you don't suspect one of us."

"Calm down," says David reaching over to give his wife baby pats on her dimpled knee.

Judith recoils from her husband's touch. "Don't you dare tell me to calm down, David."

"I'm just saying . . ."

"I heard what you said. You said 'calm down.'"

"Officers?" says Michael. "Do you really suspect that someone in this room murdered my father?"

"It's a possibility," says Ceepak.

"How can you think such a thing?" This from David.

"We have our reasons."

"Well, what are they?" demands Judith.

And since Ceepak won't tell a lie, he goes ahead and tells the truth: "The night before his murder, your father spoke with Rabbi Bronstein. Told the rabbi he was quote surrounded by assassins end quote. We suspect he meant all of you and, perhaps, his home health aides."

The Rosens shut up and sip their drinks. Silently.

Finally, Michael pipes up. "I'm due back in L.A. on Wednesday. But I could book a different flight. There are some things I need to take care of here in New Jersey."

"What sort of things?" says Judith.

"Wouldn't you like to know?"

"I would," says David.

"Production issues," says Michael, kind of coyly. "The same production issues I told you about last night, David."

David narrows his eyes. Michael narrows his. The two brothers look like they could launch into some serious neck-throttling at any second.

"Rest assured," says Ceepak, "we will do everything in our power to bring this matter to an expeditious resolution."

"Besides, Michael," says Judith, with a smirk, "you might want to be here after Dad's will goes through probate."

Michael flutters his eyes. "Why?"

"To collect your inheritance."

"Ha!" is all Michael has to say about that.

"Be advised," says Ceepak, "probate can be a long, tedious process."

David shakes his head. "Steven Robins over at Bernhardt, Hutchens, and Catherman has already paid the filing fee and given the Surrogate Court a death certificate and a copy of the will."

"Who, pray tell, is this Steven Robins?" says Michael.

"Dad's lawyer," says Judith. "You'd know that if you lived here."

"Oh, I'd know so much more than that if I lived here," says Michael.

"Steven Robins is also executor of Dad's will," adds David. "He's calling in a couple favors. Working the weekend. Pushing us to the head of the line. Says it's a very simple estate so we should be good to go tomorrow or Tuesday at the latest."

"Would this be the will he recently altered?" says Michael.

"I guess."

"Did he give you two and Little Arnie even more goodies?"

"We don't know," says Judith.

"You haven't seen these alterations?"

"Of course not. That's a private matter between Dad and his lawyer."

Michael sneers at that. "Yeah. Right."

Ceepak clears his throat. "We need to conduct a few more interviews . . ."

"Why don't you just go arrest the homicidal nurse and save us all a lot of time and aggravation?" asks Judith. "I'm sure Mrs. Crabtree's family would be happy to see Christine pay for what she did to their mother, too!"

"Trust me, Mrs. Rosen," says Ceepak. "If the evidence indicates that Christine Lemonopolous is the culprit, in this or any other murder, we will, indeed, arrest her and hold her for trial."

"Good!" shouts Judith. "Good riddance to bad rubbish!"

David is about to pat her on the knee again and tell her to calm down. But he remembers he's not supposed to do that, not if he wants to keep on living. So, instead, he fidgets with his Bart Simpson wristwatch.

"Danny?" Ceepak nudges his head toward the door.

Hallelujah.

We're done sitting shiva.

# 39

WE CLIMB INTO CEEPAK'S SHINY HOT WHEELS DETECTIVE CAR and head south.

I use my cell to contact Christine.

"We need to talk to you," I say in my most official junior detective voice.

"No problem," she says. "You guys want coffee or something?"

"Sure. Do I have any?"

Christine laughs. "No. But I'll go grab a couple cups at the Quick Pick Mini Mart."

Come to think of it, that's what I do every morning, too.

When I end my Christine call, Ceepak asks me to contact Chief Rossi. That means I get to try out the high-tech radio stashed under a sliding cover in the center console below a compact General Dynamics computer.

The Chief and Ceepak discuss putting "light surveillance" on our five suspects: Christine Lemonopolous, Monae Dunn, Michael

Rosen (currently residing at the Sea Spray Motel), and David and Judith Rosen.

"We may also need to keep tabs on a Joy Kochman, a home health aide whose job at Arnold Rosen's home was terminated. Her whereabouts, at this juncture, are unknown."

Oh, yeah. Ceepak is good.

Joy Kochman, the nurse David and Judith fired so they could plant their spy, Christine, in Dr. Rosen's house could be a disgruntled former employee, the kind that's always taking a loaded pistol back to their former workplace and wreaking revenge. Maybe Joy took a pill instead.

Ceepak parks next to Christine's VW Beetle in the Sea Village parking lot.

This is so weird.

We are going to interview Christine Lemonopolous in *my* apartment. I need to knock before I open my own door.

"Come on in, guys!"

Christine gives us our coffees, then perches on the edge of my bed. Ceepak takes my one Salvation Army chair. It cost me five dollars. The seat cushion was ripped. In two places.

I sit on the arm of my TV chair. It's a recliner. That rocks. I try to maintain my balance and a little detective-esque dignity.

Ceepak drops the first bombshell.

"We now know that Dr. Rosen was poisoned and that, in all likelihood, you were the one who gave Dr. Rosen the pill containing cyanide that killed him."

"Oh, my goodness," she mutters.

I'm studying Christine's face and hands. Looking for any ticks or tells. Some kind of body language that suggests maybe she's faking her reaction.

I get nothing except shock.

"However," Ceepak continues, "the fact that you are the one who put the tainted pill into Dr. Rosen's hand doesn't mean . . ."

"A paper cup."

"Excuse me?"

"We always took Dr. Rosen's pills out of the appropriate compartment and placed them into a small paper cup. Like a dentist uses for mouthwash. Dr. Rosen had a case of them left over from his practice."

I have a brainstorm.

"We should dust the pill organizer for prints," I say. "See who handled it."

"I'm quite certain, Danny," says Ceepak, "that each and every one of our suspects made contact with that pill organizer at one time or another."

He's right. My idea would be a waste of fingerprint powder.

Now Christine has an idea. "Monae was in charge of organizing the pills. She usually doled out the medicines into their slots early in the morning while Dr. Rosen was asleep. Said it gave her something to do besides watch TV. There's not much good on at three or four in the morning."

"We will be talking to Ms. Dunn," says Ceepak, flipping through his spiral notebook. "As I was about to say, the fact that you literally gave Dr. Rosen the lethal pill or pills does not make you the murderer or even an accessory to the crime if you had no idea that some of the medicines you were administering were actually poison capsules."

"Good. Because I didn't."

"Did you know that Dr. Rosen recently changed his will?"

"Yes. He mentioned it."

"Do you know what changes he made?"

"No. He didn't discuss any details. But . . ."

Christine hesitates.

Ceepak cocks an eyebrow and waits.

"He said Monae and I would be 'very, very pleased.'"

# 40

MONAE DUNN ACTUALLY LIVES ON THE MAINLAND, IN A TOWN called Williamsville on the far side of the causeway bridge.

Her house is kind of smallish. Which makes the silver 370-Z coupe sitting in her driveway look a little out of place. I checked out the Z the last time I went car-shopping. They start at $33,000.

We let her know that Dr. Rosen had been poisoned.

"Uhm-hmm," she says knowingly. "I figured as much."

"You did?"

"I'm semi-psychic. So, who did it?"

"That's what we're trying to determine," says Ceepak.

"Well, I know it wasn't me."

"Did you typically organize Dr. Rosen's pillbox?"

"Uhm-hmm. Doesn't mean I poisoned him."

"We know that."

"You think I murdered Dr. Rosen because I'm black?"

"No, ma'am. We're just trying to get an idea as to who might've had access to the pill organizer."

"Anyone who walked in the damn door, that's who. We just left it out on the kitchen counter. Wasn't locked up inside a safe or anything. This week, I filled up all the slots on Wednesday morning. You talk to Christine?"

"Yes, ma'am," says Ceepak.

"Good. The last old lady she worked for, that Mrs. Crabtree, she died, too."

"So we have heard. Was anyone else at the house on Saturday morning—besides you and Christine Lemonopolous?"

"David and Judy showed up. A little after eight."

Ceepak pulls out his notebook.

"Why were David and Judith there?"

"To make me work overtime."

"Excuse me?"

"David and his wife, they don't like Christine. Not since she and her lawyer put a public whooping on that Shona Oppenheimer woman—that's Judy Rosen's sister."

"Yes. We know that."

"She wants everybody to call her Judith so I call her Judy."

"I see."

"Christine can't be in the same room when David or Judy stop by. So, she has to disappear and I've got to be with Dr. Rosen in case he needs to use the bathroom."

"And why were David and Judith at Dr. Rosen's home on Saturday morning?"

"They said they wanted to see how 'Dad was holding up' after the 'ugly family dinner' on Friday night."

She makes the face she makes every time she says "Uhm-hmmm"—a look that tells you, no matter what you're selling, Monae Dunn isn't buying it.

"See, on Friday, Michael came to town with some kind of big news and wanted to take a father-son stroll on the beach with his dad, tell him all about it. That's why he bought Dr. Rosen that battery-powered beach wheelchair."

"Did they take their walk?"

"Are you kidding? Dr. Rosen told Michael his 'Mars rover' was a 'monstrosity.' That the neighbors would laugh at him if he 'so much as sat down on it.' So, when Michael gets to the house on Friday morning, after flying all night from L.A., the first thing he hears from his father is what a 'foolish wastrel and spendthrift' he is. That means he spends money like it's water."

"Yes, ma'am."

"Anyway, I like Michael, so I come out of my room to see if I can help him."

"Christine was on duty when Michael arrived at the house Friday?"

"That's right. Anyway, Dr. Rosen, he gets all snippy with his son. 'What's this big news, Michael? Just tell me!' But Michael, he says, 'No. This isn't the proper setting.' See, Michael works in Hollywood. Setting and mood are important to people in Hollywood."

"I imagine so," says Ceepak.

"That's when I pipe up. 'Why don't you make your big announcement at dinner tonight? Someplace special.' Michael? He hugs me. Says it's perfect and I should move to Hollywood and write movie scripts. I might. I got a knack for storytelling. Anyway, Michael being Michael, he makes a reservation at the fanciest restaurant in town."

"The Trattoria?" I say, remembering what Christine told us.

"Uhm-hmm. 'Let's invite David and Judith to join us,' says Dr. Rosen. 'Make it a family affair.' Michael didn't like that idea. Insisted that it just be what he called 'the real Rosens.' The two boys and their father."

"So, Saturday morning," says Ceepak, "Judith and David really came over to complain about Judith's exclusion from the family dinner?"

"That's right. Kicked Christine out of the room and made me wake up poor old Arnie. 'Aren't I family?' Judy says, getting all weepy. 'Don't I deserve a dinner at the finest restaurant in town? I gave you your only grandson. How dare you let Michael treat me like that?' On and on she goes."

"How did Dr. Rosen react?"

"Like he always does when she starts ragging on him. He just nods and says, 'Yes, dear; you're right, dear' a lot. But inside I know what he's probably thinking."

"What's that?"

Monae laughs. "'I spend too much money on your liposuction treatments for you to be stuffing your face with lasagna and cheesy bread.' But he didn't say it out loud. He only said that kind of stuff when it was just him and me in the house."

"Dr. Rosen wasn't pleased with his daughter-in-law's weight problems?"

"No, sir. Said her tuckus was too big. Tuckus is a Jewish word. Means butt."

Ceepak dutifully makes a note in his pad. "But you went to that Friday-night dinner, correct?"

"Well, I took Dr. Rosen. Drove him over. Wheelchaired him into that private room they have in the back. Then I sat by myself at a table near the kitchen and had some spaghetti and meatballs. They call it Pasta Vesuvius, but it's just spaghetti and meatballs, even if they do charge twenty-four ninety-five for it."

"What was Michael Rosen's big announcement?"

"I don't know. I wasn't there when he made it."

"Did you hear or observe anything else?"

"Just some hollering. Then the Rosen men come stomping out of that room, none of them even looking at each other. Nothin' but cold hate and old grudges in their eyes. I drove Dr. Rosen home. Never heard him be so quiet."

Ceepak shifts gears. "It seems you and Michael are on very friendly terms?"

"We sure are."

"Did he buy you your car?"

I grin. Ceepak noticed the Z, too.

"Did Michael tell you about that? Because I wasn't supposed to tell anybody. Promised him and Revae I never would."

"Who's Revae?" asks Ceepak.

"My sister. She's known Michael longer than me. Revae's the one who got me this job."

"How?"

"By telling Michael his daddy had to hire me."

"How come."

Monae shrugs. "I don't know. You'll have to ask her."

"Don't worry," says Ceepak. "We will."

# 41

CEEPAK AND I SPEND THE REST OF SUNDAY AFTERNOON
tracking down Joy Kochman and Revae Dunn.

We finally draw a bead on Joy Kochman thanks to the folks
at the AtlantiCare Home Health Aide Agency. She has taken a
live-in position with a wealthy couple up in Lavallette. That's
about an hour north of Sea Haven. You have to leave the island,
head up the Garden State Parkway, exit at Tom's River, cross
over another causeway to Seaside Heights, then drive a few
miles north.

So we call our friends in the Lavallette Police Department. Ask
them to keep an eye on 323 Bayview Drive, the waterfront home
where Ms. Kochman is currently working and living, until we can
run up and conduct a proper interview.

As for Revae Dunn, we learn she lives and works in Avondale,
the same town where Mainland Medical is located. We need to
talk to her, too. Find out what's up with her and Michael Rosen.

How come she was able to swing a job for her sister, Monae, not to mention a shiny new Z car, too.

But both Revae Dunn and Joy Kochman have to wait till Monday.

Because Sunday evening we get a call from Steven Robins, a senior partner at Bernhardt, Hutchens, and Catherman. He is the executor of Dr. Rosen's estate.

"I know this is highly unusual," says the lawyer, who Ceepak puts on speakerphone in his office, "but I was able to pull some strings at Surrogate Court and move Dr. Rosen's will through probate, post haste."

"On a Sunday?" says Ceepak, sounding impressed.

"Indeed. The judge is an old friend. From law school. Harvard."

Now the lawyer sounds impressed. With himself.

"Since this will might, I suspect, have some bearing on your current investigation into the manner of Dr. Rosen's death, I think it only prudent to invite you, or your duly authorized representative, to join me and the other interested parties at my law offices this evening. Seven P.M. Will that be convenient?"

"Of course," says Ceepak.

The law offices of Bernhardt, Hutchens, and Catherman are pretty swanky.

For one thing, the air conditioning doesn't smell like recycled mildew. For another, the walls are made out of real wood, not that paneling they used to give away on TV game shows back in the 1960s, which was the last time most of the office buildings in Sea Haven were redecorated.

A very impressive executive assistant (who's probably making double overtime for working at 7 P.M. on a Sunday and for wearing such a short but tasteful skirt) ushers Ceepak and me into an even more impressive conference room. The shiny wooden table in the center is bigger than most fishing boats. There are bottles of Fuji water and notepads in front of every seat. The water looks like it's free, too.

Since we're basically here as observers, Ceepak and I grab swivel chairs against the wall, leaving the padded table seats and free beverages for the family and other interested parties.

A few minutes later, an entire Agatha Christie novel walks into the conference room.

Michael, David, and Judith Rosen. Christine Lemonopolous and Monae Dunn. All our suspects (except the wild cards Joy Kochman and Revae Dunn) file in and find seats around the table, eager to hear the late Arnold Rosen's last will and testament. Those rewrites he made recently? Tonight the mystery shall be revealed!

Michael and Monae sit on one side of the massive mahogany table directly across from David and Judith.

Meanwhile, Christine is seated on Michael's side of the table but three chairs down, putting her at the greatest possible diagonal distance from Judith and David.

Christine shoots us a little finger wave when she sees Ceepak and me.

I wish she hadn't.

Because Judith saw her do it.

*She* shoots me a very dirty look.

Then, she narrows her piglet eyes so tight I have to wonder if the plastic surgeons who gave her those liposuction treatments also implanted bionic laser beams inside her tiny eyeballs to give her death-ray super powers like in the comic books. If so, stand by to see my head explode.

Steven Robins, a dapper little lawyer in his sixties, enters the room. He's dressed in a very nice gray suit, which is never anyone's first wardrobe choice on a Sunday night in June. Everyone else around the table is wearing what I'll call their Sunday schlub clothes. Lots of plaids, short-sleeved shirts, and frumpy pullovers.

Well, everybody except Michael. He seems to have packed the right outfit for every possible occasion. Tonight, it's another black-on-black ensemble—a black polo shirt on top of black linen pants. It's the kind of country club casual outfit you might wear to the golf course. If you were Zorro.

"Good evening, everyone," says the lawyer. "Thank you all for coming here on such short notice."

"Mr. Robins?" Judith shoots up her hand.

"Yes, Mrs. Rosen?"

"Why are Christine and Monae here?"

"They are mentioned in Dr. Rosen's revised will."

Now Judith trains her laser beam eyes on her husband. "I knew it."

"Relax, Judith," whispers David.

"Don't you dare tell me to relax," Judith whispers back. But it's a loud whisper. The kind everybody can hear.

"And the police?" asks Michael.

"The two detectives are here at my invitation," says Mr. Robins. "Since a cloud of suspicion lingers over the circumstances surrounding your father's death, I thought it best that Detectives Ceepak and Boyle join us this evening. The particulars of Arnold's last will and testament may prove beneficial to their investigation. The sooner they know about them, the better."

Content with that answer, Michael eases back in his seat. The lawyer continues.

"Now then, we don't really read the will out loud like they do in the movies. However, should you wish to delve into the details, the whereofs and wherefores, I will gladly provide a hard copy of the document for each of you."

Judith shoots her arm up.

"Yes, Mrs. Rosen?"

"These 'recent changes' to the will. Was my father-in-law of sound mind when he made them?"

Boom! She just blurts it out. Guess now that the guy is dead there's no reason for her to be subtle.

"Rest assured, Mrs. Rosen," says the lawyer, "whenever Arnold and I met to discuss estate planning issues, I was quite cognizant of his advanced age and, therefore, administered an MMSE test."

"What's that?" asks David, who always seems like the most confused person in any room. "What's an MMSE? That like the SAT's?"

"No, it's the Mini-Mental State Examination test," explains Robins. "A brief questionnaire we use to screen for cognitive impairment. Suffice it to say, despite his age, Arnold Rosen's mental state was quite sound. If you'd like to see proof, I can supply you with his MMSE scores."

"Gosh, no," says Judith, sounding all sugar-frosted corn-flakey again. "I just didn't want anybody around this table raising red flags."

"Now then," says the lawyer, before he does a good throat clearing. "To the particulars of his estate. As I said previously, Arnold's will is neither complicated nor complex. He left two specific bequests of monies to be drawn from the sale of all his investments and assets and asked that they be cited as a mitzvah. To his devoted caregivers, Monae Dunn and Christine Lemonopolous, he bequeaths fifty thousand dollars. Each."

Christine and Monae both sort of gasp.

Hey, I don't blame them. I would, too.

Then Monae starts flapping her hand in front of her face like she's about to faint. "Fifty thousand dollars?" she squeals. "This is better than hitting the Lottery!"

Judith Rosen? She's fuming.

"The remainder of his estate," says the lawyer, "which, given current market positions, land values, and comparable real estate sales in Cedar Knoll Heights, our accountants conservatively estimate at two point two million dollars, Dr. Rosen leaves to David and Judith Rosen in trust for his quote living legacy end quote Arnold David Rosen."

Little Arnie. The smiling blonde kid in all the photographs is an instant millionaire. Unless, of course, his parents blow it all on guitar lessons, Bart Simpson watches, and liposuction before he hits twenty-one.

This is why Judith wasn't pleased when Christine and Monae scored their fifty thousand dollars each. That little mitzvah cost her family one hundred thousand dollars. Still, two point one million dollars is nothing to sneeze at. It's better than beer and pretzels rich. It's practically Adele Ceepak rich.

"This isn't fair," protests Michael, his voice trembling.

"Really?" says the lawyer. "I'm surprised to hear you say that, Michael. Surely you can't begrudge your nephew his inheritance. You earn nearly that much in two weeks."

"This isn't about money." Michael says with a laugh even though I can tell he is spitting mad. "This is about fairness. This is about family."

"I beg your pardon?"

"My partner Andrew and I recently adopted a child. An African-American boy we named Kyle."

"Was your father aware of this?"

"I told him Friday night. At dinner."

"That was his 'big announcement,'" says David.

Judith sniggers.

Michael? He looks like he could weep. Or explode. Maybe both.

"I'm so sorry, Michael," says the lawyer. "Perhaps, had he lived longer, your father would've once more amended his last will and testament to include your son as well."

"No," says David. "He wouldn't have. We talked about it at dinner on Friday night. Dad thought Michael and his 'partner' pretending that they were parents was stupid. Dad didn't believe in adoption. He believed in bloodlines. And legitimate heirs."

"Dad was all about *real* family," adds Judith. "When you adopt you're not extending the family tree, you're simply taking on somebody else's problems."

"You, Judith," says Michael, sounding completely heartbroken, "are a fat, repulsive bitch."

*Yowser.*

"Watch your mouth, little brother," snaps David. "That's my wife you're talking about."

"I know who and what she is—a hideous and heartless cow."

"Gentlemen?" says the lawyer, banging the table with his fist like it's a gavel.

Michael storms out of the room.

David and Judith shake their heads as if to say, "Poor, poor Michael." Then they smile a little to savor their triumph.

Christine? She's looking at me with a very nervous expression on her face.

I'm kind of looking at her the same way.

Because I have to wonder: Did the last elderly patient she took care of, Mrs. Mauna Faye Crabtree, also leave her a little sumpin'-sumpin' in her will like Dr. Rosen did? Are deathbed bequests the bonuses of the home health aide trade?

If so, Christine might've had a solid motive for helping ease another one of her patients out the exit door.

# 42

BRIGHT AND EARLY MONDAY MORNING, CEEPAK AND I ARE IN his office sipping bad coffee from mugs we poured out of the desk sergeant's congealed pot and working the phones.

It doesn't get any more detective-y than that.

Ceepak's in his blazer and khaki cargo pants. I think there's a zipper near the knees if he wants to turn them into shorts later in the afternoon. He seldom does.

I'm in cargo shorts and my favorite FDNY Engine 23 T-shirt. It's been lucky for me in the past. Both of us are carrying sidearms.

We have a busy day ahead of us.

My first call of the morning is to Christine. I tag her on her cell because my apartment doesn't have a landline. Landlines are like e-mail: so two thousand and late.

I go over the list of all the elderly patients she's taken care of since losing her job at Mainland Medical.

"They're all dead, Danny," she tells me. "But that doesn't mean I killed them."

It also doesn't mean I won't be making a few more phone calls to the families of the deceased to see if any of Christine's other patients died suddenly or under suspicious circumstances.

Ceepak spends his coffee and phone time with Bill Botzong at the Major Crimes Unit.

They're trying to track down and trace any shipments of potassium cyanide into Sea Haven. Botzong and his team will be doing some serious data mining with all the known suppliers of the chemical compound, cross-referencing their records against the names and addresses of all our suspects, including Joy Kochman up in Lavallette, whom we will be visiting just as soon as we finish up our phone calls and hit the head.

Bad coffee? It's like beer. You can't buy it. You can only rent it.

We hop into Ceepak's Batmobile and cruise up the Garden State Parkway toward Seaside Heights.

"Fascinating," mumbles Ceepak, somewhat randomly, seeing how we're basically humming up a generic highway filled with generic cars surrounded by garden-variety Garden State evergreen trees.

"You and I have dealt with several murderers in the past, Danny. In all those instances, the killer had to brutally confront their victim. They possessed strength, skill, or, at the very least, a warped sense of courage."

"But in this case," I say, "all the killer had to do was plop a pill into a plastic box and wait."

"Precisely. It is the easiest murder to execute, perhaps the most difficult to solve."

Because there's not much evidence. When you use your strength, skill, or warped courage, you leave clues. When you plop a single pill into a slot, not so much.

Unless, of course, our killer was foolish enough to order a pound of cyanide on the Internet and have it shipped to his or her home.

"What about jewelry stores?" I say. "Should we see if any of our suspects have a connection with a business with a legitimate use for the cyanide?"

"Indeed so."

Maybe we'll get lucky. Maybe one of the cyanide buyers will be the store where Judith's sister Shona buys all her clunky gold bracelets and baubles.

323 Bayview Drive in Lavallette is a two-story townhouse in a New England-looking condo complex on the bay side of the Barnegat Peninsula.

I read somewhere that young people with kids like the beach and surf side of any island; older folks like the calmer waters and boat docks on the bay side. In Lavallette, that's the side where the sun sets, too. Makes sense, I guess. You probably watch more sunsets when you're in your twilight years.

Joy Kochman is working as a live-in home health aide for a cranky couple called the Silberblatts.

"They both have Alzheimer's," she explains when we join her in the kitchen where she's toweling up a mess that might've been breakfast. Lumpy puddles are splattered all over the kitchen table. I'm thinking oatmeal and bananas. "Mr. Silberblatt likes to sleep on the floor. His wife? She likes to wander. We had to pin her name and address on her blouse, like she was in pre-school."

"Do you have a moment to answer a few questions?"

"Yeah. The meds kicked in. They're taking naps in front of the TV. *Let's Make A Deal* is good for that."

Nurse Kochman looks to be forty, maybe fifty. Then again, she could be a lot younger. I have a feeling living full-time with the Silberblatts puts bags under your eyes. Her hair is cut short and combed to the side. Some streaks are brighter than others but you can tell she doesn't have much time to fuss with it. She's dressed in dark blue scrubs, the better to hide oatmeal splotches.

"As you may know," says Ceepak, "your former employer, Dr. Arnold Rosen, passed away this weekend."

"Yes. I read about that. Sorry I couldn't make it to the services." She opens up her arms in a gesture that takes in the enormity of her task as the Silberblatts' caregiver.

"Understandable," says Ceepak. "But you visited Dr. Rosen late last week?"

"Thursday. It's my night off. One of the Silberblatts' kids comes over, relieves me. They're great. Five sons who live in the area. They all really love their parents even though their parents hardly even recognize them any more. We're all starting to think Mom and Dad might be better off in a nursing home. But well, the boys want to keep them here, in familiar surroundings, for as long as possible."

"How do the Silberblatt children compare to Dr. Rosen's?" asks Ceepak, smoothly steering the interview in the direction he wants it to go.

Nurse Kochman makes a lip fart noise.

Sorry. She does.

"Night and day. *These* kids? They're kind and respectful. To me and their parents. Those Rosens? What a nasty pair of vipers."

Up goes Ceepak's quizzical eyebrow. "How so?"

"David wanted me to spy on his dad. Feed him medical information. I refused. Michael? He just flashed a lot of cash. Showered his father with gifts he either didn't want or couldn't use. Michael's filthy rich. Does all those 'Crime And Punishment' shows. 'Crime And Punishment New York,' 'Crime And Punishment Chicago,' Hawaii, San Francisco, Wherever.' He makes like fifty million dollars a year. I saw it in *People* magazine. He's the one who sent Monae to Dr. Rosen's house. Apparently, he owed her sister, a woman named Raven . . ."

"Revae," I say.

Kochman shrugs. "Whatever. Michael owed this Revae a favor so he insisted that Dr. Rosen hire Monae to work the night shift."

"Let's go back to David and his wife, Judith," says Ceepak. "What happened after you refused to feed them information?"

"They accused me of stealing Dr. Rosen's solid gold cufflinks."

"Did you?"

"Of course not." She holds up her arms. "I wear a uniform every day. No cuffs. Look, guys, Dr. Rosen was still with-it, but he was also old and cufflinks are small. He forgets where he put things."

"Did you protest the accusations?"

"I said I didn't do it, if that's what you mean. But let's be honest here: When you're a home health aide, it's not like you're in a union or even a regular employee. Don't call the IRS, but a lot of these families pay us off the books. When the person paying you says you're fired, trust me, detectives, you're fired."

"So Dr. Rosen fired you?"

"That's what David said. Dr. Rosen, himself, was taking a nap at the time."

"Did you meet your replacement?" I ask. "Christine Lemonopolous."

"Nope. And I didn't want to. I figured the only reason she was hired was because she said yes to everything I'd said no to. Later, after I landed this job with the Silberblatts, I asked around. Talked to a few friends. Got a pretty good picture of who this Lemono-polous girl was and what she'd do to make money."

"Care to enlighten us?" says Ceepak.

"Word is, she went nuts. Quit her high-paying job in the emer-gency room at Mainland Medical. She's been scrounging around ever since, getting by with home health aide work. My friend Bea-trice told me that this Lemonopolous gal worked for some sick rich kid at night in exchange for room and board. For cash, she did days with whatever old person she could bamboozle into thinking she was a sweetie-pie. Maybe it's a coincidence, but all the old people who hired this Christine Lemonopolous didn't live too long after she went to work in their homes. Most made it two months, maybe three. Just long enough to write her into their will."

"Dr. Rosen did that," I mumble. "Bequeathed her fifty thousand dollars."

"I rest my case. I'm surprised you guys caught her. Nobody else ever asked any questions because, from what I heard, she only takes jobs that are, basically, death watches. It's a pretty nifty little plan, if, you know, you don't have any scruples or a conscience."

Ceepak and I both nod grimly. Because, face it, neither one of us really, truly knows what makes Christine Lemonopolous tick. What kind of thoughts she harbors in her heart. We just wanted to help her when she was in a jam.

We might've also helped her get away with murder.

# 43

MEANS, OPPORTUNITY, MOTIVE.

Christine had all three.

Provided, of course, she knew how to get her hands on some potassium cyanide.

"We need to chat with Christine again," says Ceepak.

"What about Revae Dunn?" I ask.

"I think it's more important that we speak with Christine. Immediately."

"Should I set it up?"

Okay. I'm stalling. I'm half-hoping Ceepak will say something like, *"Ah, let's forget this one. Arnold Rosen was going to die anyhow and Christine is cute. So let's go grab a beer and ask Christine to join us."*

But he doesn't.

"Please do," he says. "And Danny?"

"Yeah?"

"For what it's worth, I will be greatly surprised if these rumors and accusations prove to be true. I suspect Christine is the unfortunate victim of idle gossip."

Okay. That makes me feel a little better.

Until I call Christine.

"Hey," I say when she answers the phone.

"Hey." She doesn't sound very cheery.

"You busy?"

"Sort of."

"Ceepak and I need to talk to you again."

"Danny?"

"Yeah?"

"Why are all these people calling me?"

"What people?"

"Let's see. The Bollendorfs. The Crabtrees. Janet Malone. Addie Galloway. All the people whose parents I worked for before I went to work for Dr. Rosen."

"Well . . ."

"Did you really ask Jodi Bollendorf if her dad died 'under mysterious circumstances?'"

I sigh into the phone. "It's my job, Christine."

"To do what? Ruin my life?"

"No. Find out the truth."

"I'm telling you the truth."

"Yes. I think you are."

"You *think* I am?"

Okay. Bad choice of words.

"Can you swing by the police station and talk to us?" I say. "Or, if you like, we can come back to my apartment and . . ."

She cuts me off. "The police station."

"Great. Say in half an hour?"

"No. My lawyer can't be there till three."

"Your lawyer?"

"Harvey Nussbaum."

"You hired a lawyer?"

"It is her right to consult with an attorney," says Ceepak, who's, of course, listening to my side of the conversation. "And to have that attorney present during questioning."

Great. My partner's giving *me* the Miranda warning.

"Okay," I say. "Three o'clock. Bring Harvey."

"Danny?"

"Yeah?"

"I thought we were . . ."

"What?"

"Never mind."

And she hangs up in my ear.

# 44

So, we have a few hours to track down Revae Dunn.

She works as the office manager at a place called "The Garden State Reproductive Science Center," about half a mile away from Mainland Medical in Avondale.

It's a very medical-looking building. Lots of dark windows and sterile stucco walls. The islands of grass sprinkled around the asphalt parking lot look like they get manicured instead of mowed. As we pull into a visitor parking spot, I notice that Michael has been even more generous to Revae Dunn than her sister.

In a parking slot "Reserved For Office Manager," I see a bright red Jaguar XKR convertible. Those kitty cats cost over a hundred thousand dollars. That's right. More than some houses.

"Michael Rosen sure likes the Dunn sisters," I mumble as we climb out of Ceepak's car, which, all of a sudden, doesn't seem all that super dooper any more.

"Indeed," says Ceepak, admiring the convertible. "And judging by their vehicles, I believe Revae is his favorite."

Revae Dunn agrees to talk to us.

"For five minutes. We're very busy."

We're in her nice, gray-on-gray-carpeted office. She's dressed in a crisply starched linen business suit the color of a dove. Her hair is perfectly coiffed. Her earrings match her necklace, which matches her bracelet. The woman has style.

"Ms. Dunn," says Ceepak, "given your rigid time constraints, kindly allow me to be blunt: Why did the wealthy Hollywood producer Michael Rosen buy you a Jaguar convertible worth well over one hundred thousand dollars?"

"Who said he did?"

"Me. We know that Dr. Rosen also purchased a car for your sister Monae and, at your insistence, procured her a position as a home health aide at Dr. Arnold Rosen's home in Sea Haven."

"Who are you again?"

"John Ceepak. Chief of Detectives. Sea Haven PD. This is my partner, Detective Boyle."

Revae Dunn glances at her wristwatch.

"I believe we still have four more minutes," says Ceepak.

"Look, detectives. What we do here at this clinic needs to be treated with the utmost confidentiality."

"You haven't answered my question. Why has Michael Rosen been so generous to you and your sister?"

"I asked him to look after Monae as a favor to me. She's fifteen years younger than I am. Mom and Dad called her their 'whoops baby.' I suppose I tend to mother-hen her. Anyway, a year or so ago, she was drifting. Living with me or our brother. She had no direction or goals. Finally, I encouraged Monae to take a class and obtain her home health aide license. It took a lot of effort—on my part and hers, but she did it. She was qualified to start a real career

194

with a potential for growth. However, that did not mean her struggles were over. Like many young women of color, she had trouble finding employment. So I lent her a hand. Used my connections."

"With the Rosens?"

"That's right."

"And so we come back to my original question: Why has Michael Rosen been so generous and helpful to you and your family?"

"Because we, here at the clinic, have been extremely helpful to him and his family."

"How so?"

"Dr. Rosen's only grandson. Michael's sole nephew. We had a hand in that. Fifteen years ago, Dr. Rosen paid for his daughter-in-law to undergo certain fertility treatments."

"Were you here at the time?"

"Yes. Judith Rosen and her husband, I believe his name is David . . ."

"That's correct."

"They had been trying to get pregnant with no success for several years. Judith was rapidly approaching her fortieth birthday."

"So her biological clock was ticking."

"Very loudly. Plus, her father-in-law, Dr. Rosen, desperately wanted grandchildren. So, after several unsuccessful but costly attempts at other fertility clinics, the Rosens ended up here."

"These sorts of treatments, they're quite expensive?"

"They can be. In Vitro Fertilization. Intracytoplasmic Sperm Injection. Therapeutic Donor Insemination. Controlled Ovarian Hyperstimulation. Frozen Embryo Transfer."

Man. Making babies never sounded so un-sexy.

"Each of these procedures can cost several thousand dollars."

"And Judith's father-in-law paid for it all?"

Revae Dunn finally cracks a smile. "What can I say? The man wanted a grandbaby."

"And Michael gave you a Jaguar, found your sister a job and gave her a Z-car, just to say thanks for helping his sister-in-law give birth to his only nephew?"

"Michael Rosen is an extremely generous individual."

"Then why didn't he pay for the treatments?"

"Excuse me?"

"If Michael Rosen wanted a nephew so badly, why didn't he pay for all the procedures? Surely he could've afforded the costs much more easily than either his father or older brother."

Revae Dunn's left eye twitches. Twice. She glances at her watch again.

"I don't know," she says. "You'll have to ask him. Now if you gentlemen will excuse me."

And she shows us the door.


"She's lying," I say the second we're back in the parking lot.

"Actually," says Ceepak, "I don't believe she told us any lies. However, that does not mean she has told us the entire truth."

"So now what?"

"I want to check in with Bill Botzong. See how we're doing on the cyanide search."

"And then?"

"Let's head back to Williamsville. Spend a little more time with Revae's sister."

"You think Monae knows the whole story of what went on here?"

"Doubtful. But I am certain she will be able to shed some more light on the Rosen family dynamics."

Yeah. Like why Michael was so excited about having a nephew he gave everybody involved in the process of bringing Little Arnie into the world a flashy new car—except, of course, the baby's parents.

# 45

CEEPAK LETS ME DRIVE THE BATMOBILE SO HE CAN MAKE A QUICK call to Bill Botzong.

There's nothing new to report on the cyanide front, but "they're making progress" and have initiated contact with all the major suppliers.

"They're focusing on those merchants with Internet sales sites," Ceepak tells me. "Most likely that is where our killer made his or her purchase, hoping for a measure of anonymity."

He's right. People think they can erase their on-line tracks by clearing their computer's web browser memory.

They can't.

There's always a nice trail of cookies for us to follow.

Monae offers us a cold Coke and a whole tube of Oreos.

"I'm rich," she says. "Don't have to drink that cheap Sam's Cola from Wal-Mart anymore—or their Great Value 'Twist And Shout' sandwich cookies. Can you believe Arnie left me fifty thousand dollars? From now on, boys, it's Coca-Cola and Double Stuff Oreos for Monae Dunn."

"That pretty awesome," I say. "But some people might think Dr. Rosen's generous bequest gave you a motive to murder him."

"Well, those people might also be stupid. You add up everything Michael has given me and my sister over the past year, fifty thousand dollars is what Dr. Rosen used to call bupkis. Chump change."

"Indeed," says Ceepak since I just set him up with a lob shot. "Why *was* Michael so generous to you and your sister Revae? Especially this last year?"

Monae gives us a sassy smile. "Because we're good people."

"Seriously," I say. "Why did he give you and your sister such cool cars?"

"I don't know. Maybe because we were nice to his father. See, Michael's all the way out there in L.A. It made him feel good to know that somebody with half a heart was looking after his dad."

Ceepak leans in. "What do you mean?"

"His daughter-in-law. Judy. She was all kinds of mean and nasty to that old man, even after he gave her and her husband everything. Liposuction. Tummy tucks."

"For David?" I say.

"Nuh-unh. David got guitar lessons. Can you believe that? He's fifty-six years old and still thinks he's going to be a rock star. Dr. Rosen kept giving him hundreds and hundreds of dollars so David could learn how to play 'Take Me Home, Country Roads' out of tune."

"You say Judith was 'mean and nasty' to him?" says Ceepak.

"Not in front of people like you or, you know, rich people. When she's with folks like that, Judy acts all nicey-nicey. But when there's nobody around for her to impress? Well, I heard all the horrible things she said to Dr. Rosen, especially when she'd been drinking."

"How do you mean?"

"I worked nights, Detective Ceepak. Evil people like Judith Rosen, night is when their darkest demons come out—especially if they've had a couple glasses of that Pinot Grigio."

"She said these 'horrible' things, even though you were there to witness the conversations?"

"Uhm-hmm. You ever see that movie *The Help*?"

"Yes, ma'am."

"Well, Judy and her big tuckus would fit right in down there in Mississippi; playing bridge and nibbling egg salad sandwiches with all those rich white ladies. A person like Judy, she sees a black woman in a uniform, she thinks we're invisible."

"So what exactly did you hear?"

"Things no civilized person should ever say, especially not to a ninety-four-year-old man lying in his sick bed. She'd come by the beach house nine or ten o'clock at night, before her husband came home from his office . . ."

Ceepak looks surprised. "David Rosen typically worked past ten o'clock at night? At Sinclair Enterprises?"

Monae shoots Ceepak a knowing look. "Um-hmm. Would you hurry home to a nasty piece of work like that?"

"What'd she say?" I ask, so Ceepak doesn't have to field the "nasty piece of work" question.

"'Why don't you do us all a favor and die?'"

"Judith said that?" says Ceepak. "To Dr. Rosen?"

"Several times. Then, after you people helped Christine beat that restraining order, embarrassed her sister in court? Man, oh, man. Judith tore into poor old Arnie that night something fierce. Wish I'd recorded it. Maybe you two could've arrested her for elder abuse."

"What happened?"

"She came over to Dr. Rosen's house, her breath stinking like she'd been gargling with her Pinot Grigio. I'm right there. Kind of hanging back in the shadows. I was so afraid of what that crazy woman might do, I started wondering what I could grab—a vase or a statue or a fireplace tool. Something to knock her silly if she tried to strangle Dr. Rosen right there in his hospital bed."

"And what did Judith say?" asks Ceepak.

"'How dare you let that little tramp treat my sister like that,' she says. 'You embarrassed her. You embarrassed me! I'm done, I'm done, I'm done with you.' She kept saying she was done but, believe you me, she was just warming up. 'You will never, ever see your grandson again—your one and *only* grandson—not as long as you have that, that, creature living under your roof.'"

"She, of course, meant Christine?" says Ceepak, who is furiously taking notes.

"That's right. Dr. Rosen says, 'What would you have me do, Judith? Toss the poor girl out into the streets? She has nowhere else to go.' Judy says, 'Fine. You make your choices, choices have consequences.' She was really slurring her words when she said that. 'I am so effing pissed off at you right now, I'll probably have a stroke. I'll probably die before you do.'"

"How did Dr. Rosen react?"

"He never even raised his voice. He says, 'Oh, I hope not, darling.' Judith just keeps on ranting at him. 'My death will pre-decease yours,' she says. 'You have ruined my effing life.' Judy likes to use the F-word a lot when she's been drinking. 'We're done,' she screams for the millionth time. Then she stomps toward the front door, shouting, 'I hope you're happy, Christine, wherever the hell you're hiding! You ruined my sister's life! You ruined mine. You'll get yours!'"

"You heard all this?"

"Yes, sir."

"And Christine?"

"She was locked in her room. But I'm sure she heard most of it. That Judy gets loud when she gets drunk."

Monae shakes her head.

"I sure wouldn't want to be her husband when he got home that night. Can you imagine what she said to *him*?"

# 46

WE HURRY BACK TO SEA HAVEN IN CEEPAK'S HOT WHEELS detective car because it's time to sit down with Christine and her lawyer.

"Ceepak. Boyle." This from the pit bull Harvey Nussbaum.

"Mr. Nussbaum," says Ceepak, extending his hand.

I'm checking out Christine. Her eyes are bugging out of her head like a Muppet's Ping-Pong eyeballs. She is, to quote Judith, effing pissed.

I remember something else Judith said: *"Be careful. That girl has an extremely short fuse. It's only a matter of time before she hurts somebody else."*

Is it true?

Or was Judith just saying that so we'd have our doubts about helping Christine, a woman whom Judith had vowed in her drunken rant would "get hers"?

"Couple things before we do the interview," says Nussbaum, touching the nosepiece of his designer frame glasses with his finger.

"One: You should know, Detective Ceepak, your mother is, once again, providing Ms. Lemonopolous with financial assistance. She is loaning her the money to pay my fees until Dr. Rosen's estate cuts Christine that check for fifty thousand dollars."

"Good to know."

"Is this going to create a problem for us?"

"I don't see how it can," says Ceepak. "Ms. Lemonopolous is entitled to an attorney and, if past experience is any indication, you are an excellent choice for her legal representation. I am glad that my mother has chosen to spend her money to see that justice is administered fairly, without fear or favoritism."

Nussbaum just sort of stares at Ceepak for a second or two.

"You were a Boy Scout, am I right?"

"Yes, sir. Eagle."

"Whatever. Item two." He reaches into the pocket of his creased Levi's.

And pulls out the keys to my apartment. I recognize my Mr. Mets key fob.

Nussbaum hands me my keys.

"Ms. Lemonopolous will be temporarily residing at the Mussel Beach motel until this matter reaches a satisfactory conclusion."

"Is my mother advancing money for the lodging as well?" asks Ceepak.

"You have a problem with that aspect of our arrangements?"

"No, sir. It's all good."

"Groovy. Okay, where's the interrogation room?"

"Actually," I say, "we call it the 'interview' room."

Nussbaum shrugs. "Whatever, Boyle. And remember, I get paid by the hour." He hooks a thumb in Ceepak's direction. "You're costing his mother money."

I have to go first because I was the detective in charge of calling all those families Christine used to work for.

"In cases of poisoning, when the deceased is an elderly individual," I say, trying to remember what Ceepak told me earlier in the day, "it is wise and prudent to look into the history of *all* the victim's caregivers."

I lean on the word *all* so Christine knows we're checking out Monae and Joy Kochman, too.

Well, we will be.

Eventually.

"Unfortunately," says Ceepak, who, you remember, will not lie or even fudge, "due to the time constraints of our investigation, so far we have only been able to reach out to the families of those you used to work for."

"May we ask why?" says Nussbaum, who, I'm guessing, is going to be Christine's mouthpiece today.

"Certainly," says Ceepak. "Danny?"

I hate when he does that.

"Um, Joy Kochman, and a few other individuals, suggested that your former clients died under suspicious circumstances and that you were mentioned in each of the deceased person's wills."

"You have any proof for these fairy tales?" asks Nussbaum.

"No, sir."

"Good. Get back to us when you do. Unless you want us to sue you boys, the SHPD, and all of Sea Haven Township for slander."

I wonder if Mrs. Ceepak would pay for our lawyers, too.

"What else?" says Nussbaum.

"Well," says Ceepak, "as we are still in the early stages of our investigation, we would appreciate any details Christine might give as to what life was like inside Dr. Rosen's home. I'm particularly interested in your impressions of Michael, David, and Judith Rosen."

"Why?" says Nussbaum. "Are they suspects?"

"If they are," I say, so Ceepak doesn't have to blurt out the truth again, "that would be a good thing for your client, no?"

Nussbaum squints at me. Considers what I just said.

"Okay, Christine. Tell 'em what you can."

"Well," she starts. "I guess you could say neither of his two sons really looked after Dr. Rosen all that much."

"How so?" says Ceepak.

"He used to tell me stories. How, before he broke his hip, he lived in that big house all by himself. Michael was off in Hollywood and only came home to Sea Haven maybe once a year. David and Judith lived less than five miles away, but they hardly ever stopped by just to say hello. Dr. Rosen only saw them when they needed money."

"How did that make him feel?" says Ceepak, sounding like this police psychiatrist they sent me to after I had to shoot a man to stop him from killing Rita, back before she became Ceepak's wife.

"Not seeing Little Arnie broke his heart. When I worked for him, Dr. Rosen was always asking me to clip out any newspaper stories about the Philadelphia Phillies. They were Little Arnie's favorite team. Dr. Rosen hoped to give those clippings to his grandson the next time he came over. He had a whole file folder filled with those sports stories. But Little Arnie never came to the house. Not once. Not while I worked there. He was too busy at school or with little league or soccer camp."

Christine pauses.

"What are you remembering?" asks Ceepak.

Christine scrunches up her nose and lips like she doesn't want to cry. "How David and Little Arnie always had the time to go over to Philadelphia to watch a Phillies game in person. With tickets Dr. Rosen bought for them."

Good thing there's a box of Kleenex on the table. Christine grabs a tissue. Blots her eyes.

"So has anybody told you guys about the pendant?"

"No," says Ceepak.

"You've seen the egg-shaped monitor Dr. Rosen wears around his neck?"

"Yes, ma'am," says Ceepak.

"Michael, of course, paid for it."

"And Dr. Rosen agreed to wear it?"

"Yes. But only because he agreed with what Michael said to convince him: he wanted to be around when Little Arnie graduated from high school and went on to U Penn for Dental school."

We all smile. Come on. It's sweet.

"Anyway, Michael picked the top-of-the-line model. He has all sorts of money."

"Even more than your mother," cracks Nussbaum.

We all shoot him a look.

He clears his throat. "Please continue, Christine."

"Well, what makes this particular pendant better, and more expensive, is the fact that it has a motion sensor that can detect when you've taken a fall. It has something to do with your rate of descent. If you bend over to put a plate in the dishwasher, it won't go off. But if you tumble to the floor, it'll send a signal to the control center and they'll contact you to make sure you're okay."

"Is that what happened when Dr. Rosen fell?"

"Yes. He slipped in the kitchen. Didn't answer when the pendant people tried to contact him. But they knew he was in trouble because of that sensor, so they called nine-one-one and sent in the paramedics. Like I said, Dr. Rosen was alone in that house for long stretches of time. No one came by to visit him on a regular basis. He could've been there on the floor for days. He could've died."

Christine looks down at her hands.

"Michael saved Dr. Rosen's life."

My mind drifts off to the boardwalk and that scary new ride where Mr. Ceepak works.

The Free Fall.

David and Judith got theirs; the fall that should have set them free, financially, for life. Unfortunately, brother Michael snatched away their windfall with his clever little pendant.

So maybe Judith and David decided to make Dr. Rosen take another tumble. And this time, maybe they made sure he couldn't get back up.

Maybe this time they used cyanide.

# 47

"WE UNDERSTAND YOU SAVED YOUR FATHER'S LIFE," CEEPAK
says to Michael Rosen.

We're in his suite at the Sea Spray, the highest-priced hotel in
Sea Haven. It even has bellhops and somebody to carve an S-S logo
into the sand in all the outdoor ashtrays.

"You mean the pendant?" says Michael, offering us each a
chilled bottle of Pellegrino water from his mini-fridge. I see one
of those Toblerone candy bars sitting in a wicker basket on top of
the fridge snuggled between a tiny bag of Famous Amos cookies,
a jar of cashews, and a Pringles-style can of M&M's. I'm guessing
every item in the basket costs at least ten bucks.

Ceepak raises his hand to say no-thanks to the bubbly water. I
do the same. But I'm seriously eyeballing those M&M's.

"Dad, of course, thought the monthly fee for the monitoring
service was too high. So I put it on one of my credit cards."

Michael holds a drinking glass up to the afternoon sun streaming through his twelfth-floor windows and must see a spot, because he curdles his nose.

"Filthy. Can you believe this is actually considered the 'nicest' hotel on the island?"

He shakes his head to further convey his "what a world, what a world" disdain.

After chatting with Christine and her lawyer, Ceepak decided it would be best if we spent the rest of the day talking to the Rosens: Michael, David, and Judith. He is convinced that our suspect pool is similar to a kiddies' wading pool: "very, very shallow."

"And probably full of crap," I added.

According to Ceepak, we need to look at the nurses and the family. Every single one of them, at some point in the days prior to Dr. Rosen's fatal pill pop, could've had the means and opportunity to slip a cyanide-laced capsule into the Saturday-morning meds slot.

"The key, I suspect," Ceepak told me on the drive over to Michael's hotel, "will be determining who had the strongest motivation."

And so we probe the richest son first. The one who dropped by Dr. Rosen's house on the Friday before he died hoping to take "a walk on the beach" with his father.

"Over the years, you purchased many items for your father," says Ceepak. "Is that correct?"

"Well, somebody had to," Michael answers. "He was too cheap to buy what he needed himself. And my brother was bleeding him dry. That's why I never gave my father money. If I wrote my father a check, he'd just deposit it in his bank account so he could write another check for David and Judith and Little Arnie. That reminds me. I need to hire somebody to take that 3-D TV out of Dad's house. I didn't give it to him so he could leave it to them."

"So you were angry with your father about his preferential treatment of your brother and his family?"

"I could not care less about the money. Honestly. As you gen-tlemen have undoubtedly heard, I have done pretty well for myself since leaving home thirty years ago."

"You're being modest," says Ceepak.

"You made fifty-two million last year alone," I chime in. "They put you on that list in Forbes magazine."

Michael feigns a modest blush. "Guilty as charged. But dear boy, you forgot to mention my Emmy awards."

"Sorry," I say.

He brushes it off. "That's okay. If my father were still alive, he'd tell you about each and every one of them, over and over and over again. In his eyes, that's who I was. The very wealthy, very impor-tant, award-winning son. Trust me, with Arnold Rosen, there was no such thing as 'unconditional love,' not like I finally found with my partner Andrew. With Dad-ums, you had to earn it every day. I found that wildly successful television shows, Emmy awards, and millions of dollars in the bank helped."

"When did you leave Sea Haven?"

"When I was eighteen. I went to college in California. U.S.C. Fought and scraped for everything I have. And all that time, even when I was working as a waiter in some sketchy dive to make ends meet, I never once thought about coming 'home' to sunny, funderful Sea Haven."

"Why do you think your brother stayed in Sea Haven?"

"Oh, I don't know. Maybe he likes playing miniature golf or eating pancakes the size of manhole covers. Maybe he's really Peter Pan and refuses to grow up. Of course, Dad made staying here super easy for David. All he had to do was let Daddy run his life and produce an heir to the Rosen throne."

Michael plops down into a chair. I can tell venting all this bottled-up anger is exhausting him.

"Here's another reason why David did not kick the sand of this crummy little town off his shoes and run as far away as he possibly could and still be in the continental United States: David, gentlemen, is not gay. And newsflash, thirty-some years ago, Sea Haven was not, shall we say, a safe haven for boys like me."

"And your father?" asks Ceepak. "How did he react to your sexual orientation?"

"Horribly. We're Jewish, but I think he seriously considered becoming a Born Again Christian just so he could find one of those preachers to pray my gay away. Mom was better. In fact, she's the one who told me to 'move as far away from Arnold Rosen' as I could and make my own life. She said she should've done it herself."

"When did your mother pass away?"

"Seventeen years ago. January 18th."

"She and your father weren't close?"

"Who knows? They were never very kissy or huggy, not in front of us. Dad didn't come home from the office most nights till nine. We only saw him on weekends when he'd take us fishing or to a football game up in New York or on some other god-awful manly adventure."

"But your mother and father never divorced?"

"Nope. She just did a lot of retail therapy to compensate. In the end, I think Dad just wore her out."

"How so?"

"My father—sweet and charming as he may seem when you first meet him—was a very demanding, very manipulative, very controlling, and extremely cheap, almost miserly man. Did you know, he always bought his socks and underwear at Sears because 'nobody saw the labels on your socks and underwear.' To do otherwise would be a waste of money, he'd say. So, you can imagine how disappointed he was when he heard I was spending a fortune on skivvies from Fred Segal."

"And who is this Fred Segal?"

"High-end fashion boutique in Beverly Hills."

"I see."

"My father had a set way of doing everything. And woe betide anyone who strayed off his very rigid, straight and narrow road. Drove my mother crazy. Me, too. One time, maybe twenty, twenty-five years ago, I made the mistake of going with him to the airport. We were both flying off in different directions. Anyway, we get out of the cab at Newark airport and, being a good little son, I grab Dad's bags and haul them over to the skycap.

"Well, my father pitched a fit. 'What are you doing?' he demanded. 'Checking your bags.' 'That's not how it's done!' he says, thinking I'm like David and have never flown anywhere on my own. So I say, 'Uh, yes, Dad, it is. You give this nice young fellow your suitcase and he takes care of everything for you.' My dad stomped his feet like a little boy. 'No, Michael. That is not how I do it.'

"And that, gentlemen, is the key. My father could not abide anyone doing anything in a manner that didn't conform to his well-scripted perceptions of perfection."

Now Michael pauses.

"I suppose I should've thanked him for that."

"How so?"

"Why do you think I'm such a highly paid television producer? I'm a perfectionist and a control freak. I am, gentlemen, my father's son."

# 48

CEEPAK FLIPS BACKWARD TO A PAGE HE'S ALREADY SCRIBBLED on in his notebook.

"We spent some time today with Revae Dunn," Ceepak tells Michael. "At the Garden State Reproductive Science Center over in Avondale."

"And?"

"Why were you so generous to Ms. Dunn and her sister Monae?"

"I helped Monae because Revae was helping me."

"How?"

Michael reaches into the mini bar and grabs the little blue bottle of Bombay sapphire gin. He twists open the cap and takes a bracing chug.

"You've met Judith's sister, Shona, correct?"

"Yes," I say.

"Do you remember the color of her hair?"

I think for a second. "Black?"

"Correct. Black as a raven's belly. And Judith?"

"Blonde," says Ceepak.

"From a bottle," says Michael, taking another swig on his Bombay. "Little Arnie, of course, also has blonde hair, but, unlike his pudgy mother, his roots are not jet black. And the lazy sow always forgets to do her eyebrows. They're darker than her roots."

Ceepak closes up his notebook. Leans in.

"Go on."

"Item two. Athletics. Little Arnie is very good at sports. Football, basketball, baseball—making him the first Rosen in recorded history who has ever excelled at athletic endeavors. Item three. Intelligence. Little Arnie is very smart. Straight A's. Honor roll. His poppa? Not so much. In fact, ages ago, Dad-ums had grand visions of David going to dental school. U Penn, just like he did."

"And?"

"And you don't get into U Penn or any top tier college with SAT scores in the low 400's. You go to a Community College outside Atlantic City and pick up a two-year associate degree in Hospitality Management." Michael shakes his head. "Hospitality Management. What on earth did David study? 'Reservation Taking 101'? 'Comparative Buffets'? Item four: Little Arnie has perfect teeth."

Okay. I think that's the gin talking. He's totally lost me.

"Gentlemen," says Michael, "there hasn't been a Rosen who didn't need extensive orthodontia for generations. Item five: Little Arnie's cute button nose."

Ceepak has heard enough. "Exactly what are you suggesting, Mr. Rosen?"

"Well, detective, with Revae's able assistance, I have, over the past year, been doing a little detective work of my own."

"And?"

"There is no doubt in my mind that Judith is the young Aryan lad's mother because, as she often says to Little Arnie, giving birth to him is what ruined her bikini body. That and her fondness for Mallomars, noodle kugel, and mayonnaise."

"But," says Ceepak, "you doubt the boy's paternity? You suspect that David is not Little Arnie's father?"

"All that crap about my father's 'living legacy,' the heir to the royal 'Rosen bloodline'? What if, gentlemen, at the fertility clinic, one of Judith's treatments—which of course Dad-ums paid for because he wanted a grandson so desperately—what if it was what they call Therapeutic Donor Insemination?"

"Ms. Dunn mentioned that as an option her clinic offers."

"And I suspect it's the option Judith chose."

"What is it?" I ask, because my SAT's weren't so great either.

"Artificial insemination," says David. "Using the sperm of an anonymous donor."

"And Revae has been helping you prove your hypothesis?" asks Ceepak.

"Diligently and tirelessly."

"She has been searching through confidential records, violating her patients' right to privacy?"

"Perhaps. But you'd have a very hard time proving it. The girl is good. Takes her time. Covers her tracks. She has earned every penny I have ever spent on her or her sister. You boys would get nowhere if you attempt to punish Revae Dunn for violating the sacred trust of a fat cow like Judith and some boy who jerked off in a cup fifteen years ago for seventy-five bucks a pop. The county prosecutor would laugh in your face."

"But you just told us that Ms. Dunn has been violating her fertility clinic's ethics for a fee."

"Ask me again in court and I'll deny everything."

"You'd perjure yourself to protect Ms. Dunn?"

"Yes, because you couldn't prove perjury either. It'd just be your word against mine, and I have very excellent lawyers who know how to waste time with motions and procedural maneuvering. You'd never even get me on the stand."

Ceepak is busy seething.

So I jump in.

"Did you and Revae find Little Arnie's real father?"

"As I told my brother Friday night after that god-awful family dinner: We are close. Very, very close."

"Why didn't you just run one of those Maury Povich show paternity tests?" I ask.

Michael shakes his head. "David would never consent to the DNA cheek swab. Besides, it's not dramatic enough. I wanted Dad-ums to meet his grandson's *real* father. Live and in person."

"And how did David react when you told him that you were close to identifying the sperm donor?" asks Ceepak, who's back in the game.

"He said I was just jealous because all I can do is adopt. And as you have heard from my brother and sister-in-law, adopted children, such as Kyle, don't count. They do not qualify as blood heirs. They can never be considered legitimate grandchildren."

# 49

"Do you think Michael killed Dr. Rosen because there was just no way to for him win his father's love?" I ask Ceepak when we're back in our car

I know. I sound like one of those touchy-feely dudes with afternoon talk shows on TV.

"It's a possibility," says Ceepak, which is what he usually says when he can tell I'm jumping to conclusions—especially conclusions you might find inscribed inside a sappy greeting card: *"Dear Dad, you never hugged me when I was young; So here's a poison pill to place upon your tongue!"*

It's a little after six—eighteen hundred hours in the Ceepak Time Zone. David and Judith Rosen's apartment will be our next stop.

"Oh, shoot," I mumble as we climb into the stealth-mobile. "I forgot to ask Michael about his suit."

Ceepak crinkles into the driver's seat. "His suit?"

"Yeah. How did he know to pack that black suit he wore to the funeral?"

"You're suggesting he anticipated his father's death prior to his departure from California?"

"Maybe he packed the cyanide pills, too."

"Interesting hypothesis, Danny. And your deductive reasoning is commendable as well."

Okay. I know I'm about to get a "but" or a "however."

"However . . ."

There it is.

". . . as you may have also observed, Michael Rosen is constantly dressed in black. In addition to being a fashion statement popular with those in the entertainment industry, it might also be a reflection of the frugality and parsimony Michael inherited from his father."

"You mean Michael is cheap, too?"

"Perhaps so—on a vastly different scale. Yes, his tailored suit most likely cost more than a similar, if less stylish, suit purchased at Kohl's . . ."

"They sell suits at Kohl's?"

"Indeed so."

I'm guessing Kohl's was one of the men's stores Ceepak and Rita visited back in his short-lived Chief Of Police days.

"But," Ceepak continues, "by having one very nice black suit that he can wear to any event—be it a wedding, funeral, or cocktail party—instead of a closet full of suits in various colors and textures, Michael is displaying some of the same miserliness he professed to despise in his father. It reminds of what Bruce Springsteen wrote . . ."

Hey, what doesn't? Especially when you're talking "fathers and sons."

"'Independence Day,'" says Ceepak, citing the song before quoting the lyric: "'There was just no way this house could hold the two of us. I guess that we were just too much of the same kind.'"

I remember hanging at Ceepak's place one weekend, listening to E-Street Radio, the all-Springsteen all-the-time channel on

217

the Sirius satellite radio Rita gave Ceepak for Christmas last year. (Okay, I love Bruce, but does anybody really need a 24/7 Springsteen channel just so they can hear fifty different versions of "Born To Run" every day?) The satellite station played a bootleg recording of "Independence Day" from a 1976 concert in New York City. Before he sang the song, Springsteen told the crowd a long, heart-wrenching story about coming home to his father's house.

"I could see the screen door, I could see my pop's cigarette," Springsteen said on stage. His dad kept all the lights off in the house and would sit at the kitchen table in that darkness, smoking cigarettes and working on a six-pack of beer until all the cans in the plastic rings were gone. "We'd start talkin' about nothin' much. How I was doin'. Pretty soon he'd ask me what I thought I was doin' with myself, and we'd always end up screamin' at each other."

When the song was finished, Ceepak said something that stuck with me: "Apparently, Bruce Springsteen and I grew up in the same home."

At the time, I thought, "That's impossible," because Ceepak's from Ohio, not New Jersey. Then I realized he was being meta-phorical. But still—no way are John and Joseph Ceepak "too much of the same kind."

That's when our radio starts squawking.

It's Dorian Rence, our dispatcher.

"Ceepak? Have you got your ears on?"

Mrs. Rence is still a little new on the job. Thinks she's supposed to use CB Radio jargon.

Ceepak grabs the mic.

"This is Ceepak, go."

"Sorry to disturb you, Detective. But, well, I thought you should know."

And then there's this pause.

"It's your father. Again. The gatehouse security guard at . . ."

Ceepak doesn't stay parked for the rest. He jams the transmission into reverse.

". . . the Oceanaire condo complex . . ."

Those black Nitto tires on Ceepak's slick new ride spin so fast it smells like rubber duckie burning day at the town dump.

". . . called nine-one-one . . ."

We rocket out of the hotel parking lot.

"Lights and sirens," says Ceepak.

I find the buttons. Punch them.

Cars and bikes and sea gulls scurry out of our way when all those LEDs strobe to life inside their sleek black hiding places. The Batmobile is on the move.

"We're on our way," Ceepak says into the mic. Then he tosses it aside so he can keep both hands firmly gripped on the steering wheel and drive us NASCAR-style over to his mother's condo complex.

Red lights and stop signs?

We barely even pause.

"I should have known," Ceepak mutters through gritted teeth as we whip around another corner.

"Known what?" I say, hanging on to the grab bar over my door, thinking that holding it will somehow protect me when we have our high-speed collision.

"This is Monday," says Ceepak. "Sinclair Enterprises hired a second factory-certified operator for their Free Fall who was slated to start work today."

"Giving your dad the evening off."

# 50

CEEPAK SLAMS ON THE BRAKES, CUTS THE WHEEL HARD TO THE RIGHT.

We skid sideways into the Oceanaire's entry road.

Bruce Southworth, the kid with the clipboard, is out of his guard hut.

Brian Ersalesi and John Johnston, two of our SHPD uniform cops, are standing in front of their cruiser, which has its roof bar lights swirling. No weapons are drawn. Well, except for Bruce Southworth's clipboard.

Mr. Ceepak stands between the two SHPD officers and the security guard. All smiles. He's carrying a bakery box. Guess he's bringing sweets this time instead of flowers.

Ceepak and I yank open our doors and head out.

"What's the situation?" he hollers.

"He still wants to see your mother," Southworth hollers back.

"You know this guy, Detective?" shouts Ersalesi.

"10-4."

"I'm his Papa!" wheezes Mr. Ceepak as he stumbles forward a foot or two. "And since when is paying a courtesy call to your spouse a crime, Johnny?"

"Since you were advised to stay away."

"Yeah, well, that was before your mother went bonkers. She's throwing my money down the crapper. Buying this Christine girl another lawyer? I heard all about it from Dave Rosen in H.R. at work. Your nurse pal killed Dave's dad but your mother's still bankrolling her? Adele's losing it, Johnny Boy. Someone needs to make her come to her senses."

Then he makes a big mistake.

He tucks that bakery box sideways under his left arm and balls up his right hand into a fist to show how he's going to persuade Adele to see the light.

Ceepak goes toe to toe with his old man. My hand hovers over my Glock.

The two uniforms see me make my move. Their hands are hovering over holsters now, too.

"Do you intend to beat that sense into her, sir?" demands Ceepak.

His father gets a devilish glint in his eye. "A man's gotta do what a man's gotta do, son."

Ceepak's told me stories. His father used to hit his mother. Until Ceepak turned thirteen. Then he was finally big enough to protect his mom, even if it meant taking a few punches himself.

By the time Ceepak was fifteen, his father was too terrified of his giant, muscle-bound son to even think about ever using his wife as a punching bag again. That's when Joe Sixpack shifted his rage toward Billy, Ceepak's little brother.

"Hell's bells, son. Somebody needs to teach that woman a lesson. You don't piss away a family's fortune on total strangers unless you're crazy or drunk or both. That's Ceepak money!"

"What's in the box?" asks Ceepak.

"Cookies."

"Mind if I take a look?"

Mr. Ceepak pulls back. "They're not for you."

Ceepak repeats himself. "Mind if I take a look?"

His father grins. "You got a search warrant?"

"No. However, I know you had your gun carrying rights restored. In Ohio."

"So? I worked a lot of county fairs last fall. Needed protection. Some of those carnies are tough customers."

"And you don't have a weapon in that white paper box?"

"I told you—it's a dozen damn cookies from the bakery at the supermarket."

"Then why did they forget to tie it with string?"

"Because I was in a hurry . . ."

Ceepak leans in. Sniffs his face.

"Are you drunk, sir?"

"No. I had a couple beers after work. Arrest me."

"We will. The next time you come within one hundred yards of my mother."

"What?"

Ceepak reaches into his back pocket. Pulls out a document.

"This, sir, as you might recall, is what is known in New Jersey as an emergency restraining order. They may be obtained at any police station in the state."

"What? What'd I do?"

"You foolishly threatened a family member with physical violence in front of five witnesses, four of whom are law enforcement officers, thereby giving me grounds to invoke these emergency powers as a protection against future domestic violence."

"Don't do this, Johnny."

"It's already done." He slaps the paper against his father's chest. "Judge Mindy Rasmussen signed it the day we heard you were coming to town. Just in case."

Mr. Ceepak sneers. "Be prepared, right? You overgrown Boy Scout fruitcake."

Mr. Ceepak grabs the ERO out of his son's hand. He still has that bakery box stuck sideways under his arm.

If there were cookies inside it, they would've toppled out by now.

"You're backing me into a corner, Johnny," Mr. Ceepak hisses. "You ever see what happens when you corner a hungry alley cat?"

"No, sir. I'm more of a dog person."

"Don't you give me lip, boy. I brought you into this world, I can take you out of it, too."

"I highly doubt that, sir."

Yeah. Me, too.

"However, if you'd like to continue to make threats against an on-duty police officer, once again in front of all these witnesses, we can inform your friends at Sinclair Enterprises that you will not be coming to work tomorrow."

Mr. Ceepak backs down.

"Fine, Johnny boy. Fine. You win this round. But I want my million dollars."

"I'm sure you do."

"This isn't over, son."

"You are correct. This emergency order will last until a judge of the Family Part of the Chancery Division of the Superior Court grants or denies a final restraining order. You will receive notice of that hearing within ten days."

"Okey-dokey. See you in court, Johnny—if not before."

When Mr. Ceepak says that, he gets that glint in his eye again.

Why do I think he is already hatching some new scheme to get at Mrs. Ceepak?

Probably because he is.

# 51

"Gosh, officers, I never said any such thing."

Judith Rosen is playing little Miss Nicey Nice again.

We're in David and Judith's upstairs apartment. It's getting dark out. "Little Arnie" is in his room, blasting away at zombies with robots. David is still at work. Judith is stuffing chunks of buttery fudge into her mouth and sucking on them like they were breath mints.

I see a bundled stack of moving cartons leaning against a wall. Guess David and Judith are already planning a move into the beach house they inherited from the late Arnold Rosen.

Ceepak is reading from his notepad, repeating what Judith said to her father-in-law on the night her sister was, more or less, humiliated in open court.

"So you deny ever saying 'Why don't you do us all a favor and die?'"

"To Dad? Heavens, no. Who would say such a horrible thing to a dying man?"

Ceepak cocks an eyebrow. "Was Dr. Rosen actually 'dying' at that time?"

Judith smiles and blinks. "Well, officer, we're all born with a death sentence. And the older we get, the closer we crawl to our graves."

Then she blinks some more. Just so we have time to contemplate her mind-blowing Zen wisdom.

"How's your stroke situation?" I ask because, even though I'm no Ceepak, I can tell when a witness is yanking our collective crank. I'm not buying Judith's innocent-angel act.

"Excuse me?" says Judith.

"Boss?" I say.

Ceepak refers to his notes. "During that same verbal exchange with Dr. Rosen, you told your father-in-law that the situation between Christine and your sister had made you so upset that you might suffer a stroke. That, and I quote, 'my death will pre-decease yours.'"

"Really? Somebody told you I said that? How can my death pre-decease anybody else's? That doesn't make any sense."

"No, ma'am. It does not. However, such is often the case when one speaks while inebriated."

"Excuse me? Are you suggesting that I was drunk?"

"I am simply relaying the observations of a witness to your angry exchange with your father-in-law."

I butt in. "This same witness also told us that you swore Christine Lemonopolous 'would get hers.'"

Ceepak takes over. "Were you already scheming to somehow implicate Ms. Lemonopolous in your father-in-law's death?"

"Why would I do something like that? If anything, I was encouraging Christine to keep on trying to beat her PTSD. If she did as her doctors advised, I was confident she'd 'get hers' some day—meaning her reward for all her hard work. Maybe a husband, too."

"I'm sorry," says Ceepak. "Your recollection of this incident does not jibe at all with that of our witness."

"Was it Miss Monae?"

Ceepak doesn't answer.

"That's okay," says Judith, putting on her toothy smile again. It's smudged with chocolate. "I already know the answer. It had to be Miss Monae. She works nights and you say this 'incident' took place at night?"

"No, ma'am. I gave no indication as to the time of day."

"Well, I do remember being very angry one night with Dad. I thought he was making some very bad choices. He should have fired Miss Christine the minute she attacked my sister. You don't want an individual with such a short fuse acting as your caregiver or, even worse, living under your roof. I may have raised my voice slightly but only because Dad was in imminent danger and hard of hearing. Whatever I said, I said it to protect Dad from a very volatile and violent woman with a serious medical condition."

I'm not even sure if Mrs. Rosen knows she's lying. I think she lives in some kind of a bubble where what she believes is always true.

"You gentlemen, of course, know that Miss Monae was spying for David's little brother Michael?"

"What do you mean by 'spying'?" asks Ceepak.

"Michael was jealous. Didn't like the fact that David and Little Arnie were his father's favorites."

"Speaking of spies," says Ceepak, "was it truly your intention for, first, Joy Kochman and then Christine Lemonopolous, whom you planted inside Dr. Rosen's home, to feed you information about your father-in-law's medical condition?"

"I wouldn't use the word 'spy,' but we did indeed ask Miss Joy and, later, Miss Christine to keep an eye on Dad. To monitor his physical and, yes, mental well-being. We were worried about him.

Dementia is a serious problem for senior citizens. As we age, our brain shrivels."

Yeah. Mine's doing it now.

"If you were so concerned," says Ceepak, "why didn't you visit Dr. Rosen more often?"

More blinks. "Because we respected his privacy."

"How often did your husband take money from his father?"

"Gosh, Dad was so generous. Through the years, we've all benefitted from his gifts."

"I'm told Michael never asked his father for a dime."

"And see how well he's done? With Michael, I think Dad's generosity was of the heart. It wasn't easy for Dad to accept his son's gayness."

Yes, if Ceepak says black, this lady is going to say white.

"And please, Detectives, take into consideration all that David and I did to earn Dad's generosity. The many meals we ate with him . . ."

Which, I'm guessing, Dr. Rosen always paid for.

"How we were always available to join him on a moment's notice at a Broadway show or a symphony performance."

Ditto on the tickets.

"We also surrendered a good deal of our own family life to David's father."

"How so?" says Ceepak.

"Well, not to speak ill of the dead, but Dad was a bit of a control freak. One time, right after Little Arnie was born, Dad brought over all these classical records because he didn't like the Raffi music I'd been playing in the nursery. Said it would stunt Little Arnie's 'intellectual development.'"

"So he imposed himself into your daily life?"

"Yes. Unfortunately, my husband found it very difficult to stand up to his father. I guess some boys always do. It's why we never have bottled water in our home."

"Excuse me?"

"Dad didn't believe in bottled water. Once, when he came over to visit Little Arnie, he saw a few bottles of Poland Spring in our fridge. 'Is that where my money is going?' is what Dad said to David because he had just given us a ten-thousand-dollar holiday gift. From that point on, I was forbidden to drink anything but tap water in my own home."

"So all the money Dr. Rosen gave you came with a heavy price?"

"Exactly."

Ceepak closes up his notebook.

"We may have more questions at a later time. Right now, we'd like to talk to David."

"I'm sure he's still at the office."

"By the way," says Ceepak, "I couldn't help but notice the ring on your right hand. It's quite unusual."

I check out the ring that's too tight for a finger on her right hand. It looks like a cigar band on a sausage.

"Thank you," says Judith, admiring it herself. "Believe it or not, this was a Valentine's Day gift from Dad."

"Your father-in-law gave you a ring?"

"In a way. He gave David a gift certificate worth several thousand dollars, suggested he use it to buy me something special for Valentine's Day. This was a few years ago. David and I had hit a rough patch. All marriages do, I suppose. Anyway, the gift certificate was for my girlfriend's shop. Cele Deemer. Runs the cutest little boutique—The Gold Coast on Ocean Avenue. She only sells her own incredible handcrafted jewelry. They're all one-of-a-kind items."

"It's very creative."

"Thank you. Can you see the keyhole in the center of the heart? I think that is so cute."

"Indeed. Is it gold?"

"Fourteen karat. Gold is all Cele works with. It's why she calls her shop The *Gold* Coast."

Ceepak nods.

I have to figure he's thinking what I'm thinking: Judith's friend, the local goldsmith, probably uses potassium cyanide in her work. She definitely could've loaned her gal pal a tablespoon or two last week.

Especially if Judith asked for it in her nicey-nice voice.

# 52

It's nearly eight when we climb down the back staircase from David and Judith Rosen's apartment.

Judith told us she would call her husband. "Let him know you boys are on your way."

"She's going to coach him," I say to Ceepak as we make our way around the side of the two-story building to the gravel-and-seashell driveway where the super-charged Ceepakmobile is parked.

"Such would be my supposition as well, Danny. However, at this juncture, there is little we can do to prevent spousal contact."

Judging from his speech pattern (which is beginning to mimic Data's, the emotionless cyborg from "Star Trek The Next Generation") and the fact that he said "spousal contact" (in a way that sounded a lot like "conjugal visit"), I believe Ceepak is shifting into his robotic mode because, inside his big analytical brain, the chipmunks are chugging along at warp speed on his mental treadmills.

He's starting to figure something out.

"We'll drive down to Sinclair Enterprises," he says. "Interview David."

"Have we heard anything from Bill Botzong about when his team will be done with their cyanide data mining?" I ask.

"Bill sent me a text. His forensics team has all the raw data and will work through the night to analyze the information to see if they can extract any interesting patterns or clusters that might implicate one or more of our suspects."

We cruise down Ocean Avenue.

Things are pretty quiet. There's some ambling life in the misty pools of light flooding the miniature golf courses. The summer's first lines of giddy kids and smiling parents have formed outside Custard's Last Stand and the Scoop Sloop. A few Ocean Avenue restaurants look like they're doing a brisk dinner business.

But most of the shops are closed up for the night.

Including "The Gold Coast: A Handcrafted & Unique Adornment Shoppe" at 1510 Ocean Avenue— conveniently located just five doors down from the worldwide headquarters of Sinclair Enterprises at 1500.

Why do I think Bill Botzong's MCU data miners are going to strike cyanide gold on Ocean Avenue?

The offices of Sinclair Enterprises look like one of those boiler rooms where telemarketers work; calling people at dinner time.

I think the ground-level space used to be a clothing store. Maybe a hair salon. The walls are painted the same color as guacamole. Bright green poles, spaced at intervals in tidy rows, hold up the drop-panel ceiling. A maze of gray cubicles fills most of the wide-open, industrial-strength-carpeted floor.

A few busy beavers are still clacking on computer keyboards or barking orders into phones for "ten two-pound bags of malted milk powder" and "seven sleeves of two hundred-count six-ounce snow cone cups" while saying, "no, we don't need any more multi-colored spoon straws."

The only decoration on the bare walls (where you can still see the outlines of the shelving units that used to be mounted there) are a few push-pinned posters for Sinclair Enterprises brand new thrill ride, The StratosFEAR; one or two "RE-ELECT MAYOR SINCLAIR: LEADING THE WAY TO ANOTHER SUNNY, FUNDERFUL DAY" posters; and a cartoon map of tourist attractions with gold stars slapped on top of the various outlets of the Sinclair Empire: Cap'n Scrubby's Car Wash, The Scoop Sloop, Do Me A Flavor, The Seashellerie, Sand Buggy Bumper Cars, and on and on.

The mayor must own thirty different properties up and down the island.

David Rosen is seated at a desk behind see-through cubicle walls. It looks like he's inside a ten-by-ten shower stall.

David is hunched over in his chair, rubbing the top of his bald head. A telephone is jammed tight against his ear.

"Yes, dear. Yes. Of course. Yes, dear."

We move into the open space that serves as David's door. Ceepak raps his knuckles on the closest wall.

David whips around in his swivel seat. Looks like a startled ferret.

"They're here. I know. Okay. I will. Yes. I know. Okay. Right."

He keeps inching closer to his desk where the phone cradle waits to put him out of his misery. I notice he has a Bart Simpson desk clock, too.

"Judy? Okay. Yes. I know."

And, finally, he hangs up.

"My wife," he says with a nervous chuckle. "Wants me to pick up a few things on the way home."

*"At this hour?"* I'm thinking but then I remember: most of the booze stores stay open till midnight.

"Are you free to talk?" asks Ceepak.

"Sure," says David, gesturing at the two chairs facing his desk. "Take a seat."

"Hey, Dave?"

It's that guy Bob. The manager from Sinclair's rides on the pier. He grabs hold of a panel and pokes his head into the cubicle.

"Hey, Bob."

"Heard about your dad. How you holding up?"

"I'm hanging in."

"Good. You need anything . . ."

"Thanks."

"Just wanted to pop in and say major kudos on Shaun McKinnon. He is *awesome.* Fantastic find, buddy. We should hire all our ride operators from Ohio." He makes a finger pistol and shoots it at Ceepak. "This McKinnon is almost as good as your dad."

Ceepak does not say a word.

"Oh-kay. Gotta run," says Bob. Fortunately, he leaves.

"Can I ask you a quick favor, Detective?" says David. "Could you have a word with your mother? Judith tells me she heard from a friend that a Mrs. Adele Ceepak is bankrolling Christine, again. Advancing her money to pay her legal bills?"

"And why is that a problem?"

"Because, hello? She murdered my father."

"Do you have proof to substantiate your claim?"

"Christine Lemonopolous gave my dad the fatal pill. What more proof do you need?"

"Something to establish malice aforethought. Evidence that she provided your father his morning medications with criminal intent."

"Anybody could have placed that poisoned pill into your dad's meds organizer," I explain.

"Really?" David says sarcastically. "Like who?"

"Ms. Dunn, the night nurse," says Ceepak. "Joy Kochman, the home health aide who was dismissed to make room for Christine Lemonopolous. She visited your father last week. Your brother Michael is a suspect. So is your wife, Judith."

Ceepak pauses.

"And you."

# 53

David laughs. "Me? That's rich."

Ceepak ignores him and concentrates on the scrawled questions inside his spiral notebook. "A few years ago, you purchased your wife a handcrafted gold ring, is that correct?"

"You mean that heart thing? Yeah. That was Dad's idea. For Valentine's Day. He gave me a gift certificate worth five thousand bucks from this boutique up the block called The Gold Coast. He'd heard Judith say how much she liked the rings in that shop. It's all one-of-a-kind stuff. Expensive. Dad even told me what to have inscribed inside."

"And what was that?"

"Something like 'Be mine, Valentine.' I remember it rhymed."

"Did your father often give you romantic advice?" asks Ceepak.

David bristles.

"Does this line of questioning have anything to do with your murder investigation, Detective?"

"It might," I say, so Ceepak doesn't have to break the stare-down he's got going on with David.

"So," I continue, "you guys made out pretty good with your dad's will?"

"Yeah," says David, smiling like the kid who got the biggest scoop of ice cream on his slice of Thanksgiving pie. "Of course, we could've done better if dad hadn't done that silly 'mitzvah' for those two lazy caregivers, Christine and Monae."

"Lazy?" says Ceepak.

"Come on. How hard can that job be? You push a guy around in a wheelchair. You open a can and make him soup. You change his poopy diaper. For this you should be paid fifteen dollars an hour? I've got guys working at our car washes for less than minimum wage. They're happy just to have the work and to be in America. I should've hired one of their wives or girlfriends to take care of dad."

"Are you surprised that your father didn't leave anything to your younger brother?"

"No. Michael hasn't lived here for years. He hasn't had to deal with Dad on a daily basis like I have. We earned that money, detective. We *earned* it."

Someone new knocks on David's cubicle wall.

It's Shawn Reilly Simmons. Yes, we've dated. Back when she was just Shawn Reilly. Guess she works for Mayor Sinclair now, too. She's carrying a stack of mail.

"Hey, Danny."

"Hey."

"What's up, Shawn?" says David, sitting up in his chair. Smiling. He even smooths out his goatee.

"Some mail landed on my desk for one of your new hires. Guy named Shaun McKinnon?"

"New StratosFEAR operator. Came down from Ohio." He motions for Shawn to hand him the rubber-banded bundle. "I'll take care of it."

"Thanks. Good seeing you again, Danny."

And she bops out of the office.

Ceepak's eyes follow her.

He has that thoughtful look on his face again but doesn't say a word.

For a couple seconds, the only sound in the cubicle is the BOINK-BOINK of David playing mail-stack-guitar with that taut rubber band. It could be "Country Roads, Take Me Home."

His eyes dart down to his phone like he's waiting for Judith to call and ream him out again.

"Well," he finally says. "Guess you two have heard about the big fight Michael and I had Friday night?"

Okay. David is acting extremely strange. Like a nervous guy at a party trying to make small talk with a girl he knows is too pretty to listen to him but he has her cornered behind the couch.

"See, Dad took us both to The Trattoria and Michael made his big announcement about how he and his 'partner' Andrew had just adopted an African-American baby. I guess in California gay people can do that sort of thing."

"New Jersey also encourages gay couples to adopt," says Ceepak.

"Really? Huh. That's weird. Anyway, I told Michael his adopted son wasn't really a 'Rosen.' Dad agreed. He told Michael he should send the baby back to wherever he bought it because his so-called son Kyle would never be a legitimate grandson like Little Arnie. In fact . . ." Here David snickers. "Dad said, 'given the lifestyle choices you have made, Michael, you will never, *ever* be capable of having a true family.'"

# 54

"SO WHY WAS DAVID STARING AT HIS PHONE LIKE THAT?" I ASK
Ceepak when we hit the sidewalk outside 1500 Ocean Avenue.
"Was he expecting Judith to call again?"

"My hunch is, in the conversation that ended as we arrived,
David's wife had instructed him to be sure to mention something
very specific to us. In fact, I suspect Judith told him exactly what
to say and how to say it."

"That bit about the fight at the restaurant?"

"It came out rather stilted, wouldn't you agree?"

"Yeah. Almost like he was reading a script."

"Exactly. Judith wanted us to know about that altercation
because her version gives her brother-in-law a motive for murder."

"But what if David and Judith are the ones who are lying about
what went down in that private dining room?"

"Such is our conundrum, Danny. Judith and David clearly
suspect that, in our interview with Monae Dunn, we learned

about the harsh words exchanged behind closed doors at The Trattoria. The truth of what caused that flareup, however, remains elusive."

"So we should talk to Michael again?"

"Tomorrow. He's not going anywhere tonight."

Well, if he does, or even tries, we'll hear about it. Our uniform guys are still keeping pretty close tabs on the homes and hotels of all the suspects at the top of our list: Christine, Michael, David, and Judith.

At this point, we're not really looking at Joy Kochman or Monae Dunn. Ms. Kochman really had no reason to murder Dr. Rosen because she didn't blame him for firing her. She knew her termination had been David and Judith's fault.

And Monae? The longer Dr. Rosen lived, the more presents she stood to receive from Michael.

My phone rings.

"It's Christine," I say after a quick check of the Caller ID screen.

"Interesting," says Ceepak.

I take that as my cue to go ahead and answer.

"Hello?"

"Hey."

"Hey."

"Are you guys still on the job?"

"We're more or less wrapping things up. Calling it a day."

"Am I still your number one suspect?"

"Come on, Christine."

She laughs. "Look, I know you guys have a job to do. So, I'm sorry for earlier. I shouldn't have jumped ugly in your face like that."

"That's okay. My face is used to being ugly-jumped."

Ceepak, who can only hear my side of the conversation, shoots me a very quizzical look.

"So, Danny," says Christine, "if, you know, you're knocking off for the night, you want to, maybe, hang out?"

"I'm not sure we should."

"We could meet someplace very public. Would that work? I really want to see you. Make sure we're okay."

To tell the truth, I wouldn't mind that either.

"Let me check with my boss," I say.

"Sure. And Danny?"

"Yeah?"

"Tell Ceepak I'm sorry for the things I said about him to his mother."

"You said bad things about Ceepak? To his mother?"

I'm repeating it so Ceepak can hear. He raises both eyebrows in mock surprise and cracks a funny grin.

"I think you're forgiven," I tell Christine.

"Great. So, you want to go grab a beer or something?"

"I thought you weren't supposed to drink beer."

"I'm not. But you can. I'll just watch."

"You going to be near your phone?"

"Yep."

"I'll call you right back."

I tap my phone's glass screen to end the call.

"Christine wants to get together tonight. Bad idea?"

"Not necessarily. Just make sure there are witnesses to your rendezvous. Pick a popular, crowded spot. And Danny?"

"Yeah?"

"Your 'date,' if we can call it that, should conclude in that public space as well."

Right. No hooking up, getting busy, or horizontal mambo.

I call Christine back and we agree to meet at The Sand Bar—a hot spot on the bay side of the island with three levels of party decks that overlook the sailboats in the marina.

It's always crowded.

We find a semi-quiet table on the second-floor terrace. I order a beer. Christine, a glass of ice-cold lemonade. I feel like I'm on a date with a nun, maybe a Mormon.

"I'm glad we could make this happen," says Christine.

"Yeah. Me, too."

"And I apologize if I've done anything to slow down your investigation."

Did I mention that Christine looks particularly attractive this evening? I'm guessing The Mussel Beach Motel has a better selection of toiletries and body creams than Chateau Danny. Her hair is shiny and bouncy. Her breasts in her low cut top? Well, they're not shiny.

"No worries," I say, seriously bemoaning the unfairness of Ceepak's "the date ends in a public place" edict.

"I can understand why some people might see me as some kind of angel of death. Ever since I left the ER, all I've worked with are elderly patients facing the end of their lives. And Danny?"

"Yeah?"

"It's been a blessing. Seriously. Seeing how peaceful my patients look when they pass over, well, it has really helped."

"So who's the hottie, Boyle?"

I look up.

Joseph Ceepak is standing—make that teetering—next to our table. He has a mug of beer in his right hand, which explains the wobbly legs, and a curvy redhead in a tank top hanging on to his left arm.

There's no explaining that.

"Who's your hot date?" he asks again, sounding skeevier than ever.

"None of your business," I say. "And yours?"

Mr. Ceepak turns his bleary eyes to the redhead. "What's your name again, sweetheart?"

"Joey?" she giggles. "How many times I gotta tell you? Heather. And you better remember it, because you're going to be screaming it all night!"

Mr. Ceepak turns back to me with a look of manly triumph in his bloodshot eyes. "What can I tell you, Boyle? I've still got it."

I turn to Heather. "You heard him. He's still got it. So be sure you pick up a condom on your way back to the Motel No-Tell."

Heather giggles. "That's funny."

Mr. Ceepak doesn't agree. He frowns and glowers.

"Come on, Joey. The guy made a joke. How you have like, 'it,' you know? Some kind of disease or whatever . . ."

"Yeah. I got it, babe, okay?"

The girl laughs again. "Now you said 'I got it!'"

"Right. Very funny. Ha-ha-ha."

"Relax, Joey," Heather coos into Mr. Ceepak's hairy ear. She's tipsy, too. Margaritas and high heels are never a good mix.

"Joey's gonna be a millionaire," she says, slurring most of the words. "And then, once he gets his money, him and me are gonna run down to Mexico and drink our margaritas out of glasses that look like sombreros."

"Really?" I smirk a little. "Gee, *Joey*, I thought all you wanted was beer and pretzels."

"In Mexico?" squeals the girl. "I don't think they have pretzels. Just nacho cheese Doritos."

"How'd you two meet?" asks Christine, I guess to be polite.

I forgot: she's never been formerly introduced to Mr. Ceepak. Doesn't know who this drunken old douchebag is.

"At Joey's ride," says Heather. "The Free Fall. I rode it like six times."

"In her halter top," adds Mr. Ceepak. "The StratosFEAR is a real boob-bouncer."

"Joey?" Heather acts like she's embarrassed, even though I think that might be impossible.

Mr. Ceepak ignores her. Trains his lecherous eyes on Christine's chest.

"You'd look good riding up and down on my pole, too, honey."

"Okay," I say, standing up. "That's enough."

"What? We're just having a little fun, right, Miss . . . what's your name?"

"Lemonopolous."

And Mr. Ceepak's hackles shoot up.

"You're the tramp who's bleeding my ex-wife dry with lawyer bills?" He slams his beer mug down on our table. "You murdering little slut . . ."

Mr. Ceepak lunges at Christine.

Heather shrieks and flees the scene.

I spring forward, grab hold of Mr. Ceepak's wrist, and, using his own momentum, steer him toward the nearest exit.

Yeah. He's drunk and I've been studying jujitsu with his son.

We're halfway across the floor when Mr. Ceepak plants his heels and starts thrashing at me with both his arms.

"Turn me loose, Boyle."

"Not gonna happen," I say.

So he takes a swing at me with his free hand.

Which I duck.

And once his left hook whiffs over my head, I use his inertia to spin him around and yank his right arm behind his back.

When he tries to wiggle free, I tug up. Hard.

"Hey!" he screams. "That hurts."

"That's the general idea."

Richard Lewis, the Sand Bar's main bouncer and former Mr. New Jersey bodybuilder, comes storming up the stairs, his dreadlocks swinging.

"Yo, Danny?" Richard has what I'd call a Reggae accent. "What's going on here, brudda?"

"This old fart is causing trouble. Harassing the ladies."

"Is that so?" says Richard, clucking his tongue and moving his incredible hulk across the floor.

I release my grip and shove Mr. Ceepak forward. Richard grabs him with both hands and hoists him an inch or two off the ground like he's a worthless sack of crap, which, by the way, he is.

"You causing trouble, mon?"

"No," growls Mr. Ceepak. "Not tonight anyway."

Then he turtles his head around to glare at me.

"Tomorrow? Well, like they say, Boyle, tomorrow is another freakin' day."

# 55

ABOUT THIRTY MINUTES AFTER MR. CEEPAK IS TOSSED OUT OF
the Sand Bar, Christine and I decide to call it a night.

"Big day tomorrow," I say and stretch into a pretty phony yawn.
I even pat my hand over my open mouth a couple times.

That makes Christine smile.

"Sorry," I say. "It's the hour, not the company."

I escort her down to the parking lot and her VW.

"Everything okay at the motel?" I ask.

"Yeah. Becca gave me a really nice room." She moves closer.
"Would you like to see it?" Her voice is extremely husky. And by
husky, I do not mean the size of blue jeans chubby boys wear.

"Yes," I say. "I'd love to come over. But . . ."

"I know," says Christine. "You've got a murder to solve."

"Something like that."

She shrugs. "Can't blame a girl for trying."

Then she goes up on her toes so she can kiss me.

I, naturally, kiss back.

I'll skip the juicy details but lets just say we linger.

When we finally break out of lip lock, both of us are a little discombobulated, our clothes slightly disheveled. I also notice I'm breathing a little more rapidly than when I'm, say, brushing my teeth.

"Thanks for standing up for me." Christine leans her head against my chest. It's a good fit.

"Mr. Ceepak is a nasty piece of work," I say.

"I hate when mean people like him try to push other people around. He reminds me *so much* of Shona and Judith. They shouldn't get away with the horrible stuff they do. Someone has to stop them."

"And that's why God invented cops and soldiers," I say, hoping to tamp down the smoldering anger I see burning in her eyes.

"Don't worry. I'm not going to do anything dumb or stupid, Danny."

"Good. That's *my* job."

Christine smiles.

We kiss one more time.

And then she putters away in her VW.

Tuesday morning, Ceepak and I roll in his detective-mobile to "The Gold Coast" jewelry shop at 1510 Ocean Avenue.

The store isn't open, but we press our badges against the glass-panel front door and the lone worker inside twists open the lock to let us in.

"Sorry to be intruding so early in the morning," says Ceepak. "Is Cele Deemer available?"

"I'm Cele," says the bony woman who opened the front door. Her skin is so tan and tight, it reminds me of an old leather suitcase with ribs.

"How can I help you, gentlemen?"

"Do you know Judith Rosen?"

"Certainly. We've been friends since high school. And don't you dare ask me how long ago that was."

She laughs and brings a hand up to her enormous golden necklace, which halfway reminds me of the chest pieces chariot drivers used to wear. She's also wearing enough golden rings for a solo in a Christmas carol.

"Now then, officers—what's this all about?"

"We are investigating the murder of Mrs. Rosen's father-in-law."

Ms. Deemer clucks her tongue a couple times. "Such a tragedy. How can I help?"

"You design and create your own jewelry?" asks Ceepak.

"That's right. I work exclusively in gold. Bracelets, rings, necklaces . . ."

"And do you use cyanide?"

She nods. "A liquid product called 'Twenty-Four K.' Of course, I only use it in a very well ventilated space. I have an exhaust fan and fume hood right over my workbench in the back. Plus, I always wear chemical safety goggles, neoprene gloves, and a rubber apron whenever I work with it."

"Wise precautions," says Ceepak."

"Well, it's extremely toxic. Fatal if ingested." Ms. Deemer gasps. "Is that what happened to Dr. Rosen?"

Ceepak doesn't answer. Instead, he asks, "Where do you store your cyanide solution?"

"In my workshop."

I glance toward the rear of the shop. There is a flimsy gold-sequined curtain hanging on a rod above an open doorway. Anybody could breeze through and help themselves to anything on Ms. Deemer's supply shelves. Her workshop security situation is, in a word, nonexistent.

"A while back," says Ceepak, "we understand you created a ring for your friend, Judith Rosen."

"Actually, her husband was my client." She laughs. "It was supposed to be a big, romantic Valentine's Day gift. Well, on Valentine's Day, David gives Judith a gift certificate that his father came in and bought for him. A *very generous* gift certificate, by the way. Five thousand dollars. But when David gives Judith a gold envelope with a slip of golden paper inside instead of jewelry, she hits the roof. I don't blame her. Seriously. What kind of romantic Valentine's Day gift is that? So, Judith made David come in here and tell me what to design just to prove he knows what his wife likes. Of course, he doesn't. What husband does? So, I help David out a little. Tell him how Judith has a thing for hearts. David comes up with the keyhole idea—like she has the key to his heart. A little corny, sure, but, hey, he's trying, am I right?"

"Yes, ma'am. Do you see David and Judith socially?"

"David? Not really. I see him on the sidewalk sometimes. He works just up the block."

"And Judith?"

"I see her maybe once or twice a month. Her gym is around the corner." She leans in like she's going to let us in on some big, juicy secret. "I think she only goes to the gym to get a massage. You know what I mean?" Here she uses her hands to mime her cheeks bloating up like blowfish. "Anyway, sometimes, when her son is at school, Jude drops by with pasta or pizza."

"Is David ever involved in these lunches?"

"No. Just us girls. We eat in the back and I show her whatever I'm working on."

"In your workroom?"

"That's right."

"And David?" asks Ceepak. "Did he ever spend time in your workshop?"

"Maybe. When I was doing the heart ring. I think he was back there with me once or twice so I could show him the work in progress."

So David and Judith both knew a local spot where they could pick up some cyanide.

"Has David been back in your shop since he ordered the ring?" I ask.

"No. Just Judith."

"Do you ever use powdered cyanide?" asks Ceepak.

"Not for years. Oh, speaking of Judith, this is cute."

Cele Deemer pulls a sheet of paper out from under a pile of receipts and ledger books.

"Last couple months, over lunch, we've been brainstorming a design for a big, chunky 'J' she could wear on a necklace like a rapper."

"Was this something Mrs. Rosen anticipated purchasing in the near future?"

"I doubt it. Not unless she won the Lottery. That's what we always said. When her numbers hit, we'd make the fourteen-karat 'J.'"

"How much do you estimate such an item would cost?"

"Three, four times more than her ring. But there's no harm in dreaming, am I right?"

True. Unless, of course, you take a few illegal steps to make your dreams come true.

Like poisoning your father-in-law.

# 56

"Ms. Deemer?" says Ceepak.

"Yes?"

"I would be remiss if I did not encourage you to take better security precautions and more stringently control access to your workroom. Cyanide gas, which could be generated in a simple spill, is what many states with the death penalty use to execute . . ."

The radios clipped to both of our belts start squawking.

"Detective Ceepak?" bursts out of the radio surrounded by static.

"Excuse me," Ceepak says to the jewelry storeowner as he reaches for his radio.

"Please," she says, sounding annoyed. "Be my guest."

"This is Ceepak. Go."

"Yeah, this is Officer Al Hallonquist. Me and Craig Kennedy just made our loop through the Sea Spray Motel parking lot and eyeballed that guy you asked us to keep tabs on."

"Michael Rosen?"

"Right. He just took off in his white rental car. We tailed him as he cruised out of the parking lot. Kept hoping for a busted tail light or a minor traffic infraction, but . . ."

"Where are you now?"

"Three cars behind him. On the causeway bridge. Another hundred yards, they're out of our jurisdiction."

"Stay with him."

"Okay, but like I said . . ."

"Stay with him, Officer Hallonquist. We need to know where Michael Rosen is headed. I will personally assume all responsibility for any jurisdictional blowback."

Hallonquist gives us a 10-4 and tells us he'll continue following Michael. Ceepak and I dash outside, hop into the Detective-mobile, and blast off.

And I'm hanging on to that grab handle over the passenger door again while Ceepak bobs and weaves his way through traffic.

A couple minutes later, Hallonquist radios in with Michael Rosen's final destination: The Garden State Reproductive Science Center in Avondale. I'm guessing Michael wants to chat with Revae Dunn some more.

"He went into the building," says Hallonquist over the radio.

"Roger that," says Ceepak. "We'll take it from here. Return to Sea Haven. And Al?"

"Yeah?"

"Thanks."

Riding in Ceepak's turbocharged black bullet, we're at the clinic five minutes after David.

We shove open the swinging glass doors and stalk into the medical building, making a beeline for Revae Dunn's office. We shove open her door, too. Ceepak is not in the mood for knocking, today.

When we barge into Revae Dunn's posh office, we find her and Michael sitting with an aging surfer dude with curly blonde hair. Franz Gruber. Yes. I know him, too.

"Yo, Danny boy. How fare thee, dude?"

When I was a teenager, Mr. Gruber was my surfing instructor on Saturday mornings. For a couple months, anyway. I didn't like all the wiping out or the salt water shooting up my nostrils when I fell face-first into the foam.

"I'm sorry, officers," says Revae Dunn. "This is a private meeting."

Ceepak ignores her. "Mr. Rosen? We asked you not to leave Sea Haven until we concluded our investigation into your father's murder."

"So, sue me," he says.

"We don't sue," I say. "We arrest."

"Take a chill pill, detective Boyle," says Michael, sounding all snitty. "You two are going to *love* this. Ms. Dunn has validated my substantial monetary investment in her and her sister Monae. She has, at long last, located Little Arnie's true father."

Michael happily bobs his head toward Mr. Gruber.

"Like I told you yesterday, ever since my one and only nephew hit puberty and started blossoming into a handsome young lad, I have been wondering about Little Arnie's paternity. His perfect teeth. His athletic prowess. His blonde hair and sky-blue eyes. These are not Rosen traits, gentlemen. Trust me."

Mr. Gruber grins. His teeth are perfect. His eyes sparkle like blue marbles.

Michael keeps going. "Now I knew that, in the ninth year of their marriage, David and Judith began investigating various fertility treatments. How did I know this? Because my father kvetched and moaned to me about paying for them." He turns to Revae. "How much did Dad-ums pay you people?"

"All told?" says Monae's sister. "One hundred and fifty-five thousand dollars."

"One hundred and fifty-five thousand dollars!" Michael fans his face like the number might give him a heat attack. "All that money and still Judith could not conceive. Why?"

Michael, once again, turns to Revae.

"Your brother, David, was shooting blanks."

Ceepak raises a hand. "Excuse me, Ms. Dunn. Aren't you divulging confidential information?"

She shrugs. "So? I figure Michael has a right to know the truth."

*Yeah*, I'm thinking. *Especially if he bought you a brand new Jaguar.*

Ceepak's jaw joint is popping in and out near his ear again but he doesn't stop Michael and Revae Dunn from revealing everything they've learned in their well-financed investigation.

"When Mr. David Rosen's sperm proved incapable of fertilizing his wife's eggs," explains Ms. Dunn, flipping through a stack of papers, "Mr. and Mrs. Rosen filled out a request for donor sperm. They specified that the donor be athletic, intelligent . . ."

"I'm in Mensa," says Franz. "But I find the meetings *so* lugubrious."

"She also wanted her son to be handsome and, preferably, blonde," says Revae.

"Everything her husband wasn't," adds Michael.

Franz holds up his hands. "What can I say? I was and remain the perfect package. But hey, I'm sorry the little dude lost his granddaddy." Now Franz scratches the shaggy hair behind his ear like a flea-bitten dog. "Maybe I should pay him a visit. Assuage his emotional anguish with an ice cream cone or something."

"A little over fourteen years ago," says Revae Dunn, very drily, "Mr. Gruber's sperm sample, then known as Donor One-four-three, fertilized Mrs. Rosen's egg in a Petri dish and created the child named Arnold David Rosen."

"Dig it," says Gruber, cocking a thumb toward Revae. "According to Ms. Dunn, here, I've spawned like a hundred and fifty kids. Who knew? I just did it for beer money, man. Seventy five bucks a pop for reading lascivious letters to Penthouse and, you know—choking my chicken."

I just nod and try to smile.

"After that horrible dinner on Friday night with Father, where both he and David belittled my choice of adoption," says Michael, "I warned my brother. Told him I was *this close* to uncovering the whole truth about Little Arnie."

Ceepak leans forward.

"What exactly did you say?"

"I told David that he and Dad shouldn't look down their noses at my adopted son. I also suggested that he who laughs last laughs loudest and that, judging by Little Arnie's Germanic good looks, I wouldn't be surprised if he, for all practical purposes, was adopted as well. Like I said, I let David know that I was very close to finding out the whole truth."

Franz Gruber does a little wiggle-fingered wave.

"It was me, man. And yo, if this generous Hollywood mogul is willing to provide compensation to the tune of fifty thousand big dollars, I have no qualms about totally rescinding my confidentiality agreement with the clinic and going public."

Ceepak focuses on Michael. "So on Friday night, you told your brother you knew that his son might not be his grandfather's legitimate 'bloodline heir'?"

Michael smirks. "I did indeed. Right there in the restaurant parking lot after Monae drove Dad-ums home. And you know what, detectives? It felt good. Really, really good."

"And when you heard your father's provisions for his grandson in his will?"

"That, I confess, felt horrible. It meant I had missed my deadline. I should've completed this task sooner. Before my father died. But it occurs to me, that's probably why David and/or Judith poisoned the poor bastard: to prevent him from learning the god-awful truth and completely cutting them out of his will."

"Danny?" says Ceepak.

I'm up. We need to leave. Now.

Our suspect list?

It's down to two.

# 57

MICHAEL AGREES TO RETURN TO THE SEA SPRAY HOTEL.

"I can't wait to see which one of them slipped Daddy the pill. Judith or David. Maybe both!"

"You realize, of course," says Ceepak, "that you are partially responsible for driving them to do what they did?"

"And you know what, Detective Ceepak? I don't care. I'd do it again. Gladly. I finally realized that my father never really loved me. That no matter how many gifts I showered on him, how much money I made, how many awards and honors I won, I'd never be anything to him but a big, embarrassing mistake. So I'm glad one of those two greedy ingrates finally killed him. Saved me the trouble."

When we're back in Ceepak's car, I ask how we're going to figure out which of the two Rosens killed their father or father in-law.

"They may have worked together," says Ceepak. "Co-conspirators. However, our first step is identifying which of them procured the cyanide."

Ceepak's still counting on Botzong's cyanide shipping information to fill in a bunch of blanks.

Personally, my money is on Judith in the jewelry shop with the cyanide jug.

And a funnel. She'd need it to pour the liquid into the gel caps.

But that would probably dissolve the capsules.

Okay, I'm counting on Botzong, too.

We head back to Sea Haven.

Ceepak contacts Sal Santucci—my partner the night Christine and Shona had their wrestling match at the southern tip of the island—who is stationed outside David and Judith's home.

"Kindly go upstairs and inform Mrs. Rosen that we are coming over to ask her a few questions."

We arrive at 315-B Tuna Street.

Sal Santucci and his partner, Cath Hoffner, have parked their cruiser in the only shady spot on the street. Fortunately, it's right in front of the house where David and Judith rent the upstairs apartment.

Ceepak and I make our way around the side of the building and climb up the steep back steps to David and Judith's deck.

It takes three knuckle raps on the door before somebody opens it.

"Hi." It's Little Arnie. Franz Gruber's kid.

"Is your mother home?" asks Ceepak.

"I guess."

"May we speak with her?"

"I guess." He nudges his head toward the living room. "She's in there."

His mother is seated on the sofa, sipping a glass of white wine. It's only a little after noon but I suppose it's five o'clock somewhere—as Ceepak's dad likes to say whenever he pops a brewski for breakfast.

We head toward the sofa. Little Arnie heads for his bedroom to close the door and daydream about shooting the curl and hanging ten if, you know, he soaked up any of Gruber's "surfing genes" in that petri dish.

"Why on earth do you two need to talk to me?"

Judith is not even pretending to smile today.

"And how dare you send those two police officers up here to harass me? Why haven't you people arrested Christine Lemonopolous?"

"Well, for one thing," I say, "we're pretty sure Ms. Lemonopolous didn't do anything to be arrested for."

"But you put *me* under house arrest?"

"We also continue to monitor Ms. Lemonopolous's whereabouts," says Ceepak,

"You should. She poisoned my father-in-law. She attacked my sister. She killed Mauna Faye Crabtree and all those other old people she used to work for . . ."

Ceepak cuts her off. "No, Mrs. Rosen, she did none of those things. We know about Franz Gruber."

"Who?"

"Sperm donor one-four-three, whose semen you selected when you could not conceive a child utilizing your husband's sperm."

"I have no idea what you're talking about."

"We just came from Avondale. The Garden State Reproductive Science Center."

"That's where you went for fertility treatments," I add. "Right?"

"So? We were having trouble conceiving in the traditional manner. And both David and I desperately wanted children."

*Yeah*, I'm thinking. *So they could give Arnold Rosen a grandson and cash in on his millions.*

"Highly ranked staff at the Reproductive Science Center," says Ceepak, "told us how you ended up choosing a blonde, athletic, and intelligent sperm donor when your husband's sperm repeatedly failed to fertilize your harvested eggs."

"What? Who told you these lies?"

"The same people who told Michael. Michael then told David what he had uncovered on Friday night, after that acrimonious dinner at The Trattoria restaurant."

"But," I say, "Michael didn't have his big dramatic finish until today when Franz Gruber came to the clinic and freely admitted to being your son's father."

Judith laughs. "For a multimillionaire, Michael can be such a baby. Trying to smear David and me like this? Attempting to turn his only nephew into an illegitimate bastard? Why can't he just get over the fact that, as a gay, he will never, ever be able to call himself a real father, no matter how many black babies he adopts?"

Ceepak shifts gears.

"Mrs. Rosen, we know you have spent a good deal of time with your friend Cele Deemer in her jewelry store."

"So?"

"Ms. Deemer uses cyanide."

"Really? I hadn't noticed."

"It's right there on the shelf in her workshop," I say.

"Look, detectives, how many times do I have to say this? Christine Lemonopolous did it. She's the one who gave my father-in-law the poison. I told David she was trouble. That his father needed to fire her."

"Because she wouldn't do as you requested and spy on Dr. Rosen?" says Ceepak.

"For the last time, detective, we did not ask Christine to spy on Dad. We asked her to keep an eye on David's father. There's a difference. A *big* difference. But David is such a weakling. He couldn't persuade his father to fire Christine, no matter how many times I told him he had to do it. Then, Christine attacks my sister? I tell David, 'See? The girl is violent! For your father's safety, we need to get rid or her!' David finally grows a pair and says something to his father, but his father tells him to mind his own business."

Judith shakes her head in disgust, sloshes a little more Pinot Grigio into her glass.

"Poor Arnold Rosen," she continues after a bracing gulp of vino. "One son is a bona fide homosexual, the other is such a wimp he doesn't know how to be a man. I have to hold his hand, tell him what to do . . ."

I guess Little Arnie has heard enough.

He comes marching into the living room.

"Stop saying all that bull crap about Dad."

"Go to your room, young man."

"No. I heard what you said. Dad isn't a wimp."

"Go. To. Your. Room." Judith slams down her wine.

Little Arnie flinches. Like he knows what comes next: a slap or a punch or a flying glass.

"Do we need to remove your son?" says Ceepak.

"What?" Judith acts like she's shocked.

"If you give us further reason to suspect that child abuse is taking place in this home . . ."

"Child abuse? Arnold is my son. I will discipline him as I see fit."

"No, ma'am. There are limits. Even to parental authority."

"I'm okay," says Little Arnie. "Really. I just don't like her trash-talking Dad."

Judith shakes her head. "You see what I have to deal with? I'm the only adult in the whole house . . ."

Ceepak gives me a look. "Danny?"

We've been together long enough for me to read his mind. He wants me to spend a little time with Arnie. Make sure the kid is truly okay; that the domestic violence situation is under control.

"Come on, Arnie." I nod my head toward the door to his bedroom. "Let's let these two finish up their talk. You got an X-Box?"

"PS3."

"Cool."

He leads the way. I follow.

# 58

"You okay?" I ask when the bedroom door is securely closed.

"Yeah. I guess."

"So, how much did you hear?"

"Not much. Just mom calling dad a wimp and Uncle Michael a homo."

Little Arnie sits down on the edge of his bed.

"Does your mother say mean things like that about your father a lot?" I ask, even though I don't think David Rosen is really Little Arnie's father.

"Yeah. All the time."

I can hear Ceepak and Judith's muffled voices through the door. Well, actually, I can hear Judith. She is a loud drunk.

"Hey," I say to Little Arnie, "if you ever feel like, you know, you're in danger here, that you might get hurt, you can call me." I give him one of my cards. "And right now, there's a cop parked right in front of your house. Nice guy. Sal Santucci. He'll be down there all day."

"Thanks. So, is Franz Gruber the guy who gives surfing lessons over near Veggin' On The Beach?"

"Yeah," I say, hoping I can change the subject fast. I'm not a social worker and I think Little Arnie's going to need one when he learns the truth about who his birth father really is.

I notice a photograph in a cardboard frame propped up on the dresser: Little Arnie and his dad, locked in their seats and screaming their heads off as they plummet down the StratosFEAR.

"So, how many times have you ridden the Free Fall?" I ask.

"A bunch. We get to ride for free. And they have these cameras that snap your picture when you're like halfway down."

"Awesome," I say.

There's a knock on the bedroom door.

"Danny?"

Ceepak.

"Yeah?"

"We need to roll."

I open the door.

"Everything okay?"

He nods. "Is the boy safe?"

"I think so. He has my card and knows Santucci's outside if his mom, you know . . ."

Another nod. Neither of us wants to get into gory details in front of Little Arnie.

"What's up?" I ask.

"Bill Botzong is e-mailing us a list of names and addresses."

And Ceepak's state-of-the-art cop car has a computer.

I turn around. Look Little Arnie in the eye. "You sure you're okay here?"

"Yeah."

"Remember. There's a cop right outside."

Arnie pulls back his curtains. Looks out the window. "Okay. Thanks."

"And if Sal can't help you . . ."

Little Arnie smiles. "I'll give you a call."

"Excellent."


The list Botzong and his MCU crew have pieced together is actually pretty short.

Guess there's not that big of a demand for potassium cyanide in Sea Haven. Also, Ceepak informs me that it's very expensive—over five hundred dollars for half a gram of the pure stuff.

None of our suspects' names show up in Botzong's report of recent sales:

Bobby McCue
Buggy Bobby's Fumigation and Pest Control
25 Spruce Street

Clare Thalken Harrington
The Treasure Chest
2311 Ocean Avenue

David Magayna
Dave's Roof Rat Removal Inc.
101 Swordfish Street

Cele Deemer
The Gold Coast Fine Jewelry
1510 Ocean Avenue

Bart Smith
Sinclair Enterprises
1500 Ocean Avenue

"Of course," says Ceepak.

"What?"

"We need to head over to 1500 Ocean Avenue."

"Sinclair Enterprises?"

"Yes. We need to talk to 'Bart Smith.' He is our murderer."

# 59

"So, who's Bart Smith?" I ask as we drive back to the worldwide headquarters of Sinclair Enterprises.

"If the theory I have been formulating is correct, he is an alias created by David Rosen."

I remember David Rosen's Bart Simpson watch and desk clock. Maybe he took John Smith, the most obvious alias in the world, and added a little Simpsons twist.

The compact printer in Ceepak's new ride is spitting out the details of "Bart Smith's" potassium cyanide purchase: 97% analytical grade; came from a company in New Delhi, India. Mr. Smith purchased half a gram for $499.99 and billed it to Sinclair Enterprises.

The lethal oral dose of potassium cyanide? 200 mg or 0.2 grams. A rounded teaspoon of the powder would be about two and a half times the amount needed to kill a person. Bart Smith's sample? If it really went to David Rosen, he could've killed his dad sixty times over.

"So David had the poison sent to his office but to a fake name. I can understand why. But there had to be a chance it would wind up on the wrong desk."

"Not really," says Ceepak. "Do you remember my father's 'Guns And Ammo' magazine?"

"Somebody brought it to David."

"And the stack of mail that arrived at fifteen hundred Ocean Avenue for the second ride operator, Shaun McKinnon?"

Right. My friend Shawn Reilly Simmons gave it to David Rosen.

"As head of Sinclair Enterprises' human resources department," says Ceepak, "David Rosen was responsible for making certain all the company's short-term summer hires received their forwarded mail."

"So," I say, "he knew that if he cooked up a name nobody at the company recognized and had a package sent to that name care of the office, it would eventually find it's way to his cubicle."

"Such has been my supposition, Danny."

"And he killed his father because of what Michael said on Friday night? That he was close to proving that Little Arnie wasn't his father's legitimate 'living legacy.'"

"Which," Ceepak says, "would've jeopardized David and Judith's favored state in Dr. Rosen's will—if he lived long enough to amend it in light of Michael's revelations."

"But wait a second—how come he ordered the cyanide before he knew any of this stuff? I mean, no way he ordered it after dinner on Friday night and got the package in time to doctor the pills first thing Saturday morning."

"I suspect that David had been contemplating terminating his father's life for quite some time."

"Why?"

"To free him from the unrelenting pressure of his wife's harangues. I'm sure Judith was constantly badgering David, telling him they deserved their full inheritance, *now*. That they had earned it by putting up with David's judgmental, demanding, and controlling father. We've heard how Judith talks about David. Not just today, but earlier. Imagine what she says to him in private. Late at night. After she has been drinking heavily. Undoubtedly, she hinted at how David could prove himself to be a man. How all their dreams could come true if only . . ."

I finish Ceepak's though by paraphrasing Judith's drunken late-night remarks to her father-in-law: "If only Dr. Rosen did everybody a favor and died."

"Indeed. I suspect Judith's constant, emasculating outbursts took their toll on David. He saw an easy way to slip free before his spirit was completely crushed. He purchased the cyanide but couldn't find the courage to actually do the deed until Michael's thinly veiled threats on Friday night pushed him over the brink."

"He murdered his own father."

Ceepak nods grimly. "However, I feel certain that, in David's eyes, he merely hastened his father's exit from this world; shortening the old man's life by a few meaningless months."

"But it's still murder. Right?"

"Roger that."

We arrive at Sinclair Enterprises around 2 P.M.

David Rosen is sitting on the far side of the floor in his glass box, working his phone.

"Hey, how's it going, fellas?"

Seems Bob, the manager from the StratosFEAR, is visiting headquarters today, too.

"Fine," says Ceepak, his eyes laser-locked on David. "Nice of you to inquire."

"You know, Detective Ceepak, your pops gets off work early today. Might be a good time for you two to grab a little chow, knock back a couple cold brewskis, bury the hatchet."

"Not going to happen," I say. "We're busy. Need to arrest someone for murder."

"Really?" says Bob, eagerly. "Who?"

"Danny?" says Ceepak, shaking his head.

"Excuse us," I say to Bob.

Ceepak and I march across the wide room. Bob goes over to a nearby copy machine and pretends like he's ready to collate a couple documents. But I can tell, he has his eyes glued on Ceepak and me.

"Sorry about that," I mumble in a whisper.

"It's all good," Ceepak whispers back. "However, we can only arrest David Rosen when we have sufficient evidence to press formal charges."

"So you're hoping he confesses?"

Ceepak nods. Then, outside David's cubicle, he clears his throat.

"Hugh? I'm going to have to call you back. It's those cops again. Right. I'm not sure. Okay. You're the boss. Appreciate it."

He hangs up the phone.

"Mayor Hugh Sinclair," he says like he expects us to be impressed.

We're not.

"He's in the neighborhood. Might pop in to say howdy."

Ceepak ignores what, I'm guessing, David hoped would be a threat.

"Mr. Rosen? We need to talk to an employee of yours."

"Okey-doke. Which one? I've got a million of 'em."

"Bart Smith."

"Smith? Name doesn't ring a bell . . ."

"He recently ordered half a gram of potassium cyanide from a chemical company in India."

"Coincidentally," I add, "that's the same chemical that killed your father."

David strokes his goatee.

"Smith, Smith, Smith . . ."

"*Bart* Smith," says Ceepak.

David snaps his fingers. "Right. Bartholomew Smith. One of our custodians. Said something about ordering poison to take care of rodents in the rafters over at Cap'n Scrubby's Car Wash."

"May we speak to Mr. Smith?"

"No. 'Fraid not. He didn't last very long. Liked to sleep in the dryer room with the warm towels. We had to let him go. Back in late May, I believe."

"So did the package come to your desk?"

"Pardon?"

"After you fired Bartholomew Smith, did the cyanide sample he ordered from India end up on your desk?"

"I don't think so . . ."

"Shawn Reilly Simmons signed for it," I say, placing a copy of the order form Botzong e-mailed to us on David's desk.

"Really?" David makes a confused monkey face. "I really don't recall any packages. You say it came from India? I think I would've remembered the stamps. I still collect them. How about you fellas?"

"This shipped DHL," I say, tapping the form. "No stamps."

"Did you order the potassium cyanide under an assumed name, David?" asks Ceepak.

"Me? No?"

I hear the front door whoosh open. Feel a blast of humid air.

"What's going on here?"

Get ready for a sunny, funderful day.

Mayor Sinclair is in the house.

# 60

"OFFICERS, WHAT IS THE MEANING OF THIS INTRUSION?" demands the mayor.

Ceepak gestures at David Rosen, who is still sitting trapped inside his glass cage and looking more and more like a hamster who lost his wheel.

"Your honor," says Ceepak, making a pretty loud pronouncement, "we have reason to believe that your Human Resources director, Mr. David Rosen, poisoned his elderly father, the late Arnold Rosen, with potassium cyanide purchased by Sinclair Enterprises."

Mayor Sinclair looks stunned. The other employees have stopped doing any kind of work. They're all staring at David.

I notice Bob over at the copy machine. He silently mouths something that looks like it rhymes with "moldy grit." He heads for the door like he is ready to tell everybody he knows, "Hey, guess who murdered his old man?"

I notice tiny droplets of sweat forming on top of David's bald dome.

"And tell me, Detective Ceepak," says the mayor, "do you have any proof to substantiate your accusation?"

"We are currently piecing together a trail of evidence," says Ceepak, once again telling the truth when I wish he would just say, *"Yeah, David did it."*

The mayor scoffs. "A *trail* of evidence?"

"Yes, sir. Information recently obtained by the New Jersey State Police Major Crimes Unit suggests that the poison—the murder weapon, if you will—was purchased by David Rosen under an assumed name and paid for by a Sinclair Enterprises corporate credit card. We further hypothesize that he placed the order for that chemical compound right here, from one of your computers or telephones. Therefore, we will be requesting a search warrant granting us permission to impound your computers, confiscate your files, subpoena your phone records . . ."

"Whoa, wait a second, cowboy. It's summer. Business is booming. You can't come in here and shut down my back office operations."

"Yes, sir. We can. Immediately after Judge Rasmussen signs the search documents, which I anticipate happening within the hour."

The mayor turns to Rosen.

"David?"

"Yes, sir?"

"Did you do this thing the detectives say you did?"

Sweat is dribbling down David's brow. "Of course not."

"We'll also need the complete pay records for one Bartholomew Smith," says Ceepak.

"Who?" asks the mayor.

Ceepak doesn't answer.

So the mayor turns to Rosen. "David?"

"Short-timer, sir. Worked here in May. A little bit of June. Had that rodent infestation problem."

"What? Where?"

"Cap'n Scrubby's, I think. Could've been one of the ice cream parlors, though . . ."

Panic fills the mayor's eyes. The last thing he wants is for rumors to start spreading around town about what those brown lumps really are in his Moosetracks ice cream.

"David, I'm wondering if, perhaps, you should take the rest of the day off. Maybe take a few personal days as well—until this police matter blows over . . ."

"I promise you, sir, what these detectives are saying . . ."

"*Paid* personal days, David. Okay? Go home. Spend some time with Little Arnie and Judith. Find yourself a good lawyer."

# 61

WE FOLLOW DAVID ROSEN AS HE DRIVES HOME TO TUNA Street.

On the ride, Ceepak advises Mrs. Rence, our dispatcher, to pull the cops keeping an eye on Christine Lemonopolous and Michael Rosen off their assignments.

"However," he adds, "we need to continue the twenty-four-hour surveillance detail outside 315 Tuna Street. David and Judith Rosen's home."

"Will do," says Mrs. Rence over the radio.

"Can you put me through to Chief Rossi?"

Ceepak and the Chief hammer out the details needed to get the legal paperwork moving through the system—warrants that will allow us to toss the headquarters of Sinclair Enterprises and confiscate all their hard drives.

It's a little after two in the afternoon when we reach the Rosen residence on Tuna Street.

Santucci and his partner Cath Hoffner see us pull into the driveway behind David's vehicle. The two uniforms emerge from their patrol car, most likely to find out what's up. As David climbs out of his Subaru, he sees the two officers out in the street, adjusting their gun belts.

"Why have those two police officers been parked there all day?" he asks.

"It's part of our new neighborhood watch program," I crack. "Every day, we pick one house in a neighborhood and watch it. Today is your lucky day."

"What? You think I'm some kind of flight risk?"

"Are you?" asks Ceepak.

"Of course not. I didn't do anything, why would I run away?"

"Look," I say. "We know Michael and your wife backed you into a corner. That Michael told you . . ."

He ignores me. Turns to Ceepak. "Am I under arrest?"

"No, sir. Not yet."

"Then get off of my property."

"Technically, sir, this is not your property. You are a renter and therefore . . ."

"Come back when you have an arrest warrant."

"Yes, sir. We will. We'll also come back when we have a search warrant."

"You're going to search my home, too?"

"Yes, sir."

"Several times," I add. "If we have to."

David storms around the side of the house and makes his way to that back staircase.

Ceepak waits until he hears David's footfalls climbing the steps. Then we stroll into the street to have a word with Santucci and Hoffner.

"Sal?" says Ceepak.

"Sir?"

"We have reason to believe that Mr. David Rosen murdered his father."

"I thought it was the wife," says Cath Hoffner, his partner. "She's such a witch, you know?"

I nod. Surprisingly, so does Ceepak.

"Currently," he adds, "the husband, David Rosen is our primary suspect in what might have been a conspiracy to commit murder. However, we need to gather more evidence. Right now, everything we have is solid but highly circumstantial. We need to find a more direct link."

"Don't worry," says Santucci. "While you guys are digging up your direct links and whatnot, Hoffner and me won't let the guy out of our sight."

"Appreciate it. We're working up a twenty-four/seven duty detail that should have your relief out here by nineteen hundred hours."

"Cool. You think the Chief could maybe send somebody out with sandwiches for us so we don't have to desert our post? Maybe a couple cold drinks?"

"We'll make it happen," says Ceepak.

I'm about to reach for my radio and put in the food and drink request when my cell phone starts chirping.

Ceepak nods his permission for me to answer it.

"Hello?"

"Danny?" It's Becca. "Sorry to bother you at work . . ."

"What's up?"

"Well, right after the cop car you guys had staking out my parking lot pulled away, Christine took off."

"Did she say where she was going?"

"Yeah. Down to Roxbury Drive. Isn't that where this whole mess got started?"

Becca's right.

102 Roxbury Drive is Shona Oppenheimer's address.

# 62

I TELL CEEPAK WHAT'S UP.

"Let's roll," he says, practically ripping a car door off its hinges.

"Shouldn't we be chasing down evidence against David?" I say as we blast off in reverse, slam into drive, and squeal wheels up Tuna Street.

"We are in a holding pattern until the various search warrants come down. We can spare thirty minutes to prevent Ms. Lemonopolous from doing something foolish that could haunt her for the rest of her life."

I'm remembering what Christine told me.

How she hates when mean people push other people around. *"They shouldn't get away with the horrible stuff they do. Someone has to stop them."*

Has she decided to go vigilante on us and administer a little swift and righteous justice on Shona Oppenheimer?

With Ceepak at the wheel, we race down the length of the island in about twelve minutes. The smoky black Taurus's interior no longer has that New Car scent. It smells more like a fried fan belt.

We reach Beach Crest Heights.

My high school buddy Kurt Steilberger is once again on clipboard duty inside the guardhouse.

Ceepak fishtails to a stop with the nose of our vehicle maybe one inch away from his gate. I pop out of the passenger side door, so Kurt can see something besides smoky black glass, strobing lights, and shiny black sheet metal.

"Kurt?"

"Oh. Hey, Danny. Cool car."

"Did you just let a Volkswagen in?"

"Yeah. Couple minutes ago."

"Open the gate!" I shout.

"What's up?"

"Open. The. Gate!"

Ceepak gooses the gas pedal. The engine roars. The gate still doesn't budge.

It's like Kurt can't find the button.

Finally, as I slip back into my seat, the gate arm creeps skyward. When Ceepak knows he has half an inch clearance, we blast off again.

"Hang left," I say. "One-oh-two is down the block."

We shoot up the street.

Christine's VW is parked in the driveway outside the three-story mansion.

The front door to the house is wide open.

We're up and out of the car just in time to hear Shona Oppenheimer screaming at Christine.

"Get the hell out of here!"

"B-b-but . . ."

"Leave or I'll call the police."

Ceepak takes that as his cue.

"Police!" he shouts.

Christine backs out the door.

She has something clutched in her left hand.

It glints in the sun.

"Christine?" I holler.

She whirls around.

I see what's in her hand: A slim, foil-wrapped box.

Shona Oppenheimer comes out on the porch.

"Arrest this woman!" she snarls. "She's trespassing. She should be . . ."

And then she recognizes me.

"Oh. It's you."

"Ma'am?" says Ceepak, striding up the walkway to the front steps. "What seems to be the problem?"

Shona waggles a disgusted hand at Christine. "This one. She has the nerve to invade my privacy . . ."

"It's Samuel's birthday," says Christine.

"So?" says Shona.

"I didn't want him to think I'd forgotten."

"Well, we'd all rather you did. You are not welcome here, Christine. And if you keep harassing me and my family, I will have another Restraining Order issued against you and this time it'll stick!"

Christine tries to hand the shiny package to Shona. "Will you at least give this to Samuel?"

"Hell, no. It's probably poison. Like the stuff you gave to Arnold Rosen."

"Actually," says Ceepak, climbing up the steps to put his big body between Shona and Christine, "we currently suspect that your brother-in-law, David, was the one who poisoned Dr. Rosen."

"I know. Judith called me. Are all the cops in this town as crazy as you two?"

"No," I say, hiking up the steps to stand beside Ceepak. "We're special."

I take Christine by the elbow and give her a police escort down to her parked vehicle.

"You can drop your gift off with Kurt in the guardhouse," I whisper. "He'll make sure it gets delivered."

"It's a game Samuel wanted. For his X-box."

"Awesome."

I hold open the door to Christine's ride.

"David killed his father?" she says after she slides in behind the wheel.

"Yeah. We think so."

"That's horrible."

"That it is."

While the two of us take a moment to ponder the monstrosity of what David Rosen did, up on the porch, I can hear poor Ceepak asking Shona Oppenheimer if she "wants to press trespassing charges."

"I'm thinking about it!"

"Then," Ceepak says, "you should know, since your property is not marked, fenced in, or enclosed and I observe no notice against trespassing being otherwise given . . ."

Ceepak. I love when he sticks it to people and they don't even know he's telling them to sit on it and rotate.

"Go back to Becca's," I suggest to Christine. "Ceepak and I have a bunch of loose ends to tie up."

"I have one more gift to deliver."

"For who?"

"Ceepak's mom. I know she's from Ohio and Pudgy's Fudgery does chocolate Buckeyes. There's peanut butter in the middle . . ."

"Save me one," I say.

She smiles. "I will."

I back Ceepak's ride out of the driveway so Christine can pull out, too.

As I watch her putter away in the rearview mirror, my cell phone rings.

"Hello?"

"Um, officer Boyle?"

"Yeah?"

"This is Arnie Rosen."

"Hey, Arnie. Everything okay?"

"I don't think so."

"Okay. Officer Santucci is out front . . ."

"I know. But they snuck out the back."

"What do you mean?"

"My dad and that old guy who runs the Free Fall. He's helping Dad run away."

# 63

"I GUESS I SHOULD'VE CALLED SOONER," SAYS ARNIE. "BUT that old guy, he's scary."

Yeah. Tell me about it.

That old guy is, of course, Joe "Six Pack" Ceepak.

"He said, 'Boy, you need to be a man. Don't call the cops. I heard what people are saying about your Pops. Him and me need to make a run for the border.' And then, my mother, she said, 'You heard him, Arnold. Not a word about this to anybody.' So, it took me like ten minutes to figure out what I should do. Call you."

Arnie is whispering all this. Probably doesn't want his mother to know that he did the right thing. He called the cops.

"You're in your room?"

"Yes, sir."

"Okay. Lock the door. Don't open it till you know for sure that Officer Santucci or his partner, a nice lady named Cath Hoffner, are on the other side. Can you do that for me, Arnie?"

"Yeah. I guess. But Mister Santucci doesn't even know Dad is gone because he didn't see them sneak out. See, he's out front and they cut through the backyard to our back-door neighbor's yard and then they ran up their driveway to Swordfish Street."

"You saw all this, Arnie?"

"Yeah. A while ago, I heard Mom being all sweet with Dad so, you know, I thought everything was all better. I went into the living room. Mom was hugging Dad but the Free Fall guy was in there, too."

"What did the Free Fall guy say?"

"That they'd fry Dad in the electric chair for killing his father."

Great. Mr. Ceepak couldn't be content with scarring his own son for life, now he's got to give young Arnold Rosen nightmares, too?

"I watched them run away from out on the deck."

"And then what?"

"My mother told me to get my butt in the house. That I should be proud of my father for finally doing what needed to be done."

I hear Arnie sob a little.

"Did my dad really kill my grandfather?"

I'm not Ceepak so I go ahead and lie a little. "We're not sure about that, Arnie. So, do me a favor, and stay in your room, like I said. I'm going to call Officer Santucci. He or his partner, they're going to take you and your mom to the police station."

"Why?"

"You can help us protect your dad better at the police station, okay?"

"Okay."

"Hang tight."

"Okay. Oh, Mr. Boyle?"

"Yeah?"

"I think the Free Fall guy has a gun."

"Did you see a weapon?"

"No, but he told Dad he didn't have to worry about the cops and tapped his jacket, like that tough guy does in the *Mafia 2* video game."

"Okay. Thanks for that. That's very important."

"Officer Boyle?"

"Yeah?"

"Don't let that creepy old guy shoot you. I think he's kind of crazy."

"Don't worry, Arnie. I'm very good with my gun. Check out Urban Termination II the next time you're at Sunnyside Playland. You'll see my initials in all three top scorer slots."

"Cool."

"Stay in your room. Wait for Santucci or Hoffner."

"Right."

We hang up.

I'm up and out of the Batmobile in a flash and waving my arms over my head like a lunatic at Ceepak who is still on the porch schooling Shona Oppenheimer on the burden of proof necessary to prove Defiant Trespass in the State of New Jersey.

"Ceepak?" Yes, I am shouting.

He whips around. Sees the frantic look in my eyes.

"Good day, Mrs. Oppenheimer," he says on the run. "If you have any further complaints or suggestions, please bring them to Police Headquarters on Cherry Street at your earliest convenience."

He dashes across the lawn, joins me in the street.

"What's up?"

"Your father. He just sprung David Rosen."

"Come again?"

"Little Arnie called. Said the old guy who runs the Free Fall snuck into their house and told his father that they needed to make a run for the border."

"And David fled?"

"Yeah. Ten minutes ago. Guess he admitted he's guilty with his feet."

"Roger that."

"Santucci and Hoffner didn't see the jailbreak because your dad took David out the back door and cut through the house behind them's lawn. Took him over to Swordfish Street."

"Do we know what sort of vehicle my father is currently driving?"

"No," I say.

Then I remember that night at Neptune's Nog, the package store.

"Wait. Dinged up Ford F-150. Maybe ten, twelve years old. Ohio license plates."

Ceepak raises his quizzical eyebrow.

"We bumped into each other at the beer store. Remember?"

Ceepak reaches into the car to grab the radio mic.

And my phone rings again.

Ceepak holds on. Waits to hear who is calling me. Looks like he thinks it might be Arnie with an update.

It is.

"They're heading toward the pier!"

"Arnie? Take it easy. How can you know that?"

"Dad has an iPhone and I have the 'Find My iPhone' app on my computer. I punched in his number. It's tracking them. They were in the parking lot near Pier Two; now they're heading out over the ocean. If I switch to satellite, I can tell you what they're near."

Arnie goes silent.

"Arnie?"

"Yeah. They've stopped. Right in front of the Mad Mouse roller coaster. I think that crazy old guy took Dad back to the Free Fall!"

"Okay. I'm going to call Officer Santucci right now."

"You won't hurt my dad, will you? When you catch them?"

"No, Arnie. I promise."

"Okay."

Now the radio starts chattering.

"I've got to run."

"Okay."

I end the call with Arnie.

"All available units."

It's not the dispatcher. It's Chief Rossi. This is not a good sign.

"Pier Two. Reports of a gunshot. Repeat. Reports of a gunshot and potential hostage situation. All available units please respond. Initiate lockdown protocols."

Guess Little Arnie was right.

Mr. Ceepak has a gun.

# 64

FIFTEEN MINUTES LATER, WHEN WE SCREAM INTO THE MUNICIPAL
parking lot fronting Pier Two, we enter bedlam.

The tail end of a panicked mob is still stampeding down the boardwalk access ramps like cattle through a slaughterhouse chute. I hear
screams and shouting. Freaked out tourists and locals are pushing and
shoving whoever's not running away from the danger fast enough.

Meanwhile, Ceepak and me have to run the other way.

Up into the swirling chaos and confusion.

The Murray brothers are already on the scene, trying to bring
some semblance of order to the pandemonium.

"Keep calm," shouts Dylan through an amplified megaphone
while his brother, Jeremy, stands in the middle of the swarm to
do hand signals showing people which way to head so they don't
trample each other.

"Evacuate to the far edges of the parking lot," he says over and
over and over.

"Keep calm! Do not panic!" echoes his brother with the battery-powered bullhorn.

"Move them out and lock it down," Ceepak says to the two Murrays. "Who's inside?"

"Brooks Perry and Jack Getze," says Dylan.

Ceepak and I go swimming upstream; make our way to the boardwalk.

Which is almost empty.

Ceepak grabs the radio clipped to his belt.

"This is Detective Ceepak. Detective Boyle and I are on the scene. What's our situation?"

"This is Officer Perry."

"What's your twenty?"

"We have taken up a position in the pizza stand west of the StratosFEAR ride. We have the ride operator, Mr. Shaun McKinnon with us."

I can see the Free Fall's tower rising against the early evening sky maybe a hundred feet in front of us.

"Is Mr. McKinnon injured?"

"Negative. The old guy with the gun threw him out of the control booth and told him to run away. He didn't. He found us instead."

"Maintain your position. Detective Boyle and I are on our way."

"Okay. Good. One question—the old guy with the gun. McKinnon tells us he is the day operator of the Free Fall and that his last name is Ceepak."

"Roger that. He is my father. He should be considered mentally unstable and lethally dangerous. There were reports of a gunshot. Can you clarify?"

"Getze and I were on routine boardwalk patrol, up by Paintball Blasters. Heard the single round fired. Thought it was a kid with an early Fourth of July firecracker. Mr. McKinnon found us. Told us how, uh, your father threatened him with a weapon. Described it as best he could. From our observation post, it looks like it could be a Ruger nine-millimeter pistol. Seven plus one capacity."

That means Mr. Ceepak has seven bullets left before he has to reload.

"And the hostage situation?" asks Ceepak as we crouch our way forward toward the pizza place, using the game booths and food stalls along the way for cover.

"Your father has a middle-aged bald man with him. Fifty, fifty-five. Goatee."

"It is David Rosen," says Ceepak.

"What're they doing here?" I ask.

"Unclear at this juncture."

Yeah, if Mr. Ceepak was trying to help David Rosen "make a run for the border" he's doing a lousy job, unless he's also arranged for a submarine to come pick them up at the pier.

"Hang on," says Officer Perry. "There's movement over at the base of the ride. Something's going on . . ."

Ceepak and I hustle faster.

He hand chops to the left.

We scoot up a narrow alleyway behind a row of booths and shops until we come to a service door, a rear entry into the pizzeria.

"We're coming in," Ceepak announces into the radio so Perry and Getze don't twirl around and blast us when we come sneaking up behind them.

We push the door open, keep hunkered down, and duck-walk up to the open-air front of the pizza place to take up a position behind the counter with the two cops and Shaun McKinnon, the other factory-trained Free Fall operator from Ohio.

"Does my father know you are over here?" asks Ceepak in a tight whisper.

Getze shakes his head.

All five of us are crouched behind the counter. Fortunately, the sun is setting behind us. The pizza parlor is cloaked in shadows.

Unfortunately, what we see is terrifying.

Mr. Ceepak has the snub nose of his small pistol jabbed into David Rosen's back.

He is marching Rosen up the steps to the ride.

"Sit down."

He shoves David into a seat. Tucks something into the front pocket of David's shirt.

"Don't hang up on me, Davey. If you do, you die." He cackles a laugh and backs up; keeping his pistol trained on Rosen every step of the way to his control booth.

The front window is open so he can keep his Ruger up and aimed at David. With his free hand, he raises a crinkled brown bag of something to his lips. Takes a swig.

The bottle bag goes down.

"Now we just have to wait for *my* idiot son to show up."

I hear a clunk and thud.

The Free Fall starts climbing up its 140-foot tower.

And the shoulder harness over David Rosen's seat?

Mr. Ceepak never lowered it.

# 65

THE STRATOSFEAR CONTINUES ITS EXCRUCIATINGLY SLOW ascent up its 140-foot tower.

All the foam-padded shoulder restraints are locked in their upright positions like multiple pairs of raised arms. It's almost as if the ride is surrendering.

"Okay, this is bad, man," whispers Shaun McKinnon. "Way bad."

The rest of us stay silent. Watch the Free Fall's only rider, David Rosen, climb higher and higher. It looks like he's gripping the sides of his seat with both hands. I know I would be. Imagine sitting in a chair, without a seat belt or any other kind of restraint, and being hoisted half a football field high in the sky.

"When the chairs reach the top, it'll stop," says McKinnon. "But if Joe punches the launch button, that sucker's going to plunge, man. Speeds will exceed forty-five miles per hour. No way that dude up there doesn't fly out of his seat. No way he survives a 140-foot drop."

Ceepak whips out his radio. Clicks over to the Chief's channel.

"Chief Rossi, this is Detective Ceepak," he whispers into the radio. "My partner, Detective Boyle, and I are on the scene, twenty feet away from the StratosFEAR Free Fall, with officers Perry and Getze as well as a licensed ride operator, Mr. Shaun McKinnon. We need to contact the state police. Scramble the T.E.A.M.S. emergency response unit."

The T.E.A.M.S. guys are, basically, the Navy SEALS of the NJ State Police. A full-time emergency response unit, with special weapons and tactics teams, they are prepared to handle extraordinary events, like, for instance, a screwy old drunk hauling a murder suspect up to the top of the world's tallest dunking machine.

"What's our situation, John?" asks Chief Rossi.

"My father, Joseph Ceepak, is holding David Rosen hostage on the StratosFEAR ride."

"Your father?"

"10-4. He is also a licensed Free Fall operator currently in the employ of Sinclair Enterprises."

"Your father?"

Ceepak closes his eyes for half a second. "Yes, sir. He has hoisted Dr. Rosen, without seat restraints, up to the peak of the 140-foot tower."

"What does he want? Has your father made any demands?"

"We have not yet made contact."

"Can you do so safely?" asks the Chief.

"Yes, sir."

"Do it. Buy me some time. It'll take a while for the tactical intervention team to arrive on scene—even if they chopper down."

"Roger that. Sir?"

"Yeah?"

"You may also want to grab the M-24 SWS out of the armory."

The SWS is a "Sniper Weapon System" rifle that Ceepak's first boss in Sea Haven, his old Army buddy, Chief Cosgrove, obtained for the SHPD.

I think Ceepak is contemplating using it on his old man.

"What're we doing with that kind of firepower in our arsenal?" asks Chief Rossi.

"Long story," says Ceepak. "However, it might be of use if we enter a worst-case scenario. Over."

Ceepak clips his radio back on his belt.

"Cover me, Danny."

I rip up the Velcro flap on my holster and pull out my Glock. It's a 31.357, the official SHPD service weapon. Catalog copy says the semi-automatic has "extremely high muzzle velocity and superior precision, even at medium range."

Twenty feet to where Mr. Ceepak's sitting in his control booth with the viewing window wide open? That's medium range.

I rise up out of my crouch and lean across the countertop to brace myself in a two-handed firing stance. Sighting down the barrel, I have a clean shot at Crazy Joe.

To my right, Ceepak takes off his sport coat, folds it neatly in half, and tucks it into the cleanest tomato-sauce-can shelf he can find.

He moves to the pass-through section of the counter, flips it up, and strides out of the shadows into the soft glow of what's probably another spectacular Sea Haven sunset.

While he walks away from the pizza place, I watch his Glock sway back and forth in that small-of-the-back crossdraw holster.

"Johnny boy!" cries his father. "There you are. What took you so long?"

Ceepak ignores the question. "What do you want?"

"What, you're not even going to thank me?"

"Come again?"

Mr. Ceepak nudges his head skyward. "David Rosen. He confessed. Isn't that right, David?"

Mr. Ceepak places a cell phone on the windowsill of his booth.

"David?" he shouts at the phone. "Tell my son what you did. David? Don't be an idiot. Spill your guts. Unless you want me to spill 'em for you."

"I killed my father!" I hear David's voice leak out of Mr. Ceepak's speakerphone.

"Little louder," coaches Mr. Ceepak.

"I killed my father. I put the poison in his pillbox. I had to do it . . ."

Mr. Ceepak smirks and points mockingly at the phone as if to say, *"Can you believe this guy?"*

"Michael was blackmailing us. My wife said we couldn't let him ruin Little Arnie's future. My dad should've died when he had that fall. He was ninety-four. I probably did him a favor. Kept him out of the old folks home . . ."

"Okay, David," says Mr. Ceepak. "That's enough." He taps the mute button on his phone.

"A coerced confession won't stand up in court," says Ceepak.

"Sure it will. Isn't that what you boys did over in Iraq all the time? Jammed the muzzle of your rifle right up against some sand monkey's skull and hollered, 'Talk!' Am I right?"

"No, sir. You are wrong."

"Yeah, yeah. You're such a namby-pamby pansy. You probably just asked nice. Me? I know how to get results. That boy sitting up there on top of the tower? He reminds me of you, Johnny. He broke God's holy edict. He defied the fifth commandment . . ."

Oh, boy. Here we go again. Preacher Joe is back.

"'Honor thy father and mother, that thy days may be long in the land that the Lord your God is giving thee.'"

"If David Rosen murdered his father, he will be punished," says Ceepak.

"No, he won't. They'll say, well, his father was ninety-four, he was going to die soon anyway. I guarantee you they won't give him the death penalty like I sure as hell will."

Mr. Ceepak glances at his watch.

"Hey, Johnny, remember that thing last summer at the Rolling Thunder roller coaster? How that crazy kid held us all hostage?"

"Of course."

"Well, did you know that during that whole deal, I was paying very close attention to everything that went down? It took the New Jersey State Police S.W.A.T. team a full hour to show up. Sixty freaking minutes."

"I was not clocking them. I was busy, attempting to save lives, including yours."

"Yeah, well, I clocked 'em. But hell, maybe they've been training in the off-season. Working on their speed drills. So, you and me? We've got thirty minutes."

"For what?"

"Hey, I gave you your killer and his confession. But if you want him alive enough to stand trial, you have to give me something, too."

"And what is that?"

"My one million dollars. Call your mother, tell her to grab her checkbook, and drag her wrinkled ass on over here. Now. The clock is ticking. You have twenty-nine minutes."

# 66

YES, JOE CEEPAK REALLY HAS A SERIOUS THING ABOUT BEING a millionaire.

He's like a dog with a knotted sock filled with bacon. He just won't let it go.

He leans out of the window a little.

Shouts past his son.

"You know where to find Adele, right, Boyle? That old folks condo complex. The Oceanaire with the pissant guard shack. Have one your buddies pick her up and hot-rod her over here, pronto, Tonto."

I don't take my eyes off Mr. Ceepak.

But I hear the two uniforms relaying the information about Mrs. Ceepak to Chief Rossi.

"You on it, Boyle?"

"Yeah," I shout back because, face it—he knows I'm over here, hiding in the shadows of the pizza place, covering my partner's back.

"Good. Because we're down to twenty-eight minutes till Dr. Rosen up there becomes just another greasy stain on the boardwalk. And while Adele and I work out the details on the wire transfer, you boys need to find me a helicopter. Or a boat. A speed boat. Something that'll take me and David out to international waters fast."

"You and David?" says Ceepak, taking a step toward his crazy dad.

"Yeah. He's my hostage."

Mr. Ceepak raises that brown bag to his lips again. Takes a long gulp.

"Don't worry, I'll let David go once we reach the Bahamas or the Cayman Islands."

He's starting to slur his words.

"Maybe Cuba. Hijackers used to go to Cuba all the time. Do they have banks in Cuba, Johnny?"

"Don't know. I've never been."

"You want to come with me? We could do a father-son fishing trip along the way."

"Fine. I'd much rather you take me as your hostage than David Rosen."

"Yeah, yeah. Because you're a big dumb hero. Always risking your life for schmucks like David up there, even though he deserves to die. But I'm not stupid, Johnny. The minute we boarded the boat, you'd try to jump me. Karate kick me in the nuts. Not gonna happen. Get me my speedboat. And put some food in it. Sandwiches and stuff. I like those salt and vinegar potato chips . . ."

Okay, this is why they say you shouldn't drink and try to think.

No way is any of Mr. Ceepak's fantasy escape plan going to play out the way he sees it in his booze-fogged brain. The guy probably doesn't even have a bank account. And how's he going to pilot a speedboat to Cuba? Demand that it be equipped with a GPS that'll give him turn-by-turn directions for the Atlantic Ocean?

This situation is not going to end any way but badly. The man's plans are preposterous. The scrambled brain farts of a pickled old drunk.

"Can you safely lower Dr. Rosen if mother gives you your one million dollars?" asks Ceepak.

"Yeah, yeah. The factory trained me real good. I'm pretty sure I can work him down nice and slow. But you better have a fresh pair of underpants handy because, I guarantee you, he's going to piss his pants on the slide down if he didn't already do it on the ride up."

Mr. Ceepak breaks into one of his phlegm-filled laughing jags.

As he hacks up the chuckles, Ceepak reaches behind his back for his Glock.

"Don't even think about it, Johnny," snaps his dad.

He sensed Ceepak shifting his weight, going for his gun.

Ceepak freezes. Raises both his hands to show his father that he remains unarmed.

"Good. You've got twenty-six minutes. Go find your mommy."

"Danny's on it," says Ceepak. "I think I'll stay out here. Keep my eye on you."

"What? You don't trust me to uphold my end of the deal?"

"No, sir. I do not. And if you make any sudden move toward that launch button, let me remind you that I am a very quick draw."

"Yeah, yeah. Just get me my money and my boat. Or a helicopter that'll take me to a private jet with enough fuel to fly me down to Mexico. Or like I said, Cuba. Cuba would be good. Forget the boat. I want a helicopter."

He belches.

"Any word on the SWAT team?" I whisper to the uniforms without looking over at them. I'm keeping my eye on my target. That bit Ceepak said about being a quick draw? Nobody's that quick. That was his way of telling me to take the shot if his dad makes a move for the big green button I see blinking near his gut in the center of the control panel.

"They're scrambling out of their barracks, getting their tactical gear together," says Jack Getze, who's in radio contact with the Staties. "E.T.A. thirty-five minutes."

Geeze-o, man.

"The Chief and the mayor are also on their way," Getze reports. "Officer Jen Forbus has Mrs. Ceepak and a friend. Young woman named Christine Lemonopolous."

Guess we interrupted Christine's Buckeye candy delivery plans.

"The ladies should be here in under five. By the way, the Chief says he's bringing that sniper weapon Ceepak requested. Can you handle it, Danny?"

"I don't know. Never tried. It's a military weapon with a scope. You have to set it up on a tripod. I'm better off with my Glock."

"You dudes gonna shoot Joe?" asks Shaun McKinnon.

"I hope not."

"Me, too. Dude's totally toasted. Doesn't know what he's saying or doing. That crap about flying to Cuba in a helicopter? Chopper would run out of gas, man. I think he and his son just have, you know, major issues."

Yeah. Tell me about it.

"Was Joe Ceepak telling the truth?" I ask McKinnon, keeping my focus on the control booth. "Can you bring the ride down safely and slowly?"

"Theoretically," says McKinnon. "I mean it's in the manual. But, dude, it's like you and that sniper rifle. I've never actually tried to do it."

So now I'm feeling sorry for David Rosen even though I know he murdered his father. Sitting up there at 140 feet, watching the sun go down, maybe picking up a snatch or two of the drunken crazy talk down below. He's probably wishing he had another cyanide pill.

I hear several sirens whining their way closer.

"That's them," reports Jack Getze, our radioman. "The Chief, the mayor, paramedics, dozen more uniforms . . ."

The sirens cut out.

I hear an army of booted feet charging up the boardwalk.

I take half a second to wipe the sweat off my brow.

It's almost time for the first-ever Ceepak family reunion, right here in sunny, funderful Sea Haven. Should be special.

There might even be fireworks.

# 67

"Where are we, Boyle?" asks Chief Roy Rossi.

The way he says it, I know I can't crack back with *"inside a pizza joint on the boardwalk, sir."*

So I give him the short version of what's been going down—including doing our best to stop a drunken bum from bopping a button that'll send David Rosen hurtling to his death.

"I've heard good things about your shooting," the Chief continues. "Can you handle this Sniper Weapon System if need be?"

"I could try."

"Try?" This from Mayor Sinclair. "What kind of amateur operation are you running here, Chief Rossi?"

The Chief ignores the honorable jerk.

I take my eyes off Mr. Ceepak for two seconds. Do a quick visual sweep of the room. I see the Chief, the mayor, and maybe twelve other cops plus a couple paramedics from the rescue squad.

The medics brought their big first-aid kit. And a body board with neck restraints.

But if David Rosen goes flying, none of their gear will do him any good. We're gonna need a spatula.

All the uniforms have their weapons out and up, mirroring my stance, elbows on the countertop to steady their two-handed grips on their guns. It's like we've set up a reverse shooting gallery at the front of the walk-up pizza stand. Instead of a dozen guns aiming into a booth, we're all aiming out of one at a clown whose balloon definitely needs popping.

"You have seventeen minutes, Johnny," snarls drunken Joe. "Seventeen minutes till I show everybody how that little girl up in Michigan died when she flew out of her seat on this very same ride."

"Shut him up," barks Mayor Sinclair. "What he's saying isn't true. This is not the same ride. It has been completely refurbished."

"Be careful, everyone. Joe is a very angry drunk."

I take my eyes off the target again. Glance over my shoulder.

Adele Ceepak is in the pizzeria. Christine is with her. Officer Jen Forbus escorts the two of them up to the counter.

"You okay, Danny?" asks Christine in a nervous whisper.

"Hanging in."

"Who the hell are all those people over there?" snarls Joe Ceepak, who must've seen movement in the shadows.

"Not knowing, can't say," replies Ceepak, who is still standing like a brick wall halfway between the pizza place and the Stratos-FEAR control shack.

"Is he drinking vodka?" asks Mrs. Ceepak.

One of our guys with binoculars zooms in. "Clear bottle poking out of the bag. Could be gin or rum."

"No, it's vodka," says Mrs. Ceepak. "He used to keep a bottle in the freezer. Slurp it down like it was maple syrup. How can I help here?"

"He wants one million dollars," I say.

"Then he should try playing the lottery."

Believe it or not, just about everybody chuckles a little when she says that.

"We need to buy some more time," explains the Chief. "A State Police SWAT team is on its way."

"Okay," says Adele. "Should I go out there and promise him whatever he wants?"

"No." This from Christine. "It's too dangerous."

"Not as dangerous as sitting up there in David Rosen's shoes," says Mrs. Ceepak. "And don't worry, hon. Johnny will watch out for me. He always has. My son is a very brave and courageous young man."

I'm thinking he got a lot of that from his mom.

Chief Rossi squeezes the button on the battery-powered bull-horn he probably borrowed from Dylan Murray down in the parking lot.

"Mr. Ceepak? This is Chief Rossi, SHPD. Your ex-wife has arrived. She would like to come out and discuss your financial demands."

"Hang on," says Ceepak, inching backward. "Danny?"

"Locked and loaded."

"Back-up?"

"Twelve. The target has been acquired."

"That'll work." Ceepak moves a step closer to his father. "Sir? As you just heard, you ex-wife is willing to discuss your request."

"Good. Go get her. Hurry. We're down to twelve minutes."

"If you make a move toward the control panel . . ."

"Yeah, yeah. I heard. Your buddy Boyle will blow my brains out. Now hustle, jarhead."

Ceepak hurries into the pizza parlor.

"Good of you to be here," he says to his mother. "I'm sorry we had to drag you into this . . ."

"Come on, John. Time's a-wasting."

"We need another fifteen, twenty minutes," says the Chief, getting real-time updates from the SWAT team on his earpiece.

"We'll try to buy it for you. You ready, Mom?"

"Are you kidding? I was born ready."

"Mrs. Ceepak?" says Christine.

"Yes, dear?"

"Be careful out there."

"Oh, I plan on it. And when this is all over, I want you and Danny to come over to my place for a cookout. Just the two of you."

"Yes, ma'am."

"Stay behind me at all times," Ceepak says to his mother.

"Even when I'm talking to Joe?"

"Yes, ma'am."

"I'd like to look him in the eye, give him a piece of my mind . . ."

"Mom? I need to be your shield."

"Fine. You're the boss, honey. Let's just do this thing."

And the two of them, son and mother, with Ceepak in the lead, march back out to the darkening no-man's land between the pizza parlor and the Free Fall.

I just hope nothing happens to ruin our cookout plans.

# 68

"WHERE THE HELL IS ADELE?"

Mr. Ceepak is sort of teetering in the control booth, trying to see Mrs. Ceepak, who is hidden behind the massive bulk of her towering son.

"I'm right here, Joseph."

"Step out where I can see you."

"Why? I thought you wanted to talk."

"I do."

"Then talk. You don't have to see someone to talk to them. That's why they invented the telephone."

"Still got a mouth on you, huh, Adele?"

"That's right, Joseph. And I still know to use it."

"Okay, okay. Ease up already. Seriously, babe—what the hell happened to us? Where'd we go wrong?"

Great. Mr. Ceepak's drunk has moved into the sloppy sad stage.

"I thought this was about money, Joseph, not us."

"It is, it is. But we're a team, remember? You and me against the world. What's mine is yours, what's yours is mine."

"That stopped the first time I caught you stealing beer money out of my purse."

"Why do you have to say things like that, Adele? What'd I ever do to you?"

"You mean besides murdering my youngest son?"

"That was a suicide."

"No, it was not. You just fooled everybody into thinking it was for years and years. You killed your own son."

"I had to. Billy was a weakling. Hey, I did him a favor. The world was too tough for a sissy boy like him."

"Sir?" says Ceepak, stepping forward an inch or two, his mother scooting up behind him. "Currently, you are the one wasting valuable time. I suggest we add a few more minutes to your countdown clock."

"What? No way. The SWAT team is coming . . ."

"Be that as it may, it will take considerable time for mother to organize the one million dollars you have requested."

"How long?"

"Well," says Mrs. Ceepak, "the bank's closed. But they open tomorrow at ten . . ."

"Not gonna work. I need my money, Adele. I need it now. Hell, I earned that million dollars."

"Oh, really? How?"

"Hey, I was married to you for twenty years, wasn't I? I deserve that much in hazardous-duty pay."

Mr. Ceepak wheezes out a laugh. Guzzles more booze.

"I'll give you your money tomorrow, Joseph."

"Tomorrow? I need to fly to Cuba."

"Well, what do you propose I do? Write you a check?"

"No. Because no one would cash a check for a million dollars. Not unless you had a bank account with them, and I don't have a bank account in Cuba."

Yes, the drunker he gets, the stupider he becomes.

"So, what exactly is it you want, Joseph?"

"One million dollars!"

"Will you take cash?"

"Yeah. Fine. Cache."

Mr. Ceepak sounds half asleep. His eyelids look heavy. His eyeballs blurry.

Mrs. Ceepak keeps going. "Does it need to be in unmarked bills? Tens and twenties only, like in the movies?"

"Are you mocking me, Adele?"

"You bet. Because you deserve it. Who the heck do you think you are, anyway? What you're doing here is wrong."

"No, Adele, what you did in Ohio was wrong. Taking all that money from Aunt Jennifer and not sharing it with me, your law-fully wedded husband."

"You are not my husband. We are divorced."

"We're Catholic, Adele. Divorce is against the rules."

"That's why I got an annulment, too."

"You can't annul diddly. What God has joined together . . . let no man put us under a bus . . ."

I think the alcohol has officially destroyed all the brain cells that used to be employed memorizing bible verses.

"You stole from me, Adele. That's a sin."

Mrs. Ceepak jabs up her arm to point at David Rosen's perch atop the Free Fall. "Nothing I have ever done or ever will do is half as sinful as what you're doing here."

"That boy murdered his father!"

"Then let the police deal with it."

Mr. Ceepak brings up the brown paper bag and takes yet another swig. Or at least he tries to.

He shakes the bag.

I think his bottle is officially empty and the drunken fool doesn't look happy about it.

"Why didn't Aunt Jennifer put me in her will with you?" he mutters, sounding like a mad six-year-old.

"Maybe because she hated you for killing your own son."

"Billy deserved it!"

Mrs. Ceepak disobeys her son. Steps to his side so she can directly confront her ex-husband.

"No. He deserved better. Better than you, anyway."

"Screw you, Adele. Hey, am I in *your* will?"

"Ha! Over my dead body."

"That can be arranged."

"Mother?" says Ceepak "Get behind me. Now."

Mrs. Ceepak holds her ground. "I'm not afraid of you, Joseph. Not any more."

"Mother?" Ceepak reaches for her,

Mr. Ceepak stumbles off his stool. "You ungrateful bitch. After all I did for you."

And up comes Mr. Ceepak's pistol.

Every trigger finger in the pizza parlor is ready to fire.

"Don't!" shouts Ceepak.

We all think he's talking to us.

He isn't.

He's yelling at his father while jumping in front of his mother.

A shot rings out.

Smacks Ceepak.

He goes spinning. Blood is spurting out of his thigh. As he twists around, he grits his teeth hard, grabs hold of his mother. The two of them topple in a heap to the boardwalk. My friend covers his mother, shields her from Crazy Joe's second shot.

I am so ready to take the bastard down.

But Mr. Ceepak moves his free hand over that blinking green button.

"Anybody takes a shot, David dies!" he screams.

"Stand down!" orders the chief.

"Don't shoot!" shouts Mayor Sinclair.

Mr. Ceepak's hand inches closer to the button.

And that's when my whole world goes into free fall.

# 69

THERE'S A VIDEO GAME I SOMETIMES PLAY CALLED NCAA FOOTBALL by EA Sports.

In the "Road To Glory" mode, you can flick a trigger on the game controller and enter hyper reality. The action slides into super slow motion so you can see every little detail of the play while you're in the middle of running it.

This is what happens when I tug back on the trigger to my Glock.

I can see blood arcing in bursts out of Ceepak's leg, keeping time to the thundering beats of my own amped-up heart.

His father hit him in the femoral artery.

My partner is going to bleed out, right here on the boardwalk, if those paramedics don't start administering first aid immediately. John Ceepak is going to die shielding his mom, something he has done since he was a teenager. A fitting end for such a brave man? Maybe. But this is not his time. It can't be.

I won't let it.

And so I fire at his father when Mr. Ceepak's hand moves half-an-inch closer to the green button glowing on, dimming off, glowing on, dimming off.

My first round rips across the twenty open feet of air separating us. I swear I can see the slug soaring like a guided missile to its target.

It slams into Mr. Ceepak's shoulder. Hard.

He flies backward. Looks stunned.

But his liquor-soaked brain has been numbed down to its reptilian stub. It's fight or flight time. He chooses to fight. He fires his own weapon.

"Down!" someone shouts behind me.

I hear bodies thudding to the floor.

Mr. Ceepak's bullet whizzes past my head.

Glass shatters.

Christine screams.

I cannot turn around to see if she is okay.

All I can do is line up my next shot.

Mr. Ceepak drops his pistol.

He lunges forward and fights through the pain searing his shoulder to place both hands over that glimmering launch switch. He is ready to kill David Rosen, to make that his final, dying act.

But I kill him first.

My second bullet blows through Mr. Ceepak's chest.

He glares and snarls at the world one last time.

And then, thank God, Ceepak's father finally dies.

# 70

WHEN I AM ABSOLUTELY CERTAIN THAT MR. JOSEPH CEEPAK has lost the ability to harm anyone else, I whirl around.

Christine is okay. Shocked, but okay.

I can't say the same thing for the pizza shop's Coke case. The sliding glass doors are shattered. Foamy orange soda is spewing out of the row of innocent Fanta cans that took a direct hit from Mr. Ceepak's second bullet.

I hop up and over the counter. Nearly beat the team of paramedics to Ceepak's side.

They roll him over onto their body board. Mrs. Ceepak is weeping when I help her up off the ground. She nearly faints when she sees the fountain of blood jetting up out of her son's wounded leg.

Fortunately, Christine came running out of the pizza place right behind me. Officer Getze, too. They gently take Ceepak's mother by her elbows and guide her away from the horror show. Christine automatically switches into the calming nurse mode I saw in action when that kid was choking on his seafood.

"Let's move back inside, Mrs. Ceepak," Christine says, her voice soft and soothing. "Let the paramedics do their job . . ."

"Johnny?"

"It's all good, mom," Ceepak says weakly. And even though his wound must hurt like hell, he manages a small smile for her.

I lean down near his head while the two EMTs apply pressure with a jumbo gauze square to his leg.

"Take it easy, partner."

Ceepak looks me in the eye.

"Danny . . . did you . . . were you able to?"

"Yeah."

"Thank you, my friend."

Ceepak closes his eyes as all sorts of paper cups and sandwich wrappers and scattered trash start swirling around us. I hear chopper blades thumping and whumping overhead, obliterating poor David Rosen's cries for help from the peak of the StratosFEAR.

The SWAT team has arrived.

A black-suited ninja rappels down a line.

"What's our situation?" he screams over the rotor wash.

"Secure," I say. "We need to medevac this man to Mainland Medical. Trauma unit. Stat."

"Roger that."

The armored warrior makes a series of hand gestures. The helicopter touches down in the middle of the boardwalk. Four SWAT team members hop out to make room for Ceepak, the EMTs, and all that first-aid gear.

The chopper lifts off.

I know Ceepak will be at Mainland Medical in less than five minutes.

That's how long it took for the whirlybird to make the trip with Katie Landry after she was shot.

"I'm taking Mrs. Ceepak to Mainland," Christine hollers as she leads Ceepak's mom out of the pizza place. She makes sure to steer her in a direction away from the StratosFEAR control booth where her dead ex-husband, slumped against the blood-streaked back wall, looks like a floppy scarecrow sleeping off a really bad three-day drunk.

"I'll meet you there," I shout back as they leave.

Then Mayor Sinclair gets in my grill.

"What the hell did you do, Detective Boyle?"

Chief Rossi leads a squad of uniforms over to the control booth to deal with Joe Ceepak's body. They need to remove his corpse to make room for Shaun McKinnon. Hopefully, the operator can work the knobs, feather the air brakes, and safely lower David Rosen down to the ground.

"What the hell did you do?" The mayor won't let up. He props his hands on his hips and glares at me.

"My job, sir."

"Your job? Killing that mentally deranged man on my brand new ride? Chief Rossi told you not to fire. I heard him. *I* told you not to fire. You disobeyed a direct command from your superior officer. From me!"

"If I hadn't done what . . ."

Mayor Sinclair gives me the palm of his hand.

"Save it. You're done, Boyle. Done!"

I hang around outside the pizza place for thirty minutes.

Nobody says a word to me.

The uniform cops act like I'm not even there.

Finally, after Shaun McKinnon works the controls for fifteen minutes and lowers David Rosen to within five feet of the StratosFEAR's loading dock, Chief Rossi comes over to have a word.

"Detective Boyle?"

"Yes, sir?"

"I need to notify the county prosecutor about what just happened here. It's mandatory whenever the discharge of a police officer's firearm results in a death."

Trust me: when the police chief starts reciting the Internal Affairs handbook at you, you know you're in trouble.

"Sir," I say, trying to say what Ceepak might, "I believe it was a lawful and appropriate use of deadly force."

"You killed a man, Boyle. After I issued an order not to fire."

"But he was going to . . ."

Now Chief Rossi gives me the palm of his hand.

"There will be an investigation. At that time, you will be given a chance to present your side of the story. You might want to hire yourself an attorney. I need your weapon."

I give him my Glock. It still smells like an exploded firecracker.

"You're going on administrative leave, Officer Boyle."

I just nod. I wonder if administrative leave means I get to leave early every day. Hey, I started this job as a beach bum. Guess I can end it that way, too.

I hear a commotion. David Rosen's feet have finally touched something besides empty air.

"Dude!" shouts McKinnon, relieved, maybe even surprised, to have the stranded rider safely back on the boardwalk. "Whoo-hoo!"

David Rosen is in no mood to celebrate.

His legs are so wobbly, two cops have to hold him up and walk him off the ride's loading dock.

"An ambulance is on the way, sir," says the chief.

"None of what I said can be used in a court of law," Rosen stammers. His whole body is quaking. Someone drapes a blanket over his shoulders. "I don't care if you people recorded it. You didn't have my permission. It was a coerced confession."

"Any of you would've said whatever David said in a similar situation!"

I turn around.

Judith Rosen, escorted by Sal Santucci, has arrived. They didn't bring Little Arnie with them. Good.

Judith runs over to her man. Hugs and kisses him.

"Are you okay, David?"

"Yeah. I'm fine. But you people?" He wags a finger at all the cops who just helped save his life. "I'm going to sue you! All of you! And we've got money to hire a good lawyer!"

I remember that thing Christine said about mean people. How they shouldn't get away with the horrible stuff they do.

But you know what?

Sometimes they just do.

# Epilogue

I FIND OUT THAT ADMINISTRATIVE LEAVE ACTUALLY MEANS I have to go to the police station five days a week and sit behind a desk shuffling papers.

I also replace toner cartridges and answer a ton of questions from Internal Affairs investigators about what happened in those split seconds when, going against Chief Roy Rossi's direct order, I took personal initiative and discharged two deadly rounds.

I know I did the right thing.

Ceepak agrees.

Yeah, that's the good news.

He's going to be fine. He just added another ugly scar to the collection he picked up over in Iraq. In fact, he and Bill Botzong are right now piecing together enough forensic evidence on the cyanide purchase to put David Rosen away, even without the coerced confession. They might even get his wife, Judith, as a co-conspirator. Good thing Little Arnie has all that money. He's going to need it to pay his shrink bills.

But there's more good news, too. Thankfully, Mrs. Ceepak is still in my corner. In fact, she's paying for my lawyer. That's right. Harvey Nussbaum, the Sea Haven pit bull, will be defending me at a hearing in front of the county prosecutor. According to Nussbaum, there's no question I did what "any cop with half a brain would do."

I don't know if he meant that as an insult; that I'm a cop with half a brain. Frankly, I don't care. I just want to be another one of those Wrongs that Harvey turns into a Right.

Christine Lemonopolous?

After accompanying Mrs. Ceepak to Mainland Medical and seeing her trauma team friends save Ceepak's life, she felt ready to go back to her old job. She also found a pretty cute new apartment and had her new boyfriend come over to help her paint the place.

Yep. She and I are dating. Because I have decided to officially adopt Ceepak's honor code as *my* new dating code.

If a girl won't lie, cheat, steal, or tolerate those who do, then she's all right by me. Christine was telling the truth when she swore she didn't do any of the horrible stuff other people kept saying she'd done.

Now I know exactly how she felt.

But just like Christine, I won't let them tell me who I am or what I did. I won't let them drag me down to their level.

Neither will Ceepak.

In fact, he keeps reminding me of what Bruce Springsteen sings in Ceepak's favorite song, "Land Of Hope And Dreams":

> Yeah, leave behind your sorrows,
> Let this day be the last
> Well, tomorrow there'll be sunshine
> And all this darkness past

In other words, pretty soon, it'll all be all good again.